SUSAN M. THODE

Megan,
You matter to me!
Susan Thode

Riptide

A
Do I Matter?
Series Book

By
Susan M. Thode

Reader's Group Guide Inc

This story contains mature teen subjects such as suicide, minor drug use and attempted sexual assault.

ISBN: 978-1-962168-96-0

Dedicated to my mother.
Talented writer, gifted musician
skilled nurse, tireless mother of seven.
Her cognitive life cut much too short
by early onset Alzheimer's.
I love you, Mom.

And to
Yogi, Laddie, Beauty, Shumani,
and Sunday Blessing.
The ponies and horses whose love and
companionship made childhood and adolescence
bearable.

With thanks to Emma McKeighen, my first teen
reader.
She liked the story and gave me great feedback.
And to Colleen, Judy and Sally, who wear many hats.
Friends, readers, editors, encouragers. I'm grateful to have
such lovely women in my life.

And to my husband who read ALL the versions, even
though he doesn't care for fiction let alone YA. That's
some kind of love language!

riptide
rip•tide \ rip-t $\bar{\text{i}}$ d
noun

1) A dangerous area of strongly moving water
in the ocean where two or more currents meet

2) A strong negative feeling or force that is
difficult to control

You can't go back and change the beginning,
but you can start where you are and change the
ending.
C. S. Lewis

Chapter 1

Fear has such a loud voice it drowns out truth.
Sara's Diary

"Steady, boy." I smoothed my hand down Star's licorice-black neck to calm his prancing feet. Butterflies danced like a flash mob in my stomach.

Star cocked his ears forward, eager to enter the ring. They formed a perfect frame for me to see the last obstacles to our championship. Ten fences. Ten possibilities to fly. "Or fall," I muttered under my breath. I continued stroking Star's neck in an effort to quiet both our nerves. Did it help? Nope. Not so much.

"I didn't know saints rode horses."

My hand froze midstroke when I heard the sarcastic voice raised above the noise of the crowd. My neck and cheeks felt warm and I knew a red tint would follow soon.

"No. Way. What's Courtney doing here?" I complained to Star under my breath. "She must be trolling for a guy if she came to a horse show."

I leaned forward to brush imaginary dust from Star's

neck while my gaze scanned the crowd for Courtney, who remained concealed in a sea of people and horses.

"Saint, huh?" Star twitched his ears back at my muttered question. "Let's just show her what a heavenly round we can do."

A microphone squealed before the announcer's voice rang out. "Our next contestant is Sara Mitchell riding Shooting Star. And believe me, folks, this horse definitely lives up to his name."

I nodded to the gate attendant; he opened the gate to the ring. Star's bold strides radiated confidence. I flashed a smile at the official.

"Good luck," he called. He answered my quick smile with one of his own and added a wink.

Heart pounding, I nudged Star's sides with my heels. He lengthened his strides and moved into an easy canter. I guided him in a slow circle so he could get a good look at the course then straightened him out, pressed harder with my heels and we bounded past the timing barrier. Star stretched his neck forward, eager for the first fence.

There was a sense of déjà vu when I looked at the standard four-foot white rail fence. We had probably conquered hundreds by now. The next ten jumps would seal this year's championship \ and I would finally have something the kids at school would respect—or at least notice, I amended in my mind. Respect might be asking too much, but surely a championship could rate some admiration? At the very least, a small sign that I matter in this world?

Ten fences to go. A spike of adrenaline distracted me. What if...?

What if--what? The adrenaline made my hands tighten on the reins and one of Star's ears swiveled back. But his stride stayed strong and I thrust the intruding thought away.

Leaning into Star's mane, I inhaled his clean horse scent. Wind whipped my face and I grinned when I remembered my dad's standard parting remark every time he tossed me into my saddle before a show. "Go ride the wind, Sara." A friendly slap on Star's hip would complete our ritual. Somehow Dad knew riding Star felt like riding the wind.

We sailed over the first three hurdles and I relaxed. It was easy to let Star do all the work. The few seconds we were airborne after he launched himself always sparked joy deep inside my chest.

We raced through the obstacles at the far end of the arena and I heard cheers from our fans when we approached the stands.

I reached down and patted Star's shoulder. "You love this, don't you boy?" His powerful muscles flexed and I wondered for the thousandth time why he let me control such power. He responded instantly to my lightest touch and never held back when I asked for more. Love swelled throughout my body and telegraphed through the reins. Another white blur passed beneath me and I looked up to see the combination hurdle looming.

Tricky, because it involved a four-foot fence, two quick strides and then a three-foot fence, the combination was the most difficult obstacle on the course. Timing was the key and we trained endlessly to achieve effortless harmony. Mutual rapport had never translated to fear before so what was with the moist beads of sweat gathering on my brow and along my upper lip? I licked my lips and tasted salt--tasted unfamiliar dread. Fear grew to panic when the white rails of the upcoming fence blurred and became a shapeless blob. I shook my head and blinked my eyes. My throat tightened and the reins slicked between my damp fingers.

How could I signal Star for the fence if I couldn't see? Visions of him jumping too late or too soon played tag in my mind. The right rein slipped and I struggled to grip it securely. My sudden movement jerked the rein and Star stumbled in confusion pitching me to the side. A collective gasp from the crowd echoed my own and I grabbed Star's mane to pull myself upright. The white blob of the fence appeared to rush toward us. We're too close, my mind warned. We're off balance, came the next hysterical thought.

Instinct took over. I had to trust Star's natural jumping talent and our hours of practice. I had to trust my horse. I dropped my hands to rest on Star's neck so he had free rein to recover himself. He regained his stride and launched over the first fence of the combination. My panic lowered a notch at the familiar thrill from the rush of power. His black hooves cleared the first hurdle with inches to spare. Once more I chose to trust Star's experience and balanced myself in the saddle. Two quick strides, another amazing surge and we were over. Clean. Powerful. Seemingly effortless.

When we cleared the last jump, wild applause burst from the crowd. I could barely hear the announcer's voice.

"Yes, folks, it's another perfect round for Sara Mitchell on Star! What a jumper that horse is."

Star slowed his canter to a trot while I rubbed my eyes with the back of my hand. By the time Star's head bobbed in time to his walk step, my vision swam back into focus. I spied my parents standing by the gate clapping and waving. I waved back.

The microphone clicked and the announcer's voiced resumed, "I've just verified that Sara Mitchell and Star have broken the record for the number of perfect rounds during a show season. Give this team a big hand, folks."

The crowd roared. I leaned forward and threw my arms around Star's neck. "You did it, boy! We broke the record. You're the best horse in the world."

Star's head dipped as if in agreement.

Dizzy with relief, I walked him to the winner's circle, kicked my feet out of the stirrups and dismounted to face the official. As soon as my feet hit the dirt my knees buckled and I grabbed the saddle. Star froze and I kept a hand gripped to the saddle pad until I was sure I could stand.

"What is up with this?" I grumbled to Star while we waited for the second and third place winners. "First my eyes, now my feet. Numb fingers when I saddled you. None of this has happened before." I blew out an exasperated breath and tapped my fingers against the saddle pad. Whatever it was I had to get over it quickly or clean rounds would be a thing of the past. I tested my balance. Finally. Good to go. I released my hold on the saddle pad.

Once the other riders and horses returned to the ring, I reached out to shake the second and third-place winners' hands. I forgot about my shaky legs when the judge handed out the ribbons, beginning with third place. When the judge handed me the trophy and the big blue rosette, the crowd went crazy. They really loved my flashy Appaloosa. Laughter mingled with the applause when Star grabbed the fluttering ribbon between his teeth and lifted it neatly from my grasp.

The announcer chuckled. "Star must want us to remember who does most of the work for that ribbon. Let him keep it, Sara. It looks good on him."

Heat started at my collar bone then crept up my neck and over my smiling cheeks. I looked at my feet to hide my grin. When I raised my head, my mouth turned salty with nausea and it seemed like the judge and the stands behind him were spinning. I closed my eyes and turned to lean my forehead against Star. I experimented with slitting my eyes open. Shoot. The reins in my hand were blurry strands again.

"I feel funny," I mumbled into Star's shoulder. "Like I might…" The blurry strands of rein darkened and my stomach heaved. I reached for the stirrup. It slipped through my fingers and then…nothing.

The sharp stench of the arena dirt stung my nose. I raised my head then lowered it quickly when I instantly felt queasy.

"Medical team to the main arena, please. Medics, please report to the main arena."

I rolled over on my back and tried my eyes again. Blurred shadows but no nausea. Improvement. What was that above me? I squinted and recognized Star's belly. I'm under my horse? I fell? Please no please no please no. Not with Courtney here. I'll go straight onto TikTok. Cautiously I scanned my position. Mostly under Star, kind of between his front legs which were planted like tree trunks. A horse sentinel. Great. My super power is apparently awkward moments.

"Sara?"

Dad's voice had an unfamiliar urgency.

"Yuh…" I cleared my throat. "Yeah?"

He knelt beside me. "Are you okay? What happened? Wait, just a sec. Let me move Star."

"Sir, tell your daughter not to move." A new voice. One with authority. The medic? "And could you move the horse? I can't reach your daughter."

I smiled in spite of my circumstances. At sixteen hands tall, nobody messed with Star.

Dad stood and coaxed Star a few steps to the side.

The medic swooped in and began his examination and questions. He hadn't gotten far when Mom's voice interrupted, but the medic didn't stop.

"What is it? What do you think happened?" Mom's tone sounded like Dad's.

"I'm not sure, ma'am. Possibly just a combination of excitement and heat. How old is your daughter?"

"She just turned seventeen."

"Is she on a diet by any chance?"

The medic's fingers pressed into the inside of my wrist. Reading life by my pulse like a blind person reads

Braille. Cool.

"No, she's not on a diet. Why? What does that have to do with her fainting?"

"If she's dieting inappropriately, her strength is compromised. Many girls this age don't eat properly because they're worried about their weight."

Not me. I never skip meals. I should probably tell him. I experimented opening my eyes and cleared my throat again.

"Good. She's coming around." The tech kept his fingers on my wrist.

"I did eat this morning," I told him. "Do you know how much energy it takes to do what I do?"

"Have you ever fainted before?"

"Nope. None of this has ever happened before."

"Did you hit your head before the show? Experience dizziness?"

"No."

The medic stood and brushed the dirt from the arena off his knees. "Well, Mr. and Mrs. Mitchell, her pulse is almost back to normal, her pupils aren't dilated, no broken bones. Take her home and keep her quiet. If she's not feeling well tomorrow, take her to see her regular doctor. I think she'll be fine though."

He reached out a hand to help me up, steadied me until he was sure I could stand then stepped back and picked up his bag.

I smiled and waved when the audience burst into applause. Taking the reins from Dad, I led Star toward the exit gate. My parents followed. The attendant opened the gate. I smiled a thank you and headed toward the barn. Just as we turned the corner I glanced up and froze. Courtney. Standing off to the side, phone held high in her hand. Great.

Chapter 2

They all play the same game. Unfortunately, I don't know the rules.
Sara's Diary

When we reached the barn, Dad motioned me to sit while he kept going into the depths of the barn with Star. I sank onto a hay bale jammed under the open window and blew out a deep sigh. Mom rested a hand on my shoulder.

"Are you okay?" I nodded and she disappeared after Dad to our assigned stall. Unbuttoning the top couple buttons of my formerly pristine show shirt with one hand, I tipped off my riding helmet with the other. Removing the gazillion clips and pins that kept my hair in a tidy bun took both hands and several minutes. My hair didn't conform well to the neat bun required for show jumping. Partially freed from the prison of show attire, I slumped against the window like a balloon with a slow leak.

Controlled chaos is a good description of the barn scene. Competitors and horses jostled each other for a clear path. Occasionally a horse nipped and squealed when someone, equine or human, invaded their personal space. Riders chattered about their events. Congratulations and commiserations were distinguished by high excited tones or low sympathetic murmurs. The tang of sweat and manure mingled with leather, hay, wood shavings and most of all, the sweet earthy musk of horse. Inhaling the welcome aroma loosened my tight muscles. My favorite aromatherapy. I belonged here. Every single cell of me felt at home. Exactly the opposite of school.

"She's such a drama queen. Saint turned queen, I guess."

Courtney's piercing laugh caused me to bolt upright like the hay bale was electrified. I stared out the window, then ducked down in case she could see me. I pictured her with her robo friends clustered around. I wished I had the nerve to stand, lean out the window and challenge Courtney's hypocrisy. How did she get away with calling me a saint? She went to church, too. Not that anyone would know by how she acted.

Saints were the kids who went to church or any kind of religious club. The uncool. Definitely never trending. Always on the outside looking in. That's how it felt anyway. So unfair! I didn't even like church or youth group. I wasn't a saint. Why did they have to label me?

"Falling down like that after winning." Ridicule edged Courtney's voice. "Puh-leeze. She never makes mistakes when she rides. Remember she's suuuch a horse girl."

I winced at the lash of spite in Courtney's tone. I could see air quotes around horse girl as clearly as if she was standing in front of me. I didn't expect nice things out of her mouth anymore. That's not the same as not wanting them though.

"Maybe she was really hurt." One of the other girls suggested.

Courtney sniffed. "So unlikely. She was totally grabbing attention like she always does with that horse of hers. I guess she has to have something going for her." Courtney's tone amped up another notch to cruel. "I mean, have you seen her at school? She must like shop with her mom or something. I literally don't know how she ever made cheerleader. Maybe people felt sorry for her? It must be so embarrassing to be her. That reddish-brown hair is sort of okay, I guess, and her greenish eyes. But that pale skin and freckles? Really? Hello? Make-up?"

The sound of the girls' laughter faded and I slumped in relief. They were leaving. I wanted to unhear Courtney's words, but knew they would replay endlessly on a mental loop. Familiar dark tendrils of thought slithered into my mind. You don't fit in; you don't matter; you'll never belong. I pushed against my forehead with the heels of both hands to stop the murky messages. They'd been swarming in my mind in droves during the last year. More and more they seemed like the black flies that buzzed and plagued Star. And I had been no more successful than Star at batting them away.

Sara the saint. That's who I was at school. Most kids didn't call me that to my face, but I knew. Courtney and her friends, some of the guys on the football team. They were the most vocal. My antagonists. The "in" crowd. The cool kids. Or, as my friend Tawny would say, "They're fire."

I thought when I made cheerleader I would finally be accepted. But we started cheerleading practice at the beginning of August and so far, there'd been no change. Maybe once school started on Monday things would be different. If people got to know me maybe they'd drop the label and accept me for myself. Would Courtney and her friends let that happen?

And what was up with Courtney, anyway? Courtney, Tawny and I had been inseparable until seventh grade. During the summer between sixth and seventh grade we'd hung out as usual. Courtney had even ridden Star whenever we were at my house. She liked Star. Or used to. She liked *me*. Or used to. Then in seventh grade she completely ghosted me. Like, completely. That's when the dark tendrils of thought started. That's how long I'd battled seeds of misery. Seeds that were growing.

Sometimes it seemed as though I'd been battling depression forever, but really it was hitting high school when the misery seeds grew into a dark forest. Music, clubs, boys, fashion, make-up, sports. School became a foreign country. I tried to fit in. I tried to adapt. I became an exchange student in my own town. Somehow, I got lost in translation to high school.

"Gingersnap? Feel like helping?" Dad nudged my knee with his own. He stood beside me cradling Star's saddle in one arm.

"Really, Dad? Gingersnap? Still? You know I hate that nickname. When are you going to let it go?"

"Sorry, kiddo. As long as you remind me of my favorite cookie, you're stuck."

I grinned back. It was kinda nice that Dad never changed. I reached up to grab his hand. He pulled me up and into a one-armed half-hug against the saddle.

"Hey, it looked like you kind of slipped to the side out there. What happened?"

"Just lost my balance a bit. No biggie."

"If you say so. How about you finish brushing Star down while Mom and I pack up? Sure you feel okay?"

I nodded, brushed at the arena debris on my breeches then realized it was futile since my hands were as dirty as my pants. I glanced down the corridor at Star. He stood with one hind hoof resting on point with his hip slumped down. He was dirty, too. And tired. I picked up a brush and weaved my way through riders and horses to my newly crowned champion.

I unbraided his mane and began brushing out the dirt and sweat from his neck. He'd get an all-over light grooming here and a more thorough washing once we got home. Fatigue settled on me while I brushed. I stopped to lean against Star's side. My mouth tasted sour and I flashed back on the dizzy feeling that preceded vertigo. I'd never slid down his side and collapsed under his feet before, but he had stood protectively over me while I was down. I draped an arm over his back and leaned my head against his shoulder.

"You always have my back, don't you, big guy? I never have to wonder if I matter to you." I finger-combed his mane. "Wish people were more like horses. I always know where I am with you. At school I feel like I need to wear a sign that says, DO I MATTER TO YOU? I can never figure it out."

A deep sigh escaped and ruffled Star's mane. I straightened, blew my hair off my forehead then resumed brushing Star's hide so we could load him in the trailer and head home.

Resting in the back seat of the truck, I remembered before the show began, I had trouble pinning my contestant number on my jacket. My hands were numb and tingly, uncoordinated. Like when my vision blurred, I mused. Maybe I should have told the medic?

Nah. I'd be fine. He'd said so himself.

Chapter 3

*Maybe I would be more confident if I was as happy as
I pretend to be.*
Sara's Diary

The next morning after church I headed for the barn. The kitchen door banged behind me as I clattered down the back steps humming under my breath. The sun of a perfect-rounds season left yesterday's uncertainties in shadow. Even having to go to church didn't dim the triumph of our jumping season. My good mood embraced my family and our weekly routine. I glanced around with satisfaction at the fall highlighted day.

Our family's small northern California farm is perfect as far as I'm concerned. It's not too far from Bodega Bay, and Santa Rosa is easy to get to for serious shopping. We have the pleasure of beautiful ocean and coastline with none of the heat and smog associated with the southern part of the state. Dad sometimes jokes we should sell our farm so he can retire, but I know that won't happen. He likes his job as a math professor at the community college. Plus, the rest of the family, including Grandma and Grandpa, would mutiny if he tried to get rid of the farm.

"I just don't see us going anywhere anytime soon, do you Abby?" I reached down to stroke our colorful calico who arched her back to meet my hand. Something wet pushed into my other hand and I looked down to see our old black Lab who had been my little brother's five-year-old birthday present. The dog's nose pressed insistently into my free hand. Though solid black, Ben, being Ben, had instantly named his dog, Spot.

"Saaaarrrraaa." Ben's loud yell startled every living thing within hearing distance and caused Abby to race for sanctuary under the chicken coop. One time my fourteen-year-old brother, whom I mostly call Brat, used Abby in a science experiment that involved wrapping the little cat in aluminum foil. Abby has never forgotten. I groaned. If there was anything to complain about at the farm it was Brat.

I copied Abby's quick dash for shelter and ducked inside the barn door. Maybe I could avoid him for at least a little bit. Unfortunately, Spot followed any of us when we were outside and I knew he would eventually lead Ben to my location.

Star's soft whinny caught my attention. I crossed to the stall door and ran my hand down his long face. He nudged my hand and pawed at the straw on the floor.

"Hungry?" I pulled pieces of straw out of the gleaming softness of his forelock. "Dumb question. You're always hungry." I laughed when he turned from me to go stand in front of his feed bucket attached to the wall. "Okay, okay, I get the message. Just let me get some music going and I'll get your breakfast."

I thumbed through my phone's playlists until I found the one Grandma made me. Soon her favorites from the 70's played softly through my ear buds. None of my friends, even Tawny, understood how I could listen to the moldy oldies, as they called them, but these songs reminded me of Grandma. It almost felt like she was in the barn with me while I listened. Okay by me.

Kevin, the guy who lived on the property next to us, advised me to listen to the Christian artists he liked. And though I'd never admit it to him, I like TobyMac, love Lauren Daigle and obsessively listen to the song, *Priceless,* by For King and Country. I wish I could believe I'm priceless, but if that was true it would mean I mattered.

"I mean, if I was truly priceless, like the song says, wouldn't I feel it? There's no way that song is true. But I can't get it out of my brain. The problem is, Starster, not only do I not feel priceless, I'm slipping the other way. Mostly I feel worthless."

Star nudged my arm again and startled me out of my music-inspired trance. Knowing he wouldn't move until he was fed, I left the stall door open and reached for the scoop and bucket by the feed bin. After measuring grain and grabbing a section of hay from the stacked bales, I returned to the stall and shouldered my friend aside. Grunts of eager anticipation met the flow of oat mixture into the feed bucket and Star carefully, but firmly, edged me out of the way so he could reach his food.

"All right, all right. I'll move." I slapped his shoulder affectionately. "You deserve your breakfast, boy. You did great yesterday."

While Star attacked his grain and hay, I cleaned and refilled his water bucket then grabbed a pitchfork to work on clearing out the dirty straw. Abby climbed through an open window and positioned herself like a guard on the mountain of hay bales stacked against the wall. Her eyes half closed when a shaft of sunlight shone through the window to warm her fur.

I grabbed a curry comb and brush to clean off the night's dust and attacked Star's coat. Grooming him required standing on tiptoe for much of the process, but I didn't care. I loved every inch of his sixteen-hand frame.

Carefully combing out his silky black mane, I continued down his solid black neck and shoulders. When I got to the middle of his back, I started on his blanket, snowy white hide liberally sprinkled with black dots, each spot as familiar to me as my own freckles. When I first got him, I often traced a finger from spot to spot as if to complete a picture. It made me laugh when his hide twitched at my light touch.

"You know," I addressed Star, who swiveled an ear in my direction but didn't lift his head from the feed bin, "it isn't that Ben's so bad. I only call him Brat because it irritates him. It's just with this last growth spurt there's so much more of him and he's so...so..."

"Hot? Sharp? Cute?" I startled and the pitchfork dropped from my hand at the sound of Ben's voice.

"Hey! You *are* a brat. It's not polite to sneak up on people."

"What can I say? I have mad stealth skills."

He strolled into the stall. "Hey, sis, how're you doing after your epic fail yesterday?"

An indignant protest immediately formed in my mind, but before I could complain, Ben brushed by me to stroke Star's hip. "But you, you big dalmatian, snaps to you. You were lit. You're practically blowing up social media."

My resentment melted at Ben's sincere praise of Star. "He was pretty great, wasn't he?"

Ben draped his arms over Star's back facing me. Star's tail switched in my brother's direction, as if at an annoying fly, but otherwise his attention stayed on his feed.

It bugged me that my little brother could reach all the way over Star's back when I could barely reach my horse's midback. I regarded Ben's lanky frame with exasperated affection. His hair mirrored mine, but was always a thick tousled mess. A long thick lock usually hung down his forehead and into his eyes which drove me crazy. Otherwise, there was not a lot of resemblance between the two of us. His eyes were as golden brown as a cougar's instead of my hazel-green. We both had mom's pale skin, but in the summer, his turned a deep bronze because he spent so much time at the tide pools on the beach.

"Are you kidding? You were about to be up close and personal with the turf on that combination jump and he pulled you both out of it. What you need are my ninja-like reflexes." He chopped at the air enthusiastically. Star shifted impatiently under him. "But, like I said, epic save from what would have been an epic failure. You, I mean," he nodded his head toward me. Like I didn't get it.

Ben pushed away from Star's back and moved toward the hay rack. "So, you were saying when I walked in, I'm so…what? Intelligent? Charming?"

I bumped his shoulder as he passed. "I was saying you're so sneaky and gawky, you big twit."

"Nuh-uh." Ben defended hotly.

"Yuh-uh." I insisted.

"Nuh-uh."

"Yuh-uh for sure."

"Nuh-uh, and besides, if I'm going to join the CIA I have to learn how to sneak around and listen. It's part of my skill set. Confuse and conquer is my motto." He grinned at me, but his attempt to cross his arms and lean against the hay rack failed when he missed the rack and went down with flailing arms.

Laughter bubbled out of me. "Oh, and did I mention clumsy? The CIA is going to have to wait until you're done growing. You can't take two steps without tripping. You're taller than I which is so unfair. You're my *little* brother, remember?" I leaned over and brushed the messy lock of hair off his forehead. The scent of the baby shampoo he still used filtered through the barn smells.

"I wonder if they use baby shampoo in undercover work," I teased. "And your hair's way too long to be an agent. You'll have to get a buzz cut."

"Hey. I don't like change. Why change something that's working? But you're right; the CIA might not be my best opportunity. I've been looking into Clown College, too." He swatted at my hand and struggled to his feet.

I stopped raking straw and leaned on the pitchfork. "You're kidding. Clown College?"

"Yeah, sure. I think it'd be awesome. Or maybe I'll try basketball this year. I'm almost as tall as Dad, you know. And," he pulled his sleeve back to flex his bicep, "twice as strong. Or, check it out. I could publish a slang dictionary. Tawny could help me since she knows what everything means. And I do mean everything. It's like her very own foreign language."

I shrugged. "It's just her thing. She reads all the latest magazines that come into her mom's beauty shop."

"Yeah, well, it's hard to keep up with her. Unless you're that professor guy on X-Men and can read minds. Hey, that's what I can work on. Being a super hero."

Ben spread his arms in an ungainly attempt at a Superman pose and rushed from the stall, tripping as he went. "Catch you later." Faintly I heard his shout, "Check out Snapchat."

Star lifted his head from the hay rack to watch Ben's retreat, snorted and went back to his hay.

"My sentiments exactly," I agreed.

I finished cleaning the stall then began on my saddle and bridle. Star munched his hay; one ear cocked my direction. I used a soft brush on my bridle to get rid of dried sweat and replayed yesterday in my mind. It was so weird when I couldn't pin my number on my jacket. My fingers had gone numb, kind of like when we were competing, and looked sort of pale. And when I pricked myself with the pin it hadn't hurt. That was bizarre.

A quick all-over rub with a soft cloth on my saddle finished off the tack chore and I returned everything to the tack room. I attached a hose to the indoor faucet and warned over my shoulder, "You're next, big S. Time for a shower."

Star came willingly when I grabbed his halter and clipped on a lead rope. I knew he'd follow even without the rope, but I'd learned the hard way he could be dangerously startled by the unexpected. He'd almost run onto the road at the end of our long driveway before I caught him when a chicken exploded into life with a squawk right under his feet. I didn't take chances anymore.

Singing softly along with a Linda Ronstadt song playing in my ear, I jumped when I heard a throat clearing. "Hi, Sara."

I stepped back from washing Star and glanced toward the door. The man was someone I'd seen at the horse shows, press ID tangled on the camera strap around his neck. He reminded me of my Uncle Ray. Baggy khakis, soft knit polo of uncertain age covering what Uncle Ray called his tummy cushion. I could even see he had my uncle's slightly balding hair under his worn ball cap. His smile suggested he'd make a good mall store Santa Claus.

He held out a hand and stepped toward me. "I'm Bob Walters. I'm a reporter from the County Courier. I met your mom up at the house and she told me you'd be down here. Do you have time to talk? I'd like to get some background information on you and Star. I got an action shot yesterday and meant to talk to you, but after you fainted, I thought I'd better wait."

A story about me in the local newspaper? Interesting. I stepped around Star while wiping my hands on my jeans so I could shake the man's hand. "What kind of stuff do you want to know?"

"Mostly general information and I'd like to get some pictures."

"Sure. Want to sit?" I gestured toward a hay bale.

"That would be great."

We each chose a bale and sat facing each other. Bob

pulled out a handheld tape recorder and arched his eyebrows at me in question.

I nodded permission for him to record. This was actually kinda cool.

Bob clicked the recorder on and leaned slightly toward me, elbow propped on his knee. "First I'd like to know when this year's show season is over."

"We have one more show in mid-September then we'll be done."

"That means in a couple of weeks you'll know if your championship is just countywide or statewide?"

"Yes. Last year Star and I were county champions. I'm hoping this year we have enough points for the statewide title." I shrugged. "We'll see."

"I'll keep my fingers crossed for you. Now, if you could tell me your story with Star that would be great. Like, for instance, how long have you owned him?"

"Well, Dad bought Star for my twelfth birthday. But I've been riding him since I was eleven.

"Eleven?" He straightened and pushed his cap back off his forehead. "Weren't you pretty small to ride, well, you know." He nodded his head toward Star.

"Yeah. He's pretty big."

Bob let out a low whistle. "You think?"

I grinned, leaned forward and my hands helped me talk. "See, I started riding lessons when I was eleven and Star was one of the horses stabled at the ranch. Star's owner didn't have much time to ride and Star was getting kinda mean from being cooped up all the time. My teacher, Mr. King, told the owner that somebody should ride Star before he became uncontrollable. I always stopped to see Star 'cause I really liked him, and I happened to be there when Mr. King talked to the owner.

"The owner said, 'You mean somebody like this little girl?' in kind of a mean tone of voice and before Mr. King could say anything Star's owner asked me if I'd like to ride his horse. Of course, I said yes right away. Even though Mr. King wasn't happy about it, I kept pleading so they let me try. He's so big and I was so small," I added to explain Mr. King's reluctance.

The reporter laughed. "Makes total sense."

I beamed back at him. I liked this guy. "That's when I started riding Star. Pretty soon he liked me better than his owner and wouldn't let the man near him."

"And?"

"It got kinda ugly for a while because the owner yelled a lot and tried to make Star obey, but it just didn't work. The harder he tried the more stubborn Star got. The thing is, if you try to force him, he fights back. His owner just couldn't figure that out."

Bob interrupted me, "Let me get this straight. This other guy has a horse he can't ride plus he's been shown up by what he would call a slip of a girl—that right?"

I nodded. "Pretty much. When Dad offered to buy Star, his owner figured he might as well sell. Poor guy. Can you imagine how awful it would be not to be able to ride your own horse—or like maybe any horse?"

Bob looked up from fiddling with his recorder. "I've never ridden a horse."

My jaw dropped and my eyes widened. "That's awful. I'm sorry."

A faint smile tugged at his lips. "That's okay. There are other things I like to do. Let's get back on track. How long have you been showing Star?"

"This is my third year. Dad wouldn't let me start till I was fourteen." I glanced at my watch. "Is that enough? I have to get ready for school tomorrow." Dread stabbed my stomach. Back to reality.

"I have one more question and I'd like to get a few pictures. Then we can call it a day. Tell me about Star's name."

"You mean how did he get it?"

"Yes."

"His registered name is Shooting Star. Out of Star Dreamer and Supernova. I guess the pattern on his rump reminded his owner of shooting stars.

The reporter nodded and laughed. "Thanks. Now, a couple of shots of you and then we'll include Star. Okay?"

"Sure." I pushed off the hay bale. I knew people snapped photos of me during horse shows, but posing for pictures with a professional felt strange. I crossed my arms and tucked my hands under my elbows to stop fidgeting. Then that felt awkward so I reached up to try to straighten my messy ponytail.

"Auburn hair and green eyes run in the family?"

Bob's question distracted me. "Uh, yeah. Both my parents have reddish hair and some people say I look just like my grandma."

"So, she's pretty, too?"

An unladylike snort erupted from my nose. "I wish. No, she says we're passable but no prize winners. Are you trying to distract me?"

"Is it working?"

He snapped several pictures when I smiled at him.

"Can we include Star now? I assume he's not camera shy?"

"Are you kidding? He's the biggest ham I know."

The reporter snapped several pictures of me with Star then let his camera dangle against his chest. "Thanks, Sara. I appreciate you letting me interrupt your Sunday afternoon. Good luck at the last show."

Bob wandered out of the barn while I dried Star off and put him in his stall. I followed in the reporter's steps, pulling the barn door closed behind me. My feet shuffled in some dance steps to a Carole King song as I made my way to the house. Ben joined me partway up the walk.

"So, what was up with yesterday?"

"What do you mean?" I pulled my phone out of my

RIPTIDE

pocket and thumbed my music off. Then inspected the screen for messages.

"The whole fall thing. You've never done that before."

"I didn't fall," I snapped.

"Okay, okay," Ben held up his hands. "What was up with the slo-mo float to the ground? You've never done that either."

"Oh, I don't know. I just got dizzy for a sec. No biggie. Hey," I yanked on Ben's sleeve to stop him.

He had his own phone out by now but looked up. "S'up?"

Struggling to put aside the feeling I had when I heard Courtney talking about me, I finally asked, "You know how it was in grade school when you were the last person picked for a team? Like in PE or at recess or something?"

"Picked last?" Ben's voice sounded like the confusion on his face looked. "I literally have no idea what you're talking about. Hello?" He spread out his arms and gestured to indicate his height and strong build. "Moi? Always in the highest percentile on the growth chart, as tall as you when I got to 6th grade and now taller than you." His fist knocked gently on the side of my head. "Picked last? Not likely. Like ever. But I totally get that would suck rocks. Why? Who got picked last?"

"Oh, never mind. Only, sometimes I feel like that. Like I'm the last person someone would ever pick for a team."

"No way. You've got a wicked cool horse." Ben counted off items on his fingers. "You win all the time. You get good grades. Plus," Ben paused dramatically. "You've got the hunkiest little brother ever." He punched my shoulder and turned toward the back door. "Like that is a bogus feeling for reals. Ignore it," Ben advised. He continued into the house.

My gaze followed him. "Yeah. Ignore it. Good advice. Maybe I could if I was as confident as I pretend to be."

SUSAN M. THODE

Chapter 4

I wish people would just tell me how they feel because how they act confuses me.
Sara's Diary

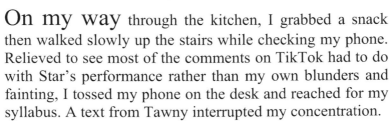

On my way through the kitchen, I grabbed a snack then walked slowly up the stairs while checking my phone. Relieved to see most of the comments on TikTok had to do with Star's performance rather than my own blunders and fainting, I tossed my phone on the desk and reached for my syllabus. A text from Tawny interrupted my concentration.

What's up, friencess?

Just finished cleaning barn. U?

Same except clean room. Come early tomorrow I have a new braid to try with your hair

K. CU

Having a best friend who planned on working in her Cuban-American mother's upscale spa and salon had its perks. Tawny liked nothing better than making me over whenever she got the chance. Fine by me since I was clueless about makeup and hair. And clothes and boys. I repositioned the giant clip I used to keep hair out of my face. I did a three-sixty of my bedroom. Pretty much crammed with trophies and ribbons. Not much time for boys with Star in the picture. Hopefully, that was changing.

I sank onto the desk chair and stared at a bright gold best in show rosette from last year. My fingers tapped a tuneless rhythm against the papers on my desk. The gold faded and Travis Baker's cocky smile seemed superimposed on the rosette. A shiver of a thrill tugged my lips into a smile when I remembered last week. How Travis made sure his shoulder and arm touched mine when we walked around town together. And in the coffee shop, he scooted up next to me so his leg and hip pressed against mine. He mentioned a picture he'd seen in our small-town newspaper of me on Star during a show. Apparently, it took being in the paper to be noticed by Travis Baker, but I wasn't complaining.

Tawny, the best person on the planet, had doubts about Travis. "He's too slick, or something," she complained a few weeks ago while we were hanging out.

A light knock interrupted my memories. Mom opened the door. "Getting ready for school tomorrow?"

"Yeah. Looking through my schedule." I glanced up at my mother whose rust-colored cords and pale-yellow shirt reflected the soft autumn colors outside. Her slightly graying hair used to match mine. We would never be mistaken for sisters, but I knew I looked like Mom. We could wear the same clothes, though we never did. Mom's pretty feminine.

I considered my mom. She's not beautiful like Tawny's, but she looks sort of nice somehow. I know she was a tomboy and hated her red hair just like me. If I looked more like Tawny and her mom, I'd probably be more popular. But I guess looking like Mom isn't bad either. Somebody has to be just ordinary nice-looking.

"How do you feel about your classes?" Mom brushed at the flour smudges on the front of her shirt. Twice a week she supplied a local deli with homemade bread and cinnamon rolls. Vanilla and cinnamon scents wafted after her wherever she went.

"I'm a little worried about chemistry. This could be one honors class I can't handle."

"Wait and see. It'll be worth it when it's time for you to pick a college. Honey, are you feeling all right?" A frown creased Mom's forehead.

"I'm okay. Guess I never quite got over that flu I had last month. I'm tired a lot and achy. No big deal, though."

"I'm worried about what happened to you yesterday. Maybe we should get you in to see Dr. Myer."

"I'll be really busy this week. I'd rather wait. We're learning a bunch of new cheers for the first game and I have that last horse show to get ready for in a few weeks. If I win all-around-champion I'll get $300. Then I'll almost have enough for that new show saddle I want. I'll make an appointment pretty soon, I promise."

Mom hesitated then sighed. "I guess so. But if you don't start feeling better, I want you to go see him, busy or not."

Studying my syllabus I mumbled, "Uh-huh."

The next morning, I met Tawny early in the parking lot at the high school. As planned, Tawny expertly braided my hair into two reverse braids caught up together at the base of my neck and finished into one fat braid. She gave the end of the braid a satisfied tug. "That's solid killer," my friend congratulated herself.

We entered the front doors where Travis's cocky smile greeted me. I skimmed Tawny's palm as thanks and waved. Travis claimed my other hand and we merged into the sea of bodies.

Travis shadowed me all week. The usual sequence involving guys with Travis in the halls was as follows; fist bump with a shoulder bump and, "S'up?" or "Trav, my man." Every once-in-a-while I'd get an uncertain chin lift and an awkward glance.

I spent a lot of time staring off into space, staring at the books propped in my grasp and my bottom lip was sore from biting it so often.

The girls were a totally different scenario. They moved in packs and clustered around Travis as if I was invisible. It was like Trav was a good luck charm they all had to touch. Or stroke. Alyssa seemed the most determined to catch his eye and ignore me. Typically, the girls looked me up and down without a word until they walked away chattering like a flock of sparrows at our birdfeeder at home.

I wondered why Travis never introduced or included me when we maneuvered through the halls and cafeteria, but figured this must be accepted cool behavior. What did I know?

It was Friday after school before I had finally had time to ride Star to the beach. After a good run, I dismounted onto the warm sand and leaned back to watch the clouds.

"See any UFOs up there?"

I had to shade my eyes when I looked up. Kevin Richards stood by Star. He's so cute, I thought looking at Kevin's sun-streaked dark hair and chocolate-brown eyes. Why does he have to be so boring?

Kevin easily fit in with the Greenies, as they were known at school. Kids who were good in science, the Greenies were college-bound students interested in climate change and the environment. Kevin was lean and fit and I knew he was strong. He helped me pile hay bales one Saturday, tirelessly tossing the bales to the top of the stack for me to position. Easy on the eyes when he got sweaty and peeled off his t-shirt, too.

Kevin, his mother and little brother had moved next door to a five-acre farm when I was ten. When Kevin's father died, Mrs. Richards had moved back to her hometown to be near friends and family. She started her own essential oil business, growing many of her own herbs, and both boys helped her. Kevin often smelled like his mother's products. Today I detected a trace of lemon and patchouli.

"Hi, Kev." I settled back down in the sand. "What do you think of your schedule? Going to stay on the honor roll?"

"Hope so. The honors classes are getting harder though, for sure. May give up band. Hey, nice job at the horse show last weekend." He stroked Star's shoulder then sat next to me.

"Thanks. Star makes it pretty easy even when I mess up. Did you catch any of the posts?"

"Yeah. The one video I saw wasn't clear."

A few silent minutes went by before Kevin asked, "Sara, are you avoiding me?"

I froze and swallowed hard. "Don't be stupid, Kev. Why would I avoid you?"

"I thought it might have something to do with Travis Baker." Kevin looked out at the waves while he sifted sand through his fingers.

I sat up and glared at him. "What do you know about Travis Baker?"

"Just that you seem to be hanging out with him tons lately."

"So? I hang with a lot of people." I tossed my hair back. I'd give anything if I could spend all my time with Travis. Would he choose me over Alyssa? What did he see in Alyssa? Please choose me, my mind begged.

"Yeah, well, he doesn't seem to be the kind of person you'd be interested in is all."

"Why not? Travis is fun. He's a lot more fun..." I bit my lip and trailed off.

"Than me?" Kevin finished. "That's pretty much what I figured. Guess I know where I stand." He got up, brushed the sand from his jeans and turned to go.

"Wait, Kev. I didn't mean..." My voice sounded lame even to me.

Kevin kicked at a rock in his way. The back of his neck flushed deep red and his body looked as rigid as Grandpa's starched shirt collars.

"Darn!" Standing up, I brushed sand off my jeans, gathered the reins and mounted Star from a nearby log. "I guess it had to happen, but it feels weird. C'mon Star, I've got cheerleading practice."

While I searched for my favorite sweats, I thought about Kevin. In the seven years I'd known him, I'd never seen him lose his temper. Until today. It had taken me hanging out with Travis to do it. The idea produced a small smile.

Last spring Kevin had walked with me around the county fair after a horse show. Partway through the afternoon he had taken my hand in his and we continued meandering around the rides and exhibits. I liked it. It was nice. But it didn't mean I belonged to him or anything. I figured he knew that now. He had to understand he was firmly in the friend category.

Except, every once in a while, I couldn't help but compare the two. Travis and Kevin. Like, completely different. One of the few times I'd been with Travis, he drank half my latte and scarfed half my scone without asking. So annoying. The times Kevin and I hung out, he always offered me some of whatever he had. Travis walked ahead of me through doorways and hopped into his car while he waited for me to get in the passenger side. Kevin always reached ahead of me to open doors and walked by my side. So why did Travis excite me while Kevin left me cold?

A glance at the clock reminded me how late I was. I zipped up a turquoise hoodie and cinched up light gray sweats, the school colors, and clattered down the stairs.

It was so nice out I rode my bike the mile into town, feeling uneasy, hoping I hadn't hurt Kevin's feelings. He had always been easy to talk to, even about youth group and church. I could tell him about my frustrations and how attending didn't mean anything anymore. He didn't agree with me, but he listened. I wasn't sure what I believed. Was all I'd been taught about God my whole life true? Kevin seemed shocked when I told him I figured I was safe because Mom and Dad are both Christians.

Parking in a bike rack, I waved to the other cheerleaders already on the football field. But when I walked over to join them, my heart pounded and I sucked in air.

"Whew." How come I was puffing? I sank down on a bench to catch my breath.

Tawny plopped down beside me. "What's up? Why are you so winded?"

"I don't know. You'd think I get enough exercise riding and taking care of Star. I just don't have much energy anymore." I checked Tawny's fingernails. "Hey, you've still got your Star nails on! And I like the new do."

I couldn't help but admire Tawny's hair. Vibrant tones of copper, teal and rich deep amethyst tinted my friend's long dark brunette tresses. A thick reverse braid began at her forehead and gathered most of the hair at the crown of her head then continued straight back and down her head to her neckline where the hair loosened and hung in relaxed waves. The dazzling colors looked incredible against Tawny's latte-toned skin. "I'm pretty sure in the spice rack of people, you're the jalapeno."

"So true, my observant friend, so true. And gracias. Mom and I worked on the color together." Tawny spread her fingers and regarded the white background with black dots decorating her nails like Star's back. "Yep. This is one of my fave designs. C'mon, we've got to hurry and get warmed up. We're ready to start working on our new stuff."

We walked toward the other girls until Courtney planted herself in my way. "Where have you been? We're all waiting."

I stiffened. No way did I have to answer to Courtney. "Not that it's any of your business, but I went for a ride when I got home. Took longer than I meant to. You don't have to wait. I'm warmed up from my bike ride. I just need to stretch."

Courtney turned on her heel and stalked toward the other girls. "We can start now that we're *all* here."

We chatted as we stretched. More than one glance strayed in the direction of the practicing football team.

"Are we going to start or not? I have to get home and get ready for a date." Alyssa sounded grouchy.

My quick side glance became an eye roll. What else is new? Alyssa always sounded grouchy. Transferred from a school in Los Angeles, she never let us forget how lame our school was and how cool her old school had been.

We began to work on the steps of the new cheer. My part included a double back flip ending in splits. After several failed attempts to complete the movement, Alyssa blew up.

"What's the matter with you? If you can't do your part, let somebody who *can* do it take over. Somebody who's actually been a cheerleader before."

"Geez, Alyssa. Judgmental much?" Tawny rushed to my defense. "Sara has always done the flips better than the rest of us even though this is her first year on cheer."

Alyssa crossed her arms. "She's not doing so great today. I say anybody could do it better than she's doing it now."

"I can do it," I shot back. Our glares held for several seconds. "I'm just having trouble with my balance is all." I backed up, took a short run and began the cartwheel that would turn into the first back flip. My arms collapsed. I literally had zero strength. I fell on my head twisting my neck something fierce. I landed on my side and curled into a fetal position from the pain.

The girls gathered around and through a fog of pain I

heard a shrill scream.

Chapter 5

One of Ben's old Dr. Seuss books says, "Why fit in when you were born to stand out?" I really just want to fit in. Really.
Sara's Diary

"What's going on here? Let me through." To my ears it sounded like Coach Shay mumbled through a mouthful of cotton. And, just to make my day even better, Travis followed close behind the football coach.

Coach knelt next to me and smoothed the hair away from my face. "What happened?" He gently examined my arms and legs for broken bones.

"For real? We don't know, Coach," Tawny answered. "We were practicing a new cheer for tonight's game and Sara just fell. Is she okay?"

The coach's thick compact body blocked out the sun when he leaned over to gently check the back of my head. For blood, I guess. I tried to lift my head to tell him I was okay, but even that effort caused a sharp stab of pain. From the sounds of shuffling feet and excited murmurs, I guessed a crowd had gathered. Great. Vultures to the carrion. Oh, how I wished they would disappear. I'd had enough of being a social media sensation. So much for fitting in. I seemed to excel at sticking out. Like a sore thumb.

The coach ignored Tawny. "Travis, go find Mr. Hamilton," he barked. "He should be in the equipment room. Get some blankets and bring them back here fast." While the coach issued orders, he jabbed 9-1-1 into his phone and explained the situation. He added the school's location then returned his phone to his pocket.

Then, blessedly, he ordered, "The rest of you go back to what you were doing. You stay," he directed the cheerleading squad.

He turned back to me. "Tell me where it hurts."

I didn't have enough breath to respond. It had exploded out of my lungs when I hit the ground. I touched a hand to my head then carefully down to my shoulder. It really hurt.

Coach glanced at the circle of girls. "If any of you have coats, bring them here, will you? We'll cover her with your coats until Travis brings the blankets. Now, somebody tell me everything that happened before I got here. Natania, how about you?"

Tawny's explanation and Travis's return with the blankets seemed dream-like as my focus faded in and out. Coach tucked blankets over the coats. He was careful not to jostle my head or neck. "Thanks, Travis. Go on back to practice now." After a quick curious glance at me, Travis gave a chin-lifted nod to the cheerleading squad and jogged off.

Coach hitched himself from two knees to one and rested an elbow on his upper knee. "Did you feel sick at all today?"

My head shake was a total mistake. I winced from the pain and switched to a hoarse whisper. "No. I've been fine. A little tired."

"She hasn't been feeling good for a long time," Alyssa volunteered. "Always complaining about headaches and stuff."

Before the coach could follow up on this report, I rasped, "But I was fine today." I frowned at the mouthy cheerleader.

"Sara," Coach Shay caught my gaze with his own. "I've known you a long time and you know you can level with me. Have you tried experimenting with drugs?"

Alyssa answered for me with a hostile laugh. "You've got to be kidding. Sara the saint use drugs? Like no way, Coach. She's just too, too good."

Coach didn't even glance at her. When he prompted me with a, "Well?" I answered, "No, Coach. I don't use drugs."

A med-aide van screamed onto the ball field. Coach Shay stood and waved his hat at the driver. The ambulance was still moving when the medical team jumped to the ground. Two of the techs organized a stretcher, gurney and other equipment while the third knelt by my side. His name tag read Jordan. He repeated the coach's questions.

I followed the path of his finger with my eyes when he asked me to and then told him how many fingers he held up. He took my pulse and blood pressure, carefully searched for obvious breaks then explained, "We're going to place you in a clam shell support to make sure your back and neck are supported while we move you onto the gurney. Can't be too careful," he added. His smile reassured me. "Cross your arms over your chest like this," the tech gently arranged my arms, "then let us take care of lifting you. Don't try to help us, okay?"

I nodded and two of the techs lifted me while a third carefully slipped what felt like a huge oblong Frisbee under my back and shoulders. Instantly I felt the pain in my neck and shoulder ease. This must be what a butterfly feels like in a cocoon, I figured. The odd contraption cradled and supported me better than our hammock at home. Jordan smiled. "And that's what we call being happy as a clam."

Through all this the cheerleaders murmured among themselves. All but Tawny who hovered just in back of the med tech. I couldn't make out what the girls said even when I strained my ears, but could easily imagine the stories they'd tell.

I couldn't physically fidget, but my thoughts and embarrassment recycled like they were on a treadmill. How could this be happening again? Why me? And why in front of the group where I so desperately wanted to belong? I didn't need to see to recognize Alyssa's strident voice suddenly carry over the others. "Some people will do anything for attention."

My eyes rolled in exasperation. Courtney and Alyssa are definitely clones. I imagined busy thumbs at their cells' keyboards.

Before I could react to Alyssa's taunt, the techs heaved the gurney into the ambulance. Another tech, Layla, according to her nametag, climbed in beside me to lock the stretcher down. She quickly ripped open a sterile package and before I could protest had a needle in my arm and hooked up to an IV. Layla fastened the plastic IV bag through a ring on the wall of the ambulance and banged her hand on the window dividing the cab from the back. The ambulance took off for the emergency room. No sirens, thank goodness.

At the hospital the med tech team raced to remove me from the ambulance. Before I could ask what was going to happen, I heard Dad's voice. "Hey, wait! That's our daughter." Then my parents' anxious faces loomed over me.

Jordan held his hand up as soon as Dad's mouth opened. "Just let us get her settled and then we'll talk. I need your daughter's permission to fill you in anyway. This will just take a moment. It would help if you use your time to fill out some paperwork."

"Stupid privacy law," Dad muttered.

"Now, Jim," Mom's voice chided. My parents sounded so normal; I relaxed.

Transferred to a bed, clamshell removed, a support collar around my neck, and the release of information signed, I listened to Layla and the ER nurse exchange information while Dad asked questions.

"We don't know, sir," one or the other would answer. Mom tried to get Dad to sit down. He paced, running his hand through his hair then finished the gesture by rubbing his neck.

A doctor replaced the med tech and explained the tests they wanted to do to rule out injuries. Mostly x-rays, but since I'd lost strength so suddenly and fainted at the horse show, they'd do a blood scan as well.

"Why don't you wait down the hall and someone will come and get you when we bring Sara back," the doctor suggested.

Mom kissed my forehead and smoothed the hair off my forehead while Dad tweaked my big toe. "See you in a bit, kiddo."

Swallowing nervousness, I summoned a smile and waved at my parents. I wished I was ten again and could ask Mom to stay.

An hour later with the tests complete, we waited in the curtained cubicle for the doctor who would explain the results of the tests. One doctor had already translated the x-rays for us. There were no broken bones or skull fractures. Only a goose egg on my head where I hit the ground and bruised muscles and tendons from wrenching my shoulder when I fell, which explained the pain. An ice pack to the shoulder and a shot of painkiller left me feeling slightly sleepy, but also with a curious sense of well-being. Kind of floaty.

Startled by the rustle of the curtain, I looked up and saw a new doctor. My parents got up to greet him when he introduced himself.

"I'm Dr. Adams. Hello, Sara. Mr. and Mrs. Mitchell." He shook hands with them both. "Sara, I'd like to talk to your parents for a moment if that's all right with you?"

"Sure. Whatever." I summoned my inner princess and dismissed them with a slight wave. Before the doctor turned, I caught the look on his face. His eyebrows frowned together; his forehead wrinkled. He turned and motioned my parents around the curtain. I blinked a few times and cocked my head with a frown. Maybe there was something to worry about?

The shadows of my parents and the doctor against the pale cream of the curtain was like watching a pantomime. I used my knees to prop up my arms and leaned forward. Chin cradled on my fist, my attention sharpened and I sat straight up when mom froze in place; Dad shifted from foot to foot and periodically ran his hand through his hair. The doctor used his hands to talk, gesturing with the test results to emphasize what he was saying.

What *was* he saying anyway? Lowering myself carefully back against the pillow, I stared at the curtain. The shadow showed Mom's hand lifted to her mouth and Dad's shadow stopped shifting. Postures straight as power poles, they leaned toward the doctor. In spite of the painkiller, my attention sharpened in response and I strained to hear the doctor.

"...tests.... serious problem indicated...need more...bone marrow...admitted right away...so sorry."

The floating feeling evaporated by what I heard—and didn't hear—I called, "Mom? Dad? Could you come here?"

Mom pulled the curtain aside and leaned through the opening. "Yes, honey?"

"Uh, could you come and talk where I can hear? I'd like to know what's going on." Mom glanced at the two men. The doctor shadow nodded and the three adults returned to my cubicle.

"Good idea, Sara. I was just about to ask your parents

for some history on you. You can help with that." Was his voice artificially hearty? Yep. For sure.

"But…wait. What were you just saying out there?"

"We can go into that later. Right now, if you could all help give me an idea of Sara's health the last several months, it would be helpful." The doctor raised the clipboard and looked from me to my parents expectantly.

"Shall we go first, Sara?" Mom asked. Fighting the drug-haze of contentment I nodded.

"She's been a bit under the weather off and on for about four months," Dad volunteered.

"She has an appointment with our doctor for a physical next week," Mom interrupted. "We were starting to worry. Especially after the horse show."

"What exactly has been wrong?" the doctor asked.

"Well," Dad glanced at mom for help. "Mostly unrelated things. She's had lots of colds this summer. Headaches."

Mom added, "And she's always tired. Sometimes she'll have a low-grade fever even after her cold symptoms are cleared up. She's been complaining about aches and pains." Mom glanced at Dad. "We thought those were probably growing pains. But she fainted over the weekend and she's never done that."

"Have you noticed whether she bruises easily?" The doctor's pen paused.

"No, but with this chilly fall weather her arms and legs are covered all the time. Does she have a lot of bruises?"

Had they completely forgotten about me? "Hello—can I say something?" I waved a hand to get their attention.

The three adults turned and stared.

"I've had a lot of colds because I'm in training or practicing at the fairgrounds all day with germy people. I'm in the glare of the sun most of the day so I have headaches sometimes. And knocking around the barn and lugging feed and tack isn't that easy, you know. I get bruised." I shrugged and winced when the strained shoulder complained. "It's what I do."

The doctor regarded me thoughtfully for a moment. "What about fainting at the horse show? What about what happened this afternoon?" He motioned toward the neck of the hospital gown, "May I?"

I nodded.

Dr. Adams loosened the tie and pulled the gown slightly away from my neck. He pointed his pen at the base of my neck and off to either side in a circular motion. "What about this? And this?" The pen moved up and repeated the circular motion around my cheeks.

"It's just a rash. Or maybe sunburn." I grabbed the neck of the gown and pulled it close again. "Isn't it?"

"That's possible, but we need to make sure it isn't an indication of something more serious. Anything you can add to what your parents have said? Anything strike you as unusual about how you've been feeling?"

"Uh...like what?" I stalled.

"Anything different."

"Like tingling in my fingers? Or blurry vision sometimes?"

The doctor nodded. "Have you experienced those things? Recently?"

"Yeah. At the horse show."

"When you fainted?"

"Well, yeah." I looked up at him, glanced at my parents then fiddled with the plastic bracelet around my wrist. "And..."

"And?" the doctor prompted.

"It sorta happened during the last round of our competition."

Mom's hand went to her mouth again as if to stop an exclamation but Dad voiced it for her anyway.

"What? You mean what happened today has happened before? Do you know how dangerous that is? Why didn't you tell us?"

"It didn't happen that much and mostly I forgot about it after it went away." I looked up at him. "I'm okay, Dad, really I am." My gaze shifted to the doctor. "Tell him."

"That's what we have to find out. These tests indicate some abnormalities. I'd like to admit you to the hospital and do some additional tests tomorrow. If you'll all excuse me, I'll go begin the admittance process."

"But I'll miss tonight's practice game." My protest was automatic. "It will be our first time trying out our cheers in front of an audience." I appealed to Dad. "I really feel okay now, Dad. Can't I go home?"

"Sorry, honey. If the doctor thinks you should stay, you have to stay. We need to get this nailed down so we know what's going on before you get any further along in school. There'll be other games."

"Not as important as this one. I'm fine," I protested again. "I really need to go to the game."

"So's your health, Sara. What's important about this game?"

"Nothing you'd understand," I mumbled under my breath.

"Sara!" Mom scolded. "Don't be rude to your father. Tell us why this game is such a big deal."

My fingers twisted the blanket. "Travis asked me to meet him after it's over. We were going to go get something to eat."

A loud silence filled the room. "Sara, you know how we feel about Travis Baker. We'd rather you didn't go out with him."

"I know, Dad, but it's so unfair. Travis is one of the most awesome guys in school and I really like him. I don't understand why you're so prejudiced. You've always said as a Christian I shouldn't judge anybody. Well, aren't you judging Travis? You haven't even met him." I couldn't control my shrill voice so I clenched my jaw instead.

My parents exchanged troubled glances. "We're just trying to protect you," Mom rationalized. "We've heard things about Travis that make us wonder if he's a good friend for you. Kelci's mother told me what he did to her in the lunchroom—teasing her about her weight and calling her names. Even filling a tray with food and putting it in front of her. He sounds cruel. Do you want to be friends with somebody like that?"

"Oh, Mom. That was no big deal. He was just joking around. Everybody laughed. It was funny."

"It wasn't funny to Kelci. She didn't want to go back to school. What happened to Kevin? Seems like you've been avoiding him."

"Oh, Kevin. He's so boring. Everybody at school laughs at him because he's so serious." My throat felt thick with unshed tears. "Do you know what the kids at school call me? They call me 'Sara the Saint' because I never do anything interesting. I'm the only one who can't go out on school nights and has to be in by midnight on the weekends. Now that Travis asked me out everybody's starting to talk to me and want to be around me. I want to ask him to go to the Turnabout with me. Please don't make my going out with him such big drama. At least meet him before you say no. Please? I'm seventeen now—I don't need you to protect me anymore. I should be able to make my own decisions."

Dad frowned. "All right. We'll meet him and talk to him, but that's all I'll promise. I don't know about the Turnabout thing—what is that?"

"It's where the girls ask the guys to a dance. It's not formal, just kind of dressy and the PTA supplies the refreshments. I could ask Travis and he could pick me up early so you have time to meet him. Okay?"

Dad glanced at Mom. I could tell he wondered if they had judged Travis unfairly. Score one for me for remembering part of a sermon about judging. But I have to admit Dad usually tried hard to be fair.

"What do you think, Shannon?"

Mom nodded. "I'd like a chance to talk to him so yes, I think it's a good plan."

"All right, we'll meet Travis before this dance thing, but your curfew stays the same. And you do have to spend the night here and follow the doctor's order."

Yes! I fist-pumped in my mind. "Tawny can tell Travis I can't come to the game."

"I'll call her," Mom promised. "Need anything else?"

"Could I have my phone charger so I can listen to music? And maybe my Kindle?"

"I'm sure that'll be all right. I'll bring them to you before dinner."

"Thanks, Mom. I'm sorry I yelled. I just get so tired of being different and not being able to do the stuff most of the other girls do."

"When you know you're doing the right thing, different isn't so bad. I think you'll find that out."

Wisely, for a change, I didn't answer.

"We'd better go now, honey. I'll come back with your things in an hour or so. Do you think you can rest?"

"Probably. I'm pretty sleepy. See you later. Don't forget to call Tawny," I reminded.

Chapter 6

It makes sense that if popular people like me, I'll be popular, too. That makes total sense. Doesn't it?
Sara's Diary

Clicking through all the channels on the TV did nothing to relieve my boredom. Nothing but sappy afternoon soaps and mindless game shows. I clicked the TV off. And what was with the thin backless nightgown? Pretty sketchy if you ask me. And the socks with weird white polka-dot nonskid bottoms kept catching against the sheet and untucking it. Monotony and irritation pretty much summed up the hospital stay. Boredom lifted the instant I heard a noise and looked up to see Travis poke his head through the open doorway.

"Hey, Sara. Heard you were at death's door and needed a dose of the master." He spread all ten fingers against his chest. "So, I stopped by."

"Hi, Travis. Sorry I missed the game last night. Did we win?"

"Did we win, she asks. Of course, we won. I wanted to, so we did."

"Just like that?"

Travis snapped his fingers. "Just like that. My old man taught me to go after what I want. He says if you don't watch out for yourself, who will? You have to go after what you want or you go without. 'Course the quarterback on the other team might not agree. He has a little problem with his leg. I'm afraid he's going to miss the rest of the season." Travis shook his head in mock sympathy.

"What did you do?"

"Now why would you assume I did anything?"

Travis's innocent expression didn't fool me. "Come on. What happened during the game? How did he get hurt?"

"Oh," Travis inspected his fingernails and moved over to perch by me on the bed. "He was a little clumsy. Tripped over my leg." He looked up from his nails with a slitty-eyed smile. The look reminded me of Abby's eyes when she had a barn rat in her sights. "He would've been okay except I sort of lost my balance and fell on him. Unfortunately, his leg was twisted underneath him at the time. Breaks of the game, I guess. Now, what's up with you?"

He leaned forward, rested against my legs and grasped my hand. I caught a whiff of his aftershave. Oh seriously, what was he wearing? It smelled yummy. I caught myself from leaning closer to take a deep breath.

I started to tell him what happened when movement caught my eye. Shoot. Mom stood in the doorway; arms folded across her chest. The expression on her face was not happy. If Mom's super power was telekinesis, Travis would be across the room in a chair. I didn't need telepathy to know why she was upset.

Travis sat on the bed, but pretty well in my lap. My hand rested in his while his thumb stroked my knuckles. Dressed in frayed jeans and a white t-shirt under a deep blue hoodie and mirror sunglasses perched on his head, he could have been posing for a magazine cover.

It didn't take a genius to recognize disapproval and I snatched my hand out of Travis's. I forced my voice to be casual. "Hi, Mom. I didn't expect you until tonight."

Travis jumped up and turned to face the door. He read Mom's emotions as easily as reading a book. Lips drawn together in a frown, eyes slightly narrowed, Mom's body had tightened into watchful stillness. When I imagined looking through her eyes, I knew why she was upset.

Travis is a tall, good-looking guy and knows it. He oozes charm. If Kevin is a candidate for the Greenies, Travis could easily be mistaken for one of the singers in a boy band. Light sandy-blonde hair worn mostly short until midway up his head, then long enough to fall forward over his eyes. It was messy on purpose. Blue eyes. Sharp and dangerous like an eagle's. His dimpled smile gives him a little boy look, but doesn't quite disguise conceit. There's nothing 'little boy' about his charm and confidence.

My body stilled and became rigid under the sheet. I knew what mom's description would be, and knew I had another battle on my hands if I wanted to keep going out with Travis. And I did. Cheerleading and Travis are key pieces of the cool camouflage I'm trying to wear so I'll at least appear cool. If I can't actually be cool or lit or dope or whatever the latest word is, at least I can try to look the part. Cool camo. My secret weapon.

Travis stepped forward and stretched his hand toward Mom. "Hello, Mrs. Mitchell. I'm glad I finally have a chance to meet you. I've been trying to cheer Sara up by telling her about the game last night. We killed 'em." He turned and smirked at me.

"Hello, Travis. It's nice to meet you, too. Would you mind if I talk to Sara alone for a minute?"

"No prob." Arrogance curved his lips. "I need to get going anyway." He turned to me. "Text me, 'kay?"

"Sure. Thanks for coming."

"'Bye, Mrs. Mitchell. Nice to meet you." Behind Mom's back Travis grinned, struck a pose with both thumbs up then left the room.

Mom perched at the end of the bed. My gaze met her steady scrutiny for a moment then dropped. My hands twisted the sheet around my sweaty fingers.

"You two seem to be pretty good friends."

"He was only holding my hand to be friendly, Mom. It didn't mean anything."

"I see." Mom excelled at 20-20 parent vision and my shoulders drooped. "He must not take touching very seriously then. Is that what you mean?"

"No, Mom." I kept my eyes from rolling, but did it inwardly. "You don't understand. He was just showing me he's concerned. It's not everybody who has to stay in the hospital, you know."

Mom pressed her lips together. "I wanted to talk to you about that, honey. You might have to stay a while longer. The doctor wants to run more tests to find out exactly why you're having problems."

"Sure, Mom. No problem." Finally, I'd have Travis's undivided attention. No other girls around, not much interference from my parents. Maybe I'd even figure out why he'd taken an interest in me. I'm no dummy. I know I'm not his normal type. Maybe this hospital stay could really change things up for me.

Now that Travis had shown up, it had become an acceptable mixture of boredom and fun. I had my own pitcher of ice water, a TV in my room and all the pop or juice I could drink just by ringing the buzzer for a nurse. The blood tests didn't worry me. I'd had them before for school physicals. The nurse pricked the end of a finger, squeezed out a few drops of blood and…done. No sweat. True, the doctor seemed worried and that left me feeling a bit uneasy, but when I weighed the unease with the prospect of visits from Travis? No contest.

"How long do you think I'll be here?"

"I'm not sure. A day or two then maybe a few more visits later."

"Okay. Think Ben can take care of Star for me?"

"I'm sure your brother will be happy to feed Star for you. He'll probably want to bargain for rides in exchange for work though."

"Yeah. Guess it's only fair to let him ride a little bit. Poor Star." Evidently, the sympathy I felt showed on my face.

"Sara!"

"Mom," I defended, "you know Star doesn't like anybody but me to ride him. Though it will be good for him," I conceded. "We have that big horse show coming up so he'll need his exercise. I want to make sure he's ready for that show with all the prize money at stake. Do you remember the saddle I want? Black with silver trim? Star will look super. Tell Ben he can ride once a day for an hour. Think that'll satisfy him?"

"I'm sure he'll be thrilled to death. You practically tear his head off if he so much as talks to Star," Mom answered.

I grinned. "I know. I guess I don't want to take the chance Star would start to like somebody else as much as he likes me."

"I don't think you have to worry about that, honey. When you're around, nobody else exists for that horse." Mom smiled.

"I know." The inner knot of stress in my chest loosened at the thought of Star. "He's pretty special, isn't he?"

I glanced at the clock on the wall. "When do they want to start this test stuff?"

"Right now," said a lab technician pushing the room door open. He wheeled in a cart. "I'm going to make like Dracula and help myself to your blood. His vampire accent made me giggle until I caught sight of the needle and glass vials he arranged on the cart. My eyes widened and I grasped the sheet to my chest. Like the sheet could protect me? This definitely wasn't anything like the tests I'd had before.

Hoping mom would tell the guy he had the wrong room I sneaked a peek in her direction. "Mom?"

"It'll be okay, Sara." Mom took my hand and turned to the technician. "Will it be all right if I stay?"

"Sure. For now. But there's a procedure we'll do after I finish here where she'll need to be in a sterile room. Sara, tell me your favorite thing in the world to do."

While he talked, he cinched some rubber tubing tightly around my arm above the elbow. He gently tapped the inside of my elbow then grabbed a syringe. I eyed the big needle aimed at my arm. The chatter meant to distract became an annoying background hum.

~ ~ ~ ~ ~ ~ ~ ~ ~ ~

Later that night I wrapped my arms around Dad like he was a life ring and my bed was an ocean. My head ached from sobbing. My hip throbbed like someone had punched a hole in the bone. Oh wait. Someone *had* punched a hole in my hip bone.

Dad sat on the edge of my bed ignoring the tear and snot stains down the front of his shirt. His hand stroked my hair. His cheek rested against my head while he kept up a low soothing litany in my ear. "That's right, honey. Go ahead and cry. I'm here; I'll take care of you. It's all right, Sara, I'm here."

I let go of him with one hand to reach for more tissues. Crumpled Kleenex littered the bed so it resembled a float in the homecoming parade. When I looked up, Dad lifted a couple sweaty locks of hair off my cheek and tucked them behind my ear.

"They gave you something for pain, Gingersnap. It should kick in any time now. Can we get you anything?"

Mom gathered up the used tissues then returned to her vigil at Dad's side.

"Oh, Dad," I whimpered. "It hurt so bad. Please don't let them do that again. Promise me."

"I can't promise you that. They have to check your bone marrow to see if it's healthy. I know it hurts but there's no other way to do it. If I could make the pain go away I would, honey, but I just can't," Dad said helplessly. His kind face, usually so quick to smile, looked pale and worried.

"But Dad, you don't understand. They put a needle through my bone to get out the marrow. I can't go through that again." Dad hugged me when I started crying again. Gradually, though, the pain med kicked in and I relaxed against him.

Mom's voice came from across the room. "How can we put her through this, Jim?"

I heard and felt the rumble in his chest when he answered. "What will we do, Shannon? What will we do if Sara has leukemia?" His voice broke.

"I might have leukemia?" I stiffened against Dad, suddenly wide awake.

Mom rushed to the bed and engulfed me in a parent sandwich. "We don't know. It's just one of the things they're looking at. Let's all do our best to stay calm and not worry about it unless it's true. Agreed?"

Dad nodded and tightened his grip. I stammered agreement.

Leukemia? Maybe not being cool wasn't the worst thing in the world after all.

Chapter 7

In fairy tales the reader always knows something important the princess doesn't. What do I need to know?
Sara's Diary

"Sara? Are you all right?" Mom asked.

"Hmmm?" My finger pressed on the crumbs scattered on the table from breakfast and placed them in a neat pile. I'd been home from the hospital for a week. Mostly I felt numb and it was hard to focus.

"I asked if you're all right?"

I looked up from the fascination of the crumbs. Worry creased Mom's forehead.

"I'm fine."

Mom's anxious gaze watched me fiddle with the tidbits on the table. Putting down the dish towel, she walked over to the table and sat down.

"Do you remember when you were little and something would go wrong? You'd come in crying..."

"...and you would hug me and say, 'tell Mommy what it is, Sara. Tell Mommy what it is.' And I would tell you what it was and you would make everything right again."

My brief smile must have encouraged Mom. "I know

you're older now and we don't always agree, but you do know you can always tell me what's bothering you, don't you?"

"Yeah. I know. I'm just kinda tired. Don't worry about me."

Mom sighed and went back to the dishes. She was almost done when there was a knock on the back door. "Get that, will you? My hands are wet."

I pushed up from the table like I had weights on my back, slouched to the door and opened it.

"Oh. Hi, Kev."

"Hey. I heard you were sick and it must be true because you sound like you have zero energy. How are you?" Kevin's clear brown eyes looked concerned.

"I'm fine. Just tired." A spicy scent teased my nose. "Mmmm—is that vanilla and what?" I drew in a deep breath. "Orange? Smells good. Is that what your mom's blending today?"

Kevin blushed while he brushed at his clothes like he could stroke the scent away. "She's trying a new mix for fall and I was helping her. Sorry. My bad. Should have changed my clothes."

"No, it smells great. I like it."

"Are you too tired to go for a short walk?"

I hesitated. "No, I guess not. Mom? I'm going for a walk with Kevin. Be back in a while."

Mom came out of the kitchen wiping her hands. "Hi, Kevin. It's nice to see you." Her face beamed with pleasure.

I smothered a groan.

"Where have you been? We haven't seen you for a while." Mom sat down in a nearby chair.

Kevin glanced at me. "Oh, I've been pretty busy with school and stuff. I'm doing some extra credit for biology-- keeps me down on the beach a lot."

"I see. Well, come by anytime for a visit. We miss you, don't we, Sara?"

My gaze fixated on the floor. "Yeah, sure. Can we go now, Mom?"

"All right. Don't overdo it though."

"Don't fuss, Mom. I won't."

"Bye, Mrs. Mitchell."

"Good-bye, Kevin. Remember what I said."

I pushed the kitchen door open. My footsteps veered automatically toward the barn and corral.

"So, do you have mono or something?" Kevin asked.

"Or something. They're not sure what it is. I was in the hospital for a few days while they took tests. Tomorrow we find out the big verdict."

We got to the pasture gate and leaned over the top rail. Star heard our voices and trotted up.

Kevin commented, "I still think he's completely classic. He's so big and sort of, I don't know, interested in things."

I tipped my head and glanced at Kevin in surprise. Star's curiosity about everything had sometimes gotten him into trouble. How did Kevin sense that about my horse? He must've paid attention the times he'd been around. A warm feeling of appreciation spread through my chest.

Star greeted me by gently lipping the hair brushing my shoulder. I reached up and hugged him, enjoying the sun-kissed horsy smell of his mane.

Kevin reached over to stroke Star's muscular neck. "Hi, guy. Remember me? I cheered for you at the horse show."

Again, to my surprise, Star turned his head and nudged Kev's arm in a friendly hello. Usually, my horse was tolerant but a little standoffish with people. I pulled an apple out of my pocket and offered it to the big Appaloosa. He crunched and slobbered with obvious enjoyment. My mouth stretched into a smile.

Watching me, Kevin burst out, "Sara, when you smile it's, I don't know, it's..." his voice trailed off and he tried again. "It's like, well, you know, you're not really beautiful..."

I stiffened. "Well, thanks a lot. I totally needed to hear that. As if."

"No! That is, what I mean is..." Kevin blew out a breath and looked to the sky then at his shoes. "It's like, when you smile you sort of light up all over and you really *are* beautiful." His voice faded.

My jaw literally dropped. I could not believe quiet Kevin Richards actually said I'm beautiful.

A car screeched to a stop behind us. Travis called, "Hey, Sara! What's up? Is that your horse? Kinda big for you, isn't he?" He jumped out of his car and sauntered up to us. "Oh, hey, Kev. Didn't know you'd be here. What's happening?" Travis slid his arm across my shoulders.

The possessive movement wasn't lost on Kevin. He grimaced, looked away and gave Star a final pat. "Not much, Travis. I was just leaving. See ya, Sara, hope you feel better." He turned toward the path that led to the beach and his house.

Travis smirked. "Killer Kevin. What was he doing here? What was that I smelled? What a dweeb. You don't hang around with sissies like that, do you? Do you know he even goes to Sunday school and church? How lame can you get?"

Since Kevin and I went to the same church, I actually could imagine. I sidestepped the question. "No, really?" Then I changed the subject. "What are you doing here, Travis?"

His arm tightened around my shoulders. "I came to see you, of course. And meet this wonder horse you keep talking about. Hi, big fella!" Travis slapped Star on the shoulder. Star snorted, rolled his eyes and jerked back from the fence.

"Not very friendly, is he? C'mon boy, come back here!" Travis clapped his hands.

The sound spooked my horse. He shook his head, turned and trotted away.

"Don't, Travis! You're spooking him," I protested.

"What? A big horse like that? C'mon, don't tell me he's a sissy too."

"He's not a sissy. No horse likes a loud clapping noise."

"Okay, okay, didn't mean to upset you. I wanted to get a selfie with him is all. I can do it later. How about if you show me the barn?"

"All right. But there's not much in there, it's just a barn."

"You've got hay in there, don't you?" Travis grinned.

My heart did an unfamiliar shiver. What was that? What was I missing? "Well, sure. Straw, too."

He laughed, dimples flashing. "Well, come on. What're we waiting for?"

We walked toward the barn. Travis slipped his arm around my shoulder again and pulled me against his side. Oh, that aftershave. Not vanilla, that was for sure.

I opened the big sliding door and flicked the light switch. The barn was only four stalls with a small tack room and hay storage at one end. I walked over to the biggest stall. "This is Star's. He's usually only in here at night, though. He'd rather be outside."

Travis moved in front of me, slipped his arms around my waist and tugged me close. "Well, I'd rather be inside with you." He lowered his head and kissed me. He used enough force that his teeth clacked into mine and I involuntarily ducked back.

It may sound unlikely, but I have been kissed before. So far, they'd been quick nervous kisses at the end of a couple dates. Never like Travis just kissed me. It seemed a little rough and I wondered if that's how it was supposed to be. He gripped my waist again to pull me against him. "C'mon, Sara. You can do better than that."

My eyebrows frowned in concentration. What did that mean? What was I supposed to do? The groan of frustration that started up my throat didn't make it past my clenched teeth. I didn't have a clue. He'd never stick around if I didn't up my game. The girls he normally hung out with had tons more experience at this than I did. I chewed at my lip and glanced up at him.

He grinned. "Shy, huh? That works for me." He reached down, drew my arms up around his neck and kissed me again. I did better this time. Releasing my lips, he looked down and said, "Smile for me, Sara. You have a sexy smile, you know that?"

Unlike the comfortable warmth I experienced when Kevin commented on my smile, nerves shimmered throughout my body. It startled me. At the same time, I liked it. Still, was I ready for this? I didn't even know if he really liked me. Or why. But if I didn't keep going, would he leave?

That thought did it. I smiled and raised my gaze to his. He laughed softly and lowered his head toward me. His lips had barely touched mine when I heard mom calling.

"Sara? Saarraa--bring Kevin in, I've made you hot chocolate."

Frantically, I pushed Travis away and put my hands to my cheeks to cool their flaming heat. "Oh no! It's my mom. We better get out of here!"

Travis caught my arm. "Chillax." He spoke softly in my ear. "Don't hurry or she'll know something's up. Ease up and walk to the door."

I gulped in air and blew it out then side-stepped away from Travis just as the door opened.

"Hi, Mrs. Mitchell. Kevin had to leave, but I'll make sure his hot chocolate doesn't go to waste if that's okay with you."

Mom looked from Travis's smile to my blushing face and frowned. "Travis. When did you get here? Sara, where did Kevin go?"

"He had to go home." I ducked my gaze to avoid Mom's sharp scrutiny.

"I think it's time for Travis to go, too."

Travis smirked. "Sure thing. I've got stuff to do anyway. Later, Sara. 'Bye, Mrs. M." Whistling, he left the barn and drove off.

"Sara? What was Travis doing here? Why did Kevin leave? You weren't rude to him, were you?"

Nudging past Mom I muttered, "Oh, Mom, just stay out of it. You don't understand anything." Guilt chased me into the house.

I reached the sanctuary of my room and flopped onto the bed. Kevin's shy but genuine compliment made me feel good. The sincerity of it warmed me even now. Travis's glinting blue eyes and confident smile broke into my thoughts. My pulse pounded and confusion returned. I puzzled over my different reactions to each boy. They had both complimented me though Travis exuded charm and confidence. It was almost like he rehearsed and polished what he said and did. Did that mean Kevin was more authentic? When I was around Kevin, I felt safe. That is not the word I'd use to describe Travis. Defiance egged me on. "I don't care," I declared to my room. "He likes me and I'm going to have some fun for a change. I can handle him."

Chapter 8

Is it possible to drown from holding in too many tears?
Sara's Diary

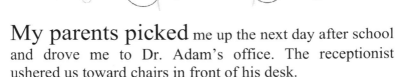

My parents picked me up the next day after school and drove me to Dr. Adam's office. The receptionist ushered us toward chairs in front of his desk.

"Sara, with the results of our tests we've been able to find out why you haven't been feeling well. We're almost certain you have a chronic, sometimes disabling autoimmune disease called 'systemic lupus erythematosus', or SLE as it's known." The doctor paused.

My heel bounced against the floor. I imagined an eye roll emoji. Big deal. Sounds like terminal bad breath.

Doctor Adams cleared his throat and continued. "This is a disease of your immune system. In your case, it resembles the effects of leukemia. Most likely when you get dizzy or feel faint, it's due to anemia or possibly respiratory problems. We'll do more tests to fine tune our diagnosis."

Whoa! My eyes stretched wide open. I glanced sideways at Mom first, then Dad. I know about leukemia. People die from that. I hard-swallowed against the lump in my throat.

The doctor continued to explain the disease and I understood at last this isn't a joke. My eyes blinked and I rubbed my hands up and down my thighs. The fabric quickly warmed my palms. I snuck a peek at Dad and caught the shine of tears in his eyes before he glanced down at his tightly clasped hands.

Mom reached over to still my restless leg bouncing. Immediately I felt like I had to move or I was going to explode. I grasped the arms of my chair and pushed myself up off the seat.

"Ah, can I…I think I need to go to the restroom."

"Of course, Sara. Right through the door over there." The doctor's voice sounded kind.

Once in the restroom, I held a paper towel under the cold water then wiped my forehead and neck. The water gurgled down the drain while I peered at my reflection in the mirror. My cheeks looked awfully red. What was that anyway? I leaned forward and studied the rouge-like blush of my cheeks. There was a faint butterfly pattern and I remembered the doctor talking about that in the ER. I traced the outline of butterfly wings and remembered feeling superior to the girls who always had their compacts out adding blush to help them look healthy.

"I didn't have a clue," I whispered to the healthy-looking Sara in the mirror.

The drone of the doctor's voice wasn't super clear through the slightly open door, and every so often an announcement over the PA blotted out all other sound, but I was pretty sure I heard most of what the doctor said. I turned the faucet off and thought I heard, "I'm sorry to have to tell you there is no cure for lupus, but there is medication Sara will take to help control the symptoms of the disease." I strained to hear the rest while a plea for housekeeping to report to the ER rang out over the PA.

Did he just say there was no cure? Had I heard

correctly? I willed the PA to silence so I could be sure. Dad asked a question, but I didn't hear it or the answer. I moved over to the crack in the door.

"What do you mean no cure?" Dad sounded angry, but I figured it was more accurately freaked out.

"I mean," the doctor explained gently, "this can be a life-threatening chronic illness. I should say it depends on how lupus affects Sara because SLE is different in every patient. It can be fatal, but it's unlikely with good care."

I gripped the doorknob. Wait. Life-threatening? Fatal? That came through loud and clear. Does that mean I'm going to die from this, this, whatever it is? My mouth dried up and my stomach fluttered. The doorknob felt slick under my hand. Was I really going to die? I moved my ear directly in line with the small space in the doorway.

"We can't let Sara know." That was Mom. Dad agreed. Wait. What? They weren't going to tell me what was going on? That can't be right. How could they do that? I pressed in closer to the door. The doctor said several things I couldn't quite hear. Something about the nature of the illness, my age and ethics of disclosure. Whatever that was.

Nature of my illness. If Mom and Dad didn't want to tell me what it was, then for sure I was probably going to die. They persisted in protecting me to ridiculous degrees. Like I couldn't Google this and find out all about it? What were they thinking? How did other kids get their parents to let them grow up?

The silence in the other room spoke loudly and I knew I had to leave the sanctuary of my safe place. Doctor Adams smiled at me when I sat down. I'm pretty sure he sees a child even though I'm seventeen. He continued talking before I could make sense of my jumbled thoughts to ask questions. He described the medication I would start taking and warned until they got the correct dose the medication itself could make me feel sick. There was a pill for that, too. He handed me a couple of slips of paper and arranged another appointment for two weeks away.

"We need to continue monitoring the course of the disease," he explained. "We'll examine you every two weeks for three months then cut it down to once a month. One of the things we'll track is your bone marrow and other blood samples."

I couldn't help it. My eyes flooded with tears and my body tensed at the mention of bone marrow tests. Dad radar guided him to reach out and unerringly grab my hand. His tight grip helped center me.

The doctor's voice droned on. "You've already experienced a few of the symptoms of lupus, and you may develop others. This particular disease attacks the body in a variety of ways so there are many things we have to watch for."

"Will I always feel sick? Until I, ah, I mean, will I always feel sick?" Can brains develop static? It felt like I couldn't get my mind clear enough to think.

"No. Many SLE patients go into remission. If that happens, you'll feel normal with few to no symptoms. But while it's encouraging to be in remission, it's important to remember remission doesn't mean cured. SLE is a chronic illness so there is no cure. Many things can trigger a new phase of lupus, but chronic isn't the end of the world," he assured me.

For who? I wondered. Sounds like the end of my world. I stared unseeing at the doctor while my brain scrambled to make sense of what I'd heard. It didn't help that my mind raced with fear. The doctor kept talking. Blah, blah, blah. Would he ever shut up? Then one sentence sharpened with crystal clarity.

"You're too young to worry about this now, but childbearing sometimes has an adverse effect on lupus patients. It would be best to avoid pregnancy. We'll address that when we need to…" He murmured on.

"I'm not listening," I wanted to shriek. My brain would explode if I had to hear any more. My mind finally cataloged what I thought I'd heard so far. I was going to die and maybe pretty soon. This disease was going to kill me. And not only was it going to kill me, I was going to feel rotten until it did. And I couldn't have kids. Who would want to marry me if I couldn't have kids? If I even lived long enough to get married. Did I want to get married? I didn't even know. An overwhelming sense of loss caused my body to sag into the chair. Could I ride? Would I have to give up Star? If I had to give up Star, I might as well be dead.

My mind reeled with assumptions that solidified into fact. The black pinprick thoughts of a few days ago suddenly merged and became a suffocating blanket. And now I knew for sure Kevin was wrong. There was no way God could care about me if He'd let something like this happen to me. Bitterness soured my mouth. And my parents? My parents didn't even want me to know? What was even up with that?

I blinked when Doctor Adams pushed back his chair and stood. "That's it for now. I'll see you again in two weeks, Sara."

We could have been in a silent movie for all the conversation there was on the way home. I went straight to my room, changed into jeans and hurried out to the barn. Not bothering with the saddle, I used a handy stump to leap onto Star's bare back. We were hardly out of sight of the barn when I urged him into a headlong gallop toward the beach. Right now, I needed a big dose of Star medicine.

His powerful strides carried me easily and quickly. I concentrated on Star's strength and speed, letting him transport me away from reality. By the time I noticed his labored breathing my cheeks were numb and my eyes blurred with tears from the cold wind. I immediately pulled him down to a walk and let him amble until his breathing slowed. Then I picked a sheltered spot between some rocks on the beach and slipped from his back, dropping the reins. I stumbled when my feet hit the ground so I let myself drop onto the sand. The weight of the news I'd just received flooded over me and I broke into sobs.

Star stood over me, a comfortable looming presence, and nudged my back or lipped at my hair every so often. The storm of crying finally died away and I laid back, knees up, arm over my eyes, hiccoughing in shuddering breaths of air. Star's feet shifted uneasily and I knew he could read my distress loud and clear.

"Sara?"

My head jerked up. I glanced around and groaned. Great. Just great. Kevin. He peered at me from a perch on one of the rocks I sheltered behind.

"Are you okay? Did you fall?"

"No, I didn't fall!" I wiped at the tears on my cheeks with the back of my hand. Seriously? Like I needed someone witnessing my ugly cry and raccoon eyes. I licked a finger and rubbed under my eyes.

"Is there anything I can do?"

"No. Yes. You can leave me alone."

"I mean, is there anything I can do to help?"

"No. There's nothing anyone can do."

He jumped down from the rock and walked over to me. He held out a hand toward Star's nose then ran his hand down Star's neck. Sitting not far from me, he crossed his legs and rested his arms across his knees.

I straightened up, sucked in a big breath and blew it out while I brushed at the sand on my sleeves and legs. Every fiber of my being wanted to jump on Star's back and race away. Instead, I fake-coughed. "What're you doing out here?"

He shrugged. "I'm doing an extra credit report on marine life for biology. These rocks are a good place to find tide pools." He fell silent and we both stared out at the waves endlessly washing the beach.

"No riptide today," I offered. I sifted sand through my fingers while I kept my gaze firmly on the gently breaking waves.

"Nope. Not the right time of day. Later on, when the tide goes out maybe."

"Did you get the riptide lecture from your mom?"

Kevin snorted. "Only almost every day." He settled further into the sand, leaned back against the rock then asked. "What're you doing out here?"

I stalled. Sighed. Gave up. "I just got back from the doctor's office. He had the results of the tests."

Kevin waited.

My gaze took in the water. Then the sky. Then my tightly clasped hands. Then the words burst out like from a broken dam. "I'm going to die, Kevin. I have something called lupus and I'm going to die."

I started to cry and Kevin shifted forward, gently grasped my shoulders and drew me toward him. I collapsed into him, turned my face into his shoulder and clutched the front of his jacket. He didn't say anything. He didn't need to. He simply stayed close, holding me while I cried as if my heart would break.

Chapter 9

Kevin says I shouldn't cross bridges until I get to them. Easy to say when your bridges aren't on fire beneath you.
Sara's Diary

"Here," Kevin held out some tissues. "They're crumbly from my pocket, but clean."

Nodding my thanks, I sat back from Kevin and turned my head to wipe my eyes and blow my nose. Star snorted and jerked his head when I blew my nose. Kevin and I both laughed at Star's head jerk and wide-eyed surprise at the weird noise.

"Never thought I'd find anything to laugh about today. Good old Star." I stuffed the used tissue into my pocket and leaned back, hands propped onto the sand behind me.

Some people might be uncomfortable at a tall horse towering over them, but Kevin just looked up at Star with a smile on his face. "He must be a pretty good friend for you."

"My best friend," I vowed.

Kevin stared quietly at the waves. The wind tousled his hair into an attractive mess. And those eyelashes.

Wasted on a boy. Tawny would pay big bucks for those lashes. "Sara, are you sure the doctor said you're going to die?"

"I heard him tell my parents lupus is life threatening. What else could that mean?"

"I don't know. Maybe you should talk to them about it and make sure."

"I don't need to. I'm going to die and my parents are going to lie to me and not tell me anything. And they preach to me about being truthful. Ha!" Kevin looked surprised and I wondered if I should dial down the scorn.

"So how long do you have to live?"

"Not sure. Sounds like the medicine will keep me going for a while."

"So that means you're not going to die right away."

"I don't know. Does it matter? The stupid disease is going to kill me."

"Or you might get hit by a bus tomorrow and die that way."

"Well, gee, Kev. You're loads of comfort. You'll be wasted as a biologist. You should definitely consider counseling as a career." Sarcasm soured my tone and matched my mood. Hopefully it would render him nonverbal.

Kevin's neck flushed a dull red, but he stayed stubbornly on point. "What I mean is we're all going to die sometime. Usually none of us know how or when. You know something that might kill you at some point, but you're really not that different from anybody else. Doesn't seem to me like this makes much difference."

For the record, I honestly tried to stay cool. But, really? My news didn't make much difference? That's crazy. "I don't believe this. Didn't you hear anything I said? I have a fatal disease, I have to take tons of medicine that's going to make me feel even more sick, my parents are lying to me. No difference," I snorted. "That's a good one."

Evidently, my sarcasm hit hard because Kevin's posture stiffened defensively. Eyes narrowed; his hands gestured with some kind of angry sign language. "So why are you so freaked out about dying anyway? You're going to Heaven, after all. Right? You *are* going to Heaven, aren't you Saint Sara?"

My scuffed boots suddenly became intensely interesting and I studied them carefully.

"Sara?"

I leaned forward and grabbed some sand to toss back and forth between my hands. My concentration shifted to my sand game. "Well, sure. Of course. I go to church most of the time and I try to be good. I even pray every day. Well. Most days. I ask God to help me and stuff."

Kevin crossed his arms and smirked. "That is so not what makes you go to Heaven."

Anger flushed through my body and my heart pounded. "Who's asking you? Just. Knock. It. Off. What are you? Some kind of religious fanatic or something?" I continued in a singsong voice, mocking him. "Haven't seen you in church lately, Sara...I can pick you up for youth group, Sara...don't forget how much God loves you, Sara. You know what? If God is as pushy and preachy as you, I don't even want to know him."

I gulped in air and tried to calm down. "I'm sorry, Kev, but I'm tired of it. You and my parents just keep at me about what I believe and what I should do. I don't know what I believe and church is boring. God's not real to me and church isn't helping me know him any better. It's just a bunch of rules. And I really, truly do not get how you all can keep saying how much God loves me when I have this creepy illness that's going to kill me. He loves me so much he let me get this stupid disease. Seriously? If that's love, you can have it. There's no way I matter much to God if this is happening to me."

Kevin shifted in the sand and leaned toward me. "Don't you remember in youth group when we studied about bad things happening to good people?"

The burst of anger left me exhausted and I slumped, shrugged my shoulders and sighed. "Kinda."

Kevin groaned.

"What? I don't remember everything the pastor said, okay? He talks like a lot."

"It was the time he told us about how much God loves us."

"Hello—you're not listening. If God loves me so much then how come I'm sick?"

"Because people get sick in this world. And they have problems. God didn't say everything would be perfect. He just said if we belong to him, he'll take care of us no matter what happens. It's kinda like your horse shows with Star. If you tried to do all those events, like jumping those fences, by yourself you'd never get anywhere. You need Star to get anywhere in a horse show. Well, God is the Star of your whole life. You need him to get you through all this stuff. Even the lupus thing."

I thrust my open palm in his face. "I don't want to hear it. I don't know what I believe. I just know I have no idea if I really matter to God or...or to anybody."

I jumped to my feet. "What I believe is none of your business, Kevin Richards. And I'm pretty sure you shouldn't be comparing God to a horse." Anger rushed back and made my voice shrill. "Thanks for the tissue," I yelled while I led Star to a rock and mounted, "but you can keep your sermon." I dug my heels into Star and we cantered away.

Later that week at the dinner table, I picked at the pot roast and vegetables on my plate. My parents kept exchanging worried glances, but didn't say anything. When my cell phone vibrated, I pulled it out of my pocket to check the screen. I looked up at Dad. "It's Mrs. Hughes.

Can I answer it?"

He nodded. "Since it's job-related." Usually, my parents are pretty strict about the no cell phones during dinner rule.

Pushing back my chair, I thumbed the little green phone symbol and walked into the living room. "Hello? Oh, hi, Mrs. Hughes."

"Hi, Sara. Do you have a minute to talk?"

"Sure. Do you need me to babysit an extra night this week?"

"No. I actually, well, the truth is I'm worried about what happened the other night and think maybe it's better if you don't babysit for us until you feel better."

"Oh, I'm sure I'll be okay. I just need to learn to time when I take my medication better. I'm sure it won't happen…"

"Sara," Mrs. Hughes interrupted. "I'm really not comfortable using you as a sitter right now. It will work better for us to find someone else until your health improves. I hope you understand."

"Oh. Well, sure. That's okay. I understand."

"We've been happy with you until now. This situation just makes us nervous. No hard feelings?"

"Sure, Mrs. Hughes. That's okay. No hard feelings."

"Thank you, Sara. Bye now."

"Bye." I stared at my phone. Sure, no hard feelings, Mrs. Hughes, I mocked under my breath as I jammed my phone back into my pocket. I stared out the window while my fingers twisted at the ring on my little finger. My hands had swollen so much the ring pinched my flesh.

"Sara? Everything okay?" Dad called from the kitchen.

I swiveled back toward dinner and slumped onto my chair. "It was just Mrs. Hughes wanting to talk about babysitting. She called to tell me she's sorry, but they want to hire another sitter. Guess it made her nervous that I was asleep when they got home last night. She had trouble waking me up."

Mom's forehead furrowed sympathetically. "Oh, honey. I'm sorry."

"It's okay, Mom. What's one more thing wrong with my life? Mrs. Hughes isn't the only one who doesn't appreciate my falling asleep. My algebra teacher had to shake me awake in class the last two days. I've only been taking my medicine a little over a week and not only is my face breaking out, my hands and feet swelling, but I had to stop cheerleading, I'm gaining weight and falling asleep a half hour after I take the stupid pills. And now my best babysitting job is gone. What else can go wrong?" I knew my tone was lemon-bitter, but I didn't care.

I soon discovered what else could go wrong the next afternoon during my after-school ride. Star veered toward our favorite route along the beach, and I let him go. The rhythmic rumble of the ocean never failed to soothe and it did its job. Unfamiliar relaxation felt great, until suddenly it didn't. Serenity jolted into fright when the numbness and tingling in my hands returned with a vengeance. The tingling stung and I remembered Dr. Adams explaining it was called Raynaud's Syndrome and was part of the SLE. I looked at my hands and my chest tightened in fear. All my fingers were white. White and numb. I could see I was holding the reins, but couldn't feel the leather between my fingers. How could my hands feel numb and throb at the same time? I didn't want the reins to slip out of my hands so I fumbled them into a knot.

No sooner had I tied the loop than the strands of leather blurred into shapeless brown. Frantically I blinked my eyes to focus. Nothing. The world around me appeared like a blurred watercolor. Then nausea hit my stomach. The world spun around me. I clamped my eyes shut to control the sensation, but that made it worse because then it felt like I was spinning myself. I swayed on Star's back. Queasiness slammed my stomach and I tasted bile on the back of my tongue. I slid off Star's back in a controlled fall. Instantly he stopped.

Slumped in the sand, I wrapped my arms around Star's front leg and gradually tried to stand. Every time I moved, the vertigo increased until I finally collapsed to my hands and knees. Between dry heaves I gulped in air and tried to calm growing panic. Star nudged my back and I sensed him shift his weight toward me. I carefully cracked my eyes open and saw Star had his head down, his mane right in reach in front of me. Would it work? I had to try.

Slowly, and I do mean like the world's most relaxed snail, I eased myself to a kneeling position with my knees braced apart for balance. I rubbed my hands together to force circulation back into my fingers and blew into my cupped hands to warm them. When I could see a faint pink tinge and could flex them a bit, I wrapped my hands in Star's mane and held on for dear life. Star raised his head and I closed my eyes at the stab of nausea when he pulled me to my feet. I leaned against him, renewed my grip on his mane, fought the nausea and vertigo and nudged him down the path toward home.

Halfway dragged and mostly stumbling alongside Star, we made it to within sight of the barn. Ben's irritated voice called my name and then abruptly he came into view. A few more steps and he turned toward Star's movement.

"Sara, Mom wants to know where you've been. What are you even doing? How come you're not riding? Why is Star walking so slow?"

The barrage of questions was the final straw. I let go of Star's mane and crumpled like a torn kite.

"Hey! Are you all right?" The concern in his voice triggered tears and, for a change, I was relieved when he skidded to a stop beside me and knelt down.

"I need help...can you get me in the house and take care of Star?"

"Well, yeah. I mean, sure. Here." His arms closed

around me and he lifted me like I was a baby. Gratefully, I leaned against his shoulder and closed my eyes.

"Hey," I mumbled into his shoulder, "you really are strong."

"Don't sound so surprised." I could hear the grin in his voice. "Told you."

We reached the back door which Ben kicked a few times while he called, "Mom! Mom? Come and get the door. Hurry!"

Chapter 10

*It doesn't matter which direction I choose because I
don't know where I'm going.*
Sara's Diary

Mom's face drained to the color of my fingers
when she came to the door. "Sara? Ben—what in the
world—what are you two—what happened?"

Ben interrupted. "Mom, open the door and move out
of the way, please. I'm strong, but I have to put her down."

Mom opened the screen door and backed up to make
room. "Take her into the living room and put her on the
couch." She closed the door and hurried after us.

The couch felt great after sand and hard ground. I
curled up on my side and pressed my palms over my eyes.
"Ben? Don't forget Star."

"Aye, aye, captain." The screen door slammed and he
clomped down the back porch stairs.

Mom sat by me on the couch. Her gentle touch
smoothed my ponytail off my neck and rubbed my back.

"What happened? Are you hurt? Should I call the
doctor?" She tugged my hands away from my face.

I jerked my arm away and shifted back from her. "Go

away." Angry sobs punctuated my demand.

She persisted. "Sara. What happened?"

"Just go away, Mom. I don't want to talk about it."

"If you're hurt, I want to know. What happened?" Her soft touch returned to my shoulder.

After several deep shuddering breaths, I turned on my back and stared at the ceiling. "Do you remember when I started riding lessons?"

"How could I forget? We almost had to peel you off the ceiling you were so excited."

"And remember when Mr. King told you I was naturally talented and you might want to consider having me train for the junior Olympics?"

"Yes, I remember. We were proud, but didn't want to push you into anything."

"Then I found Star." My voice quivered. I couldn't continue.

"You found Shooting Star," Mom took up the story, "and you came home with stars in your eyes. You looked like a queen whenever you rode and your father and I knew there was no way we could separate you two. You were made for each other." She ended the story with that simple truth. Then paused. "What happened today?"

Gulp-talking around my tears I burst out, "I can't ride him anymore. I fell off. My hands and feet went numb and I couldn't feel what I was doing. Then I got so dizzy I couldn't get back on. And I felt so sick. This can't be right. I have to stop taking those pills, Mom. I'd rather die than have to stop riding Star."

"Sara, don't even think that," Mom scolded. "You don't know what you're saying."

"I do. And I mean it. With all the lousy things happening to me, Star is the only good thing in my life. If I can't ride him, I don't want to be alive. You don't understand, riding Star is the only time my life feels okay. Everywhere else I have to watch what I say and what I do. I feel like if I don't always do everything just right, I'll turn the corner and be in this dark place. It's just there…waiting. Except when I'm riding. That's the only time I feel safe."

Through eyes swimming with tears, I glanced up at Mom. "Have you ever felt like you're right at the edge of just losing it?"

Mom continued smoothing the hair back from my tear-stained face. "What are you talking about? A dark place? And lose what? You'll never lose important things like your family, your home, your faith. Those things are a foundation for your life. Just rest a bit. I'm sure you'll feel better soon."

My breathing was almost normal when she spoke again. "I'll call the doctor and explain what's happening. We'll see if one of the medications is causing the numbness and if it can be decreased a little. Remember he said there would be a few problems until he got the right dose. It's not forever, Sara. Things will get better." She briefly cupped my cheek then left the room to call the doctor.

I stared at the ceiling. "I wish I could believe you, Mom. I really wish I could."

After a few minutes the worst of the dizziness passed and I could focus again. I slid my phone out of my pocket to check messages. Just as I pressed the home button, my cell chimed the opening chords to Taylor Swift's, *Shake It Off*. Tawny. Even though it was an old song, Tawny made it her mantra.

WU?

Typing quickly, I answered Tawny's "what's up" with a list of my current woes then slowly backspaced. I had to decide how much to tell my friend. Did I really want to tell her what was up? As far as I knew, Tawny was my best friend and had been since grade school. But so had Courtney. And Tawny really liked to talk. I didn't want my SLE diagnosis getting around school. It felt embarrassing. I decided to wait.

Not much. U?

Epic boredom. Can I come over?

Please! Best offer in a long time

That's sad. Be there in a flash.

Pushing up from the couch, I tested my balance. Whatever the problem had been, it had passed so I walked upstairs checking my phone. I stopped to splash some cold water on my face and press a cold washcloth to my eyes for a few minutes to get rid of the red, then headed to my room. It wasn't long before I heard Tawny tease Ben then she pounded up the stairs and into my room.

"Hey! What is up with you? I haven't seen you around at all and even at school you're hard to catch. What gives? Does this have anything to do with the fainting thing? That was so awkward." Tawny slipped off her shoes and hurled herself on the bed next to me. Her sudden weight caused us to bounce against each other.

Laughing, I rolled back to the side of the bed. "I don't know. Just been busy I guess."

"Busy with what?" Tawny nudged me with her toe. "Not Travis Baker is it? It is mad cool that your parents said you can invite him to the Turnabout. Ask him yet?"

"Yeah, a few days ago."

"For real? What'd he say? What is up with you anyway? You've turned into a clam or something. We used to talk every day and suddenly you're GWOP or something."

"GWOP?" I frowned in confusion. More slang I didn't know?

"Yeah. Gone Without Permission. Isn't that an Army thing or something?"

"That's AWOL—Absent Without Official Leave—you twit."

Tawny snorted and hugged a pillow to her chest. "Whatevs. Means the same thing. The point is you're never around anymore. Are you mad at me about something?"

"No," I assured her. "I've just had a lot going on." I decided to tell Tawny at least a little bit of what was going on. "Remember after I fainted and had to go to the hospital? The doctor did a bunch of tests and I have to take pills. They make me feel crummy."

"For real? That's so wrong. You're only in high school. Only old people have to take pills and stuff." Tawny lay flat on her back with a pillow hugged to her chest. "Travis has been telling everybody how he came to visit you at the hospital to make sure you were all right. That's crazy romantic. Maybe he's good boyfriend material after all."

"What do you mean, after all? Did you think he wouldn't be good boyfriend material?"

"Seriously, you have got to get more in tune. He's pretty much done all the things."

"What does that mean?"

"I literally don't know how you can be so clueless. Are you telling me you didn't know he's a catch-and-release kind of guy?" Tawny grabbed a lock of hair and examined it for split ends.

"Catch-and-release? You mean like in fishing? You know I don't keep up with how everybody talks."

Tawny's gaze rolled toward the ceiling. She groaned. "I've like become your own personal Google," she complained. "It's so hard to talk to you. It's like…it's like…well, you know how we're always bugging my dad to get rid of his old flip phone and get a smartphone?"

"Yeah. He loves that old phone. So?"

"Your vocabulary needs some serious software upgrades."

"Are you saying I'm a dumb phone?" I swallowed a giggle while she struggled to keep a straight face.

"Exactly." Tawny shrugged. "You are the flip phone of language."

Tawny struggled to a cross-legged position and pulled me around by my shoulders to face her. She leaned toward me with a serious expression. "Catch-and-release means he's into the chase, but once he's caught what he wants he drops the relationship. Classic player. Though he is seriously hot."

"Caught what he wants? What does he want?"

"Hello? What planet do you live on?" Tawny knocked her fist gently against my head. "Oh, I forgot, you live in Star world. You know, if you spent as much time with people as you do riding your horse, you'd know what we're talking about. It means he's trying to hook up with as many girls as possible. Sometimes a few at a time. He has the personality of a bulldozer. Slime," she added as commentary.

"Hook up? What happened to hang out?"

Tawny took my hands in hers. "Honestly. You're so cute. Hanging out is what our parents would have called dating. Hooking up is what they would have called going all the way."

My mouth literally dropped open. "But...but...that's...eeeewww."

"I know. Right? Disgusting. I was going to talk to you about it, but, hello, you've disappeared. Anyway, maybe he's changing. Maybe you're his BAE. What'd he say when you asked him to the Turnabout?"

"Wait. BAE. Is that good?" Slang truly is a foreign language for me.

"Duh. Before anyone else? That's fire. The closest he's come to making somebody his BAE was when he did a slow fade with Alyssa. Which is why she's such a troll with you all the time, by the way. She thought she had him locked in."

"Slow fade? Boy, I wish you would talk English."

"He broke it off gradually instead of just letting her know he was moving on. She caught him with Angie and found out that way. It was mad intense. The sad thing is I think she was really into him. Travis doesn't stick long with anybody. Like, ever." Tawny gathered her hair into a long ponytail and began to braid it behind one ear. "Girl, I hate when it's horse show season. You are just so out of it. What happened when you asked him? C'mon, give."

"The day after I asked him, I found a carnation in my locker with a note. One side of the flower was dyed turquoise and the other side was silver. The note said, 'You and me.' I guess that means yes?" I looked at my friend for confirmation.

"That. Is. Hot. Maybe you really are his BAE. I've never heard of him giving anybody else a flower. What are you going to wear? I'm wearing the most awesome silver dress. Can I do your hair? Please, please let me do your nails, too. You have to let me do your nails to match your shoes. You should wear teal. We would totally kill it."

We happily discussed dresses, shoes and whether we should tan or not—Tawny, yes; me, no—before the dance. But I didn't forget about what Tawny told me about Travis. Was it true? I tucked it away to think about later.

Chapter 11

Sometimes lies are told by staying quiet.
Sara's Diary

In the doctor's office the next day, I discovered one of the medications had to be increased not decreased.

"The numbness is due to poor circulation. That's the Raynaud's we talked about. The blood isn't reaching your hands and feet so they get cold and go numb. I'll increase the dose of this medication," he held up a peach-colored pill, "and we'll see what happens. It'll take a week or so to notice much change. Don't get discouraged. We'll figure this out."

"Okay, Dr. Adams. Thank you." Even I knew my voice sounded dull. More medicine, not less. I joined my father in the waiting room.

"All set?"

"Yeah, Dad. He increased one of my meds and said that should help. He said I'll notice..." My voice trailed off when I remembered the upcoming championship show. It was only a few days away. If I told Dad the medicine wouldn't do much for at least a week, he wouldn't let me ride in the show.

"Notice what?"

"Huh? Oh. I'll notice a change when I take more of this one pill. That's all."

"That's great. Glad to hear the problem is easily solved. Let's get home." He ushered me out the door and toward the elevator.

It's not a real lie, I assured myself as I got in the car. I will notice a change. And surely if I start more medication right away it'll do something by Saturday. "I hope," I muttered to the passing scenery.

Unfortunately, I wasn't noticing much difference by Saturday.

"Gingersnap, are you sure you should be riding in this show?" Dad asked Saturday morning.

"Dad, I have to! You know how long I've been saving for this new saddle. With the prize money from today I'll finally have enough to get it. I have to ride in this show," I insisted. Possibly rudely.

"But, honey, even I can tell you're having trouble with your riding. I'm not sure it's safe."

I laughed. "Oh, come on, Dad. You know Star would never do anything to hurt me."

"I know he wouldn't," Dad agreed. "What I'm afraid of is you hurting yourself. There will be plenty of shows next season. Why don't you wait until the doctor gets your medication stabilized? Then you won't have so much trouble."

"I'm fine. Star and I can ride rings around any of those other kids, medication or not. I promise I'll cut down on my riding as soon as we win this show. Okay? Please?" I put every ounce of pleading I possessed in my tone.

Still, Dad hesitated. I held my breath. "All right. One last show then you'll take it easy. But promise me, Snap, you'll stop if you start feeling sick. Promise?"

"Sure, Dad," I grinned in victory. "But I'll be fine. You'll see."

The day was clear and crisp. "Perfect for our last show," I confirmed to myself as I headed to the barn. "And in our own fairgrounds two miles from home. We are gonna kill it. New saddle, here we come."

I shivered as I wrestled with the barn door and realized clear and crisp also meant cold. I slapped my hands together in an effort to get circulation going. I couldn't afford numb hands today.

Our first event went fairly well. We came in second, but equitation was not our specialty. I wasn't worried. "Just wait 'til we get to jumping, Star. We'll show them." I patted his neck while I walked him to keep him warmed up for the jump event.

While we waited for the jumping class, the weather turned cloudy and gloomy. And colder. I dismounted to walk beside Star hoping that would help the circulation in my hands and feet, but it didn't. By the time Dad boosted me onto Star's back, I had to fumble for the stirrups because I couldn't feel my feet. I had to lean over and guide each foot into the stirrup. By the time they called our number, I had to look down and make sure I was holding the reins. I had no feeling in my fingers. Spikes of pain shot up my legs. Dad's words echoed in my mind, "I'm afraid you'll hurt yourself...promise me you'll quit if you feel sick..."

"Sorry, Dad," I said under my breath as we walked into the ring. "Can't quit now."

At the starting gate, I pressed my heels into Star and he shot forward like an arrow released from a bow. I grabbed his mane to keep from falling off. Holding on as best I could, I directed him toward the first hurdle. "C'mon, boy. We've done this a million times. One more round and we're done."

Star seemed hesitant. Not his style at all. Did he sense something was wrong with me? Probably. I hoped the numbness in my legs and hands that kept me from signaling him for the jumps wouldn't mess us up. I felt my lack of balance and did my best to stay centered. Counting on our experience, I urged him forward with my voice.

Halfway through the course, I slipped to one side after we landed a jump. Star slowed and would have stopped if I hadn't urged him on. His gait became tentative and I knew we were in trouble. Still, I couldn't give up. That sealed our fate. I should have guided him to the side, but my brain froze in determination. We approached the next jump too slowly. To compensate, Star bunched his hindquarters and gave a tremendous leap to clear the jump. That powerful leap was my undoing. My balance vanished and I lurched over Star's shoulder. I fought to right myself, but looked down and saw my foot had slipped out of the stirrup. My leg was so numb I hadn't felt it.

I fell.

I hit the ground and all the air rushed out of my lungs. Stunned, winded, aching, I lay on the ground and wished desperately it would open and swallow me up. Embarrassment burned through my body. My dad, my coach, all the people in the stands…how could I ever face any of them again? I hadn't fallen off a horse since I was twelve-years old. Only truly inexperienced riders fell off in the middle of a championship show. The best of the best. Supposedly. Whistles and cheers usually greeted our performance. Now the stands were as silent as a battery-dead phone. Shame curled me into a fetal position and escaped through a soft moan.

Star nudged my shoulder. I looked up. His feet shifted uneasily. "It's okay, boy," I soothed. "Not your fault."

Dad's voice interrupted me. "Are you all right? Does anything feel broken?" He gently felt my arms and legs while he questioned me.

"I'm fine, Dad," I wheezed. "Just winded"

"Are you sure, honey? Here, let me lift you up and help you out of here." He moved toward me silently signaling his intent to lift and carry me off.

"No!" Urgency sharpened my voice. "No. I rode in and I can ride out. Help me up, will you please?"

Tears threatened, but I fought them back. I. Would. Not. Cry in the ring. I struggled up on an elbow and held out my hand toward Dad. If nothing else I would leave the ring with whatever dignity I could manage.

Dad's hand reached to meet mine. He clutched my hand with both of his and tugged carefully until I stood. Not steady, but standing. He gestured a thumbs-up toward the approaching medical team and they backed off. Grabbing me firmly around my waist, he boosted me effortlessly into the saddle.

My hands fumbled the reins. I gripped them as tightly as I could in one hand and lifted the other to wave toward the crowd. Applause rewarded my show of good sportsmanship. As soon as we cleared the exit gate, tears brimmed and overflowed through my blinking eyes. It didn't matter. Nothing mattered.

When we reached the barn, I slid off Star's back and caught my breath at the sharp stab of pain from my feet. I would have fallen but for two hands grasping me in a steady hold. "Thanks, Dad," I said before I realized it wasn't him.

"Here," Kevin's eyebrows drew together in a frown of concern. His hands gripped both my elbows firmly. "Sit over here." He helped me to a nearby bale of straw. "Can I do anything?"

"Yeah. You can turn back time a half hour and let me begin again." I used my forearm to wipe tears off my face.

"Sorry. That kind of stuff is out of my league. I know it's a poor substitute, but how about a drink of my pop instead?" He picked up a lidded ice-filled plastic cup off the ground and offered it to me.

"You mean to wash the dirt of the arena out of my mouth? I just blew my chance at the championship by plowing the arena on my face." Bitterness left a sharp taste on my tongue.

"Nope. Just thought you might be thirsty. Star sure is." Kevin nodded toward Star who was busy gulping water out of a trough. He finished his drink and walked over to me, dribbling water down the legs of my pants as he stood over me.

Kevin joined me on the straw. He stared at the drink held lightly between his hands then said, "You should have seen Star twist himself in the air to avoid stepping on you. I've never seen a horse do that. He looked like a giant fish flipping around on the end of a fishing line. I was afraid he was going to fall, too."

I stared into space. Too numb to answer. Tears dripped off my cheeks to the ground below.

Kevin tried again. He placed a tentative hand on my shoulder. "It's not the end of the world, Sara. Lots of people fall off horses. Especially during jumping. You ever watch the Olympics? Even those guys fall sometimes."

I shrugged off his hand. My mind replayed the memory of falling over and over.

Kevin rubbed his hands up and down his thighs, looked at the ground then outside the window, then rubbed the back of his neck. He blew out a breath of air on a long sigh then glanced at me. "You know how there's a right time to say stuff?"

A rock might have been more responsive than I.

"That never happens to me," Kevin continued. "I never know what to say at the right time. I wish I did. I wish I could say whatever would make you feel better, but since I can't, how about if I take Star's saddle off? He's still breathing pretty hard."

A stone statue had nothing on me for cold silence. The enormity of what happened rolled over me in endless waves of despair. No championship, no prize money, no saddle. No more riding, I knew, not now I was outed about how bad the numbness was.

Kevin moved over to Star and fumbled with the cinch. Before he could figure it out, Dad rushed in, his face ashen with fear. He took in Kevin's actions and relief lit his face. "Thanks, Kev. I promised the medical team I'd take Sara directly to the emergency room, but I had no idea what to do with Star. Can you see to him while I get Sara checked out?"

"Yes, Mr. Mitchell. I'd be glad to. Would it work if I just walk him home along the back road? It's not that far. I could put him in his stall."

"Thanks, son. That would be great. Can I borrow your car? We'll come back and get the truck and trailer later."

Kevin tossed him the keys. "Sure."

Dad turned to me, leaned down, pulled my arm up around his neck and grasped me firmly around my waist. He stood slowly, watching me anxiously the whole time. With slow steps he walked me out of the barn toward Kevin's old Jeep.

I guess I have a never-ending supply of tears because they kept rolling down my cheeks. A few slipped into my mouth where they left a salty tartness. My throat felt too thick for me to swallow, and I didn't think anything could get by the heavy lump in my chest. Every part of my body felt heavy, and I leaned hard on Dad. In spite of the chilly air, sweat gathered under my arms and along my forehead. I gulped in air, but couldn't get it into my lungs. Frantic, I clutched at Dad.

"Honey? Sara? What's wrong? Here," he yanked the door of the Jeep open and lifted me onto the seat. He pressed me back and grabbed both my hands in his. "Take a deep breath," he directed, firmly but calmly. "I think you're having a panic attack. You're going to be okay. Just hold onto me. Take a deep breath through your nose then let it out through your mouth. Keep doing that and concentrate on letting your shoulders relax."

My brain felt like it was full of buzzing bees. I could barely hear Dad saying something about breathing. Duh, Dad. I know I need to breathe. I can't…I can't breathe…I'm going to pass out. Terror tightened my throat even more. Can't breathe, can't breathe, can't breathe, can't breathe. In blind panic I grabbed my throat.

Amazingly, through the buzz of bees a quiet voice in my mind suggested, "Sure you can. Just take a breath."

And then, with no trouble at all, I could. One breath, then another. Gradually I could feel the warmth of Dad's hands holding my own. The steady repetition of his voice broke through the remaining panic, "Breathe, Sara. Just take a deep breath slowly through your nose." And I did. Breath after breath feeding my oxygen-starved body. Adrenaline backed off.

I know Dad's voice. What was that other one? Who talked through the chaos and confusion? My heart rate slowed and panic retreated. Misery remained. It overshadowed my curiosity about the unknown voice.

Without Star, I had nothing. Now I didn't fit in anywhere. I didn't belong. I'd never belong. I might as well be dead. The lament became a recording on repeat in my mind. This time I made no effort to chase the depressing thoughts away. Despair settled over me like a heavy blanket.

Chapter 12

Kevin is wrong. Hope doesn't come from God. It comes from me making something happen. And I will.
Sara's Diary

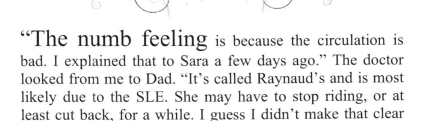

"The numb feeling is because the circulation is bad. I explained that to Sara a few days ago." The doctor looked from me to Dad. "It's called Raynaud's and is most likely due to the SLE. She may have to stop riding, or at least cut back, for a while. I guess I didn't make that clear the other day, did I Sara?"

I ignored him. I leaned down to force my feet back into my boots. Never! Despair flared into anger. I'd never give up riding Star even if I had to tie myself on.

"For today, nothing that a hot bath and rest won't cure," Doctor Adams said. "As I explained to Sara, the increase in this one medication will help with the numbness, but it will take a week or so to notice a change. For now, though, just take her home."

"You're sure?" Skepticism tinged Dad's voice.

"Yes. Nothing broken, no internal injuries. But she'll be sore and probably have some nasty bruises. Keep her quiet for a few days and she should be fine. And you, young lady," the doctor directed his gaze at me, "no more horse shows for now. Once we get your medication stabilized things will be different, but for right now go easy on the riding, okay?"

I avoided his gaze and didn't answer. I looked at Dad instead. "Can we go now? I have to make sure Star's all right."

Dad glanced at the doctor and shook his head with a small grimace. "Thank you, Doctor." Then he directed a pointed gaze at me which I ignored. I was done.

We accomplished the journey to the Jeep in silence, but once we got in, Dad hesitated before he turned the key. Hands on the steering wheel, he looked over at me. "You were pretty rude to the doctor. Next time you see him I want you to apologize."

Dad excels at dad voice. I groaned.

"I mean it. He made a special trip in to see you on a Saturday and didn't deserve that kind of rudeness. Your illness doesn't give you a free pass on good manners. You know better."

"Okay, okay. I'll apologize. Brother. You'd think I'd murdered somebody or something."

"That's enough." Dad spoke sharply. "I know you're disappointed about the horse show, but I won't have you taking it out on everyone else. I also don't want any more lying from you. You knew the medication wouldn't do any good by today, didn't you?"

"Yes, but I didn't lie." I mumbled.

"What   did   you   say?"

I raised my voice. "I said, yes, but I didn't lie. I told you the doctor said I would notice a change. That's true. He did say that."

"Don't fence with me. You knew if you told me the medicine wouldn't take full effect until after the horse show I wouldn't allow you to ride, didn't you?" Dad demanded.

I had definitely done it now. His hands tightened on the steering wheel until his knuckles whitened.

"Do you realize you could've been seriously hurt or even killed today because of your stubbornness?"

My breath caught. I had a sudden vision of Star falling and breaking a leg. "Star," I whispered. "I could've hurt Star."

"That's true, though I wish you'd think of yourself first. Star almost flipped completely over to avoid stepping on you. It's a miracle he didn't fall right on top of you."

"He could've broken a leg." I stared out the window. "I'm sorry. It's just that I was so sure we would win. I really wanted the championship and that saddle." Tears welled up again. "I know I should've been more careful. It's just that things seem so lousy right now; I wanted to have something wonderful happen."

"I know, honey." Dad became his usual kind self. "And you'll get your saddle, you'll see. When the shows start up again in the spring you'll be back on top. For now, I think we need to have a serious talk about whether you should be riding at all right now."

"Dad! I can't stop riding. No more shows, yeah, but please don't take riding away completely."

"If today is an indication of how safe it is, I think it would be better for you to stop for a while. We'll talk about it later. We're almost home."

I slumped against the seat and leaned my head against the window.

Dad turned the Jeep into our driveway. I sat up straight and squinted. "Look. Kevin got Star home. I'm glad the fairgrounds are so close. Looks like he's brushing him." Surprise brightened my voice.

"So it does," Dad agreed. "He's a nice boy."

"Yeah." I absolutely did not want to talk about Kevin. "Can I go make sure Star's okay, Dad?"

"Yes, but don't take long. Remember the doctor said

you should rest. And Kevin and I need to go get the truck and trailer at some point." He parked the Jeep and walked into the house.

"Thanks for getting Star home, Kev." I joined him at the corral. He climbed the fence and handed me the brush he'd been using.

"No problem. He sure is a nice horse. I felt kinda stupid leading him so I rode him most of the way home. We just walked. I hope that was okay."

"Star let you ride him?" Surprise widened my eyes.

"Yeah. I was a little nervous because I haven't ridden much and he's pretty big. But he didn't seem to mind I didn't know what I was doing. Sorta made me feel like royalty or something sitting up there," he admitted with an embarrassed laugh. "Know what I mean?"

Budding indignation, partly jealous, calmed down and I smiled. "Yeah, I know what you mean. I feel like that every time I ride him."

"Yeah. Well. I guess I better get your dad and take him back to the fairgrounds. See ya." He patted Star one last time and headed toward the house. He and Dad took off together in a cloud of dust.

I watched him go with mixed feelings. If he was so boring, how come I felt lonely every time he left? I did like Travis better. I definitely did. And yet…I sighed and turned my attention to Star. I had ducked under the corral fence to check his legs when a car roared down the driveway. Straightening up I watched Travis get out of the car and wave.

"Hey, Sara. What's going on? You all done with the big show? Sorry I couldn't make it. Didn't get up in time."

He let himself through the gate and sauntered over to Star and me. He reached for Star's halter. Star jerked away.

"Come on, boy. Don't be so shy." Travis grabbed for the halter. I opened my mouth to warn him, but was too late.

Travis's fingers connected with the halter and he yanked. Eyes rimmed white, Star pivoted. His muscled shoulder caught Travis a solid blow. He sprawled backward in the dust. Star snorted, trotted away shaking his head and switching his tail.

Travis struggled to his feet slapping at his jeans to brush off dirt. He stood, hands curled into fists, and cursed loud and long at Star. His face bloomed beet red.

"Are you all right, young man?"

I froze. Great. Mom. I bit my lip, and my stomach clenched. Hands jammed into my pockets, I turned to see Mom with her hands on her hips. Clearly, she had seen and heard the whole thing.

"Yes, ma'am," Travis muttered, not meeting her gaze.

"Then perhaps it would be best if you went home. It's time for Sara to come in." Her tone was deceptively soft.

Travis left.

"Put Star up, Sara. Then it's time for dinner."

Her lack of lecture didn't deceive me one bit. I knew it was coming.

During dinner that evening Dad cleared his throat. "Sara."

I glanced up.

"Your mom and I don't want you to get together with Travis anymore. He's proven what a bad influence he is."

"But, Dad…"

"No, Sara. You asked us to meet him before we made a decision. We've met him and know he's not the kind of boy we want you to date. From his behavior we've heard about from other parents and his behavior in front of your mother, he's just not the influence we believe is right for you. That's final. I know your plans are all set for the Turnabout and we're not going back on our word so you can keep that date. After that, no further dates."

"That's so unfair. I can't believe you're doing this." Even I could hear the whine in my voice.

"That's enough, Sara."

"I'm old enough to figure out who I can be friends with and who I can't. You and Mom can't just order me who to see and who not to see. I'm not a kid anymore." I punctuated my tirade by shoving back from the table and turning to leave.

"Sara." The unfamiliar command in Dad's voice made me pause. "Sit down. Our family is not finished and we stay at the table until we're all through with dinner." His stern gaze pierced my rebellion. I froze. It felt like two separate people in my mind fighting for mastery. Unusual fury wrestled with obedience. A tense silence arrested the scene until I slumped back onto my chair. Sullen, but compliant. For now.

Dinner became a hushed affair. The clink and clatter of utensils on plates became the only sound. The clash of a spoon against a serving bowl the only conversation. When everyone appeared done with the meal, I, in a tone that made it clear to my parents their IQs had dropped several points, enunciated clearly, "May I be excused?"

"Yes."

Gathering my dishes, I placed them in the kitchen sink and walked quickly from the room. I hurried up the stairs and took some frustration out on my bedroom door by giving it a satisfying slam. I threw myself on the bed and grabbed a pillow, punching it into submission.

"I don't believe it," I fumed. "I finally get to go out with a cool guy and now I've been forbidden to see him." I turned over on my back. My glance took in all the trophies and ribbons arranged around the room, but my mind fixated on anger at Mom and Dad. I remembered Travis's theory when I was in the hospital. His words, 'You have to go after what you want or you go without,' echoed in my mind.

"Fine," I muttered. "It's obvious Mom and Dad don't think they have to be honest and tell me everything, I guess that means I don't have to tell them everything either." I grabbed my phone and found Travis in my contacts.

U okay?

I'm cool. What's up with the fam?

Nothing. They're just lame.

Seriously lame, dude. Put a dent in our ship?

I thought feverishly trying to decipher the unfamiliar language. Ship? Oh, duh. Relationship.

No. They're just being parents.

Not into being treated like a kid. Up for WIT to hang?

Falling behind in translation again, I racked my brain for what he meant. Where had I heard WIT? It was like a bolt of energy when I remembered Tawny using it a few weeks ago.

Whatever it takes, I agreed, my thumbs flying over the small keyboard.

A smiley face with sunglasses answered me.

Chapter 13

I won't let my past define my future. I will definitely do whatever it takes.
Sara's Diary

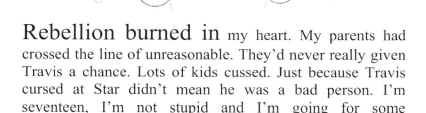

Rebellion burned in my heart. My parents had crossed the line of unreasonable. They'd never really given Travis a chance. Lots of kids cussed. Just because Travis cursed at Star didn't mean he was a bad person. I'm seventeen, I'm not stupid and I'm going for some happiness. I'm overdue to break my nice girl mold.

Travis and I met every morning before school and at lunch. I still felt at the edge of his group, but at least the girls had mostly stopped sniping at me. If looks could kill I'd be dead, but, oh well. As long as Travis kept his focus on me, I could stand their attitudes.

Because of my parent's antiquated rules about school nights, it was tricky when Travis wanted to get together during the week. I invented a school project with Tawny to get around their questions. I felt a little guilty, but figured Tawny would have covered for me if I asked.

"Hey, Sara," Tawny's arms grabbed me in a bear hug. "I haven't seen you in weeks it seems. Want to come over tonight and watch a new streaming series I found? It's pretty dope."

"Ah, no, Tawny. I can't. I have to study." My gaze couldn't quite meet hers.

"Oh, sure. Study. With Travis, I suppose. You call that studying?" Tawny asked with a giggle.

"What'd you mean?"

"Come on, Sara. I've seen you hanging around with Travis. He's such a cool guy." She paused then added, "Even though he's mad sketchy in a ship."

"I have no idea what you're talking about. Ship? Sketchy? Are we talking about a human person?"

"Okay, check it out." Tawny clasped her books to her chest and leaned against the lockers. "Sketchy is phony-like. I don't mean to be rude, but he's dodgy-dude kind of guy. Know what I mean?" Tawny examined her violent green purple-slashed finger nails.

I leaned my hands on the shelf of my locker and glanced at her. "Come again?"

"Look, I tried to warn you about his being a catch-and-release kind of guy, but I don't think you're getting it. A dodgy dude. Sneaky. As long as he gets what he wants, he doesn't care how he does it."

"And what he wants is to hook up?"

Tawny threw her hands in the air. "That is literally what I mean."

"Jeez. Judgmental much?"

"Sorry. But I know what I know."

"But he could change, right? Everybody can change."

Tawny looked skeptical. "I guess. But he's got a solid rep."

I knew that one. Travis's reputation was so deafening even my parents had heard about it.

"I've gotta jet." Tawny turned to go then peeked back at me over her shoulder. "Have fun studying." Big emphasis on studying. "But come over soon. I miss you."

She waved and warned in a singsong voice, "Be careful."

Doubt poked at my mind. After all, Tawny had her fingers on the heartbeat of the school, but my resolve hardened and beat back the uncertainty. There was always a first time for change. I determined to be the one around when Travis's time came.

One thing that nagged at my thoughts was my failure to tell Travis anything about my diagnosis. He never asked how I felt or what had happened at the horse show. He didn't really ask me questions about anything. He did notice I was gaining weight though. He slipped up beside me and placed his hand casually around my waist.

"Hey. Quite an overhang you're getting here." He squeezed the inch or two of extra flesh around my waistband. "You been sharing Star's feed?" He smirked at his own joke.

I turned my head so he wouldn't read the pain and embarrassment on my face. I forced out a laugh, but it was shaky. "No way. Star doesn't share his food with anybody. Not even me."

It was hard to laugh off his teasing. I knew I wasn't as fit as I used to be. The darn medication caused weight gain and my face had started to break out. There wasn't anything I could do about the changes in my body as long as I had to take the prescriptions. Was that all he cared about? How I looked? When he teased me about my weight, little black thoughts of shame piled onto the other dark feelings in my mind. I'm such a fat loser, joined the other messages I believed were true about myself.

Before long, Travis stopped meeting me every morning before school. Several days went by with no text from him to meet up. Sometimes I saw him in the halls with an arm draped over another girl's shoulder. At lunch there wasn't an empty seat for me by him anymore. I tried sitting further down the table, but being obviously pushed out of the circle was just too humiliating. No matter how hard I pretended I belonged, it was a show. Then came the day I watched him leave the cafeteria with Robyn Larsen, a new girl at school.

Robyn looked like she could be on the cover of a fashion magazine. She was in my English class, but so far, we hadn't talked. Everybody thought Robyn was exotic because she bragged about her Norwegian mother and Italian father. How was that any different than any of the other biracial kids at school? What made her so special?

I watched the cafeteria door close behind them and determination fueled my decision. I hurried to catch up with them then glanced over as I was about to pass.

"Oh, hi Travis. Hi, Robyn." My gaze zeroed in on Robyn. "I'm in your English class, but we haven't met yet."

Robyn's eyes lifted briefly to my face. "Oh yeah. You're the one with all the answers. What are you, a genius or something?" She smirked softly with Travis.

Why, oh why, couldn't I control the self-conscious blush I felt creeping up my neck? "Uh, no. I just like English, I guess. Anyway, it's nice to meet you." I switched my gaze to Travis. "Can I talk to you for a minute?"

He looked at Robyn before he answered. "Robyn and I are just figuring out a road map for later. Catch you on the rebound?"

"Sure, that'd be fine. At my locker? After our next class?" I had to pin him down.

"Yeah. Sure. Whatever." What little I had of his attention returned to Robyn as they continued wandering down the hall.

Cheeks flaming hot, I backed away then pivoted and rushed the other way. I looked back and saw Travis and Robyn whispering, heads close together. His hand rested on her slender hip.

An hour later, I leaned against my locker, books hugged tightly to my chest. My fingers beat an irritated tempo against the hard surface of my history text. My next class would start in a few minutes. Where was he? I pushed off my locker to head to class when he sauntered up.

"Hey. S'up?"

"I hoped I'd have more time to talk to you." I couldn't keep the irritation out of my voice.

"Sorry." His careless attitude made him sound anything but. "I got held up. What's the LD?"

The blank look on my face must have been obvious.

"What's shakin', what's up—what do you want?" he finally enunciated as if to a child.

"I wanted to tell you my parents are upset about my seeing you. They just don't understand…"

"Yeah, your fam is a real trip," he interrupted. "They must not be into quality." He laughed. "Whatevs. Guess that means you can't do the Turnabout with me, huh?" He turned and walked down the hall, talking over his shoulder. "Too bad we can't hang, but can't go against Mom and Pop, right?" He laughed. "Sucks. We would've been able to party. Buh-bye." He saluted then walked away.

The bell rang, but I stood frozen. "Wait…Travis," I called. I was talking to air. I finished in a whisper to myself, "That's not what I was going to say. I can go to the dance with you."

After school I rushed to find Tawny. "It was almost like he was relieved I couldn't go with him," I protested to my friend. "And what does LD mean anyway?"

While she checked her phone, Tawny answered absently, "Low down. I wish you'd pay attention when people talk. It's lame to have to translate for you all the time," she complained. "And anyway, why would he be relieved? Everybody knows he's hot after you."

"I thought he liked me, too, but it really sounded like he was looking for an excuse to break our date. He wouldn't even listen when I tried to explain that even though my parents aren't sure about him, I still get to go to the dance. I wanted him to talk to them a little before the dance this weekend. They really don't like me seeing him, but maybe he'll change if he hangs out with me. I could even invite him to church. I could help him change his behavior. What do I do?" I wailed.

"Honestly? I don't know. It'll be such a bust if you can't go. What about our plan?"

"I know. I have my dress and everything. Maybe I should text him and explain."

Tawny looked up from her phone screen. She put a perfectly manicured finger on my wrist to stop me from using my phone. Her frown made me pause. "I don't know. Makes you seem kind of despo. Desperate," she added without being asked. "Not sure that's a good idea." Then her face brightened. "Hey! You can ask Kevin. Chelsea asked him to go, but she's got the flu. Her mom already said she won't be well enough to go to the dance. Why don't you check with Kev? He's hot in a greenie kind of way."

"I don't know, Tawn. I haven't seen much of him lately."

"Much of who? Or should it be whom?"

Tawny and I jumped at the sound of Kevin's voice.

"Oh, hey, Kev," we said in unison.

"Sorry to hear Chelsea's sick," I offered tentatively.

"Yeah. She's pretty depressed. I feel bad for her. It would've been fun going to the dance with her. I'm on my way to take her homework to her and visit if her mom will let me. So far, her mom only lets me drop off her homework. What's up with you two?"

"Not much. I gotta beat feet. I'll catch you later, Sara." Tawny gave me a hard stare when she turned to go.

An uneasy silence filled the space Tawny left. Finally, Kevin asked, "How's Star? Has he been asking to see me?"

I laughed. "Sorry. Mostly he's interested in his hay and oats. That's about all he asks for."

Kevin shifted his backpack to his shoulder. "Uh, how have you been? I haven't really talked to you since you told me about the doctor visit. Are you okay?"

He really sounded concerned; like it mattered to him if I was okay or not. I swallowed hard. "I'm having problems with the meds, but doing all right. I have trouble sleeping sometimes." I shrugged. "It is what it is."

"I'm sorry to hear that. I hope everything works out for you." He looked around as if searching for something else to say. "Ah, I guess I better get to Chelsea's. Want to go with?"

What did I have to lose? "I can go part way, but then I better get home and get going on my homework."

We started down the sidewalk. Working up courage, I blurted. "So, are you disappointed to miss the dance?"

"Not really. How about you? I figured you'd be asking Travis, but then I heard Robyn's taking him. She beat you to it, huh?"

I froze. "Travis? And Robyn? To the dance? Are you...how do you know...where did you hear that?"

Kevin stopped walking and looked back at me. The curious tilt to his head prompted me to keep catch up with him. He reached up and batted a leaf from a low hanging branch.

"Just now. They're in the cafeteria planning on matching outfits. Guess they want to show everybody up or something."

My mind reeled. I wondered how long Travis had been planning to ghost me and go with Robyn. Would he eventually have told me or just stood me up if I hadn't conveniently given him an out? We had talked about matching outfits, too. It was my idea. A different plan formed in my mind. Maybe I could teach Robyn a lesson.

"Actually, Kev, I wondered if you'd like to go to the dance with me."

He stopped mid-step and stared at me. "You're asking

me? Why now? The dance is in a few days."

"I just found out you can't go with Chelsea. I didn't know she was sick." True as far as it went, but my conscience squirmed.

"Oh, yeah. Well. I guess I could. Sure. That'd be fun." He started walking again.

I took a deep breath. "We could wear coordinating outfits. Not matching, exactly, but same colors." I shrugged. "Since you heard Travis and Robyn talking, we could take advantage of knowing their plan and surprise them." And Robyn will freak when she sees we've gone them one better. No need to tell Kevin about that part.

Kevin didn't answer. I wondered if he heard me. "Kev?"

"You want to do a variation of what they're doing? Why?"

"I don't know. It could be fun. Maybe we could start a new tradition. Think of it. Us. Fad creators." I grinned at him. "I'm wearing a teal dress with black trim. You could wear a black jacket and shirt with a teal tie and vest. What do you think?"

"I guess it'd be okay. Be the first time I've ever been in Travis's league before, that's for sure. Not that it bothers me. Not much about him I like. Have you ever noticed how he always seems to get his way? No matter what?"

Kevin shook his head. "I imagine you have to be pretty careful to be his friend. I don't think I'd ever trust him very far."

I ignored what Kevin said. It made me squirm. "You want to stop by later and I'll show you my dress? I can give you a color swatch so you can find something to match."

"Yeah, sure. I'll come by after I visit Chelsea. See you later." He gave a casual wave and continued on while I turned toward home.

Chapter 14

Here I am, treading water in my own personal ocean of denial.
Sara's Diary

Star's wide back offered such a comfy seat I couldn't resist. I clambered up on the rim of the hay rack, grabbed his mane and edged my foot over his back to straddle him. Leaning forward, I let my arms droop down each side of his neck and rested my cheek on his withers. His ears flicked back, but his steady munching didn't miss a beat.

"I wish people were as easy as horses," I complained. "You wouldn't believe how complicated tonight is going to be. It's either going to ease me into popularity or sink me beyond hope."

Suspicious that if I voiced my biggest concern, it might come true, I didn't mention the fact that Kevin might not be okay with my plan. Worry that everything would blow up in my face had my stomach in knots. Apparently, my conscience wasn't okay with gray-tinged honesty. My constant self-assurance that I didn't exactly lie wasn't helping.

With a glance at my watch, I swung my leg over Star's back and slid down his side. "Wish me luck, big guy. I'm going to need it."

After dinner I stared uneasily at my reflection. Was tonight going to be okay? Had I chosen poorly with my suggestion to Kevin? Would Travis and Robyn be upset we copied their idea? Wait. Their idea? It was *my* idea in the first place. They had no right to be upset. Too bad if they were.

Tawny had come and gone so my hair and nails were unbelievable. No problem there. We agreed to meet later at the dance, and that was also a good thing. I liked Tawny's boyfriend, Ryan, though it was a mystery to me how they stayed together.

Ryan didn't go out of his way to impress anybody. He got decent grades, had gone to state in cross country the last two years, wore old jeans and t-shirts most of the time and was unfailingly nice to everyone. I had never heard him raise his voice in anger, never heard of him doing anything connected to drugs or alcohol, and he never seemed to care that he looked sort of messy most of the time. He didn't fit in any category at school and was as low-key as Tawny was flashy.

I knew Tawny would flit around like a butterfly at the dance, but she would always end up back at Ryan's side. I envied Tawny her boyfriend. Not because I liked Ryan myself, but because it was clear Tawny mattered a lot to Ryan. You could see it in the way his gaze followed her and how he always seemed to know where she was. Like he had Tawny radar or something. Nice, I decided.

My reflection stared back at me in the mirror. Even with my weight gain I knew I didn't look too bad. Teal is a good color for me and Tawny had gathered one side of my hair in two French braids that connected then wound around my head blending into the rest of my hair loosely curled and touching my shoulder. She had looped a black ribbon through the braids to match the black trim of beads on the bodice of my dress.

I remembered what Travis planned to wear to match my outfit and an uneasy chill shivered through me. Kevin was right. Travis did like things to go his way. What if tonight backfired? The memory of Travis's anger when Star embarrassed him at the corral multiplied my edginess. I'm pretty sure Trav doesn't take a joke very well. I shrugged my shoulders. "Too late to do anything about it now," I addressed the girl in the mirror. "That's Kevin at the door and it's time to go."

I hurried down the stairs. Admiration stopped me midway when I saw Kevin waiting. "That's brilliant," I exclaimed, and rushed down the rest of the stairs.

Kevin's suit and shirt were black, but his tie and vest matched the color of my dress. Sewn carefully along the edges of the V-neck of the vest was a pattern of black beads, a simplified version of the beads on my dress. The vest buttons were black to further pick up the contrast of colors. Kevin self-consciously smoothed his hands down the front of his jacket.

"Mom took the swatch you gave me and found material to match. She made the vest and did the beads after I described your dress to her. She thought if you wanted us to coordinate this would work. It's okay?" He tugged at his tie and shifted his feet.

"It's perfect," I assured him. I knew what Travis was wearing and Kevin looked way better. Ditch me, will you, Travis? Let's see how that works for you, I thought with a spiteful spike in my emotions. No more Sara the Saint, I decided with satisfaction.

After pictures, we got in Kevin's car and headed for the dance. We entered the gym, Kevin laughing and talking with friends, but my eyes searched restlessly for Travis and Robyn. It wasn't long before I spotted them talking to the DJ. I was right. They had kept to the plan of matching outfits I originally worked out with Travis. Robyn wore a teal dress and Travis had on a teal suit with a black tie and vest. It looked fine until compared with how classy Kevin looked in his black suit with teal accents.

My confidence began a slow leak. Travis was going to be furious at being shown up. I turned toward Kevin hoping to detour and maybe even persuade him to leave. Instead, just as I opened my mouth to distract him, Kevin caught sight of Travis and Robyn. He raised his hand in greeting and called, "Hey! We're sorta quadruplets. Great minds, huh? We all came up with the same plan."

Heart thudding, I turned to face Robyn and Travis. When I saw Robyn's face, rigid with anger, my hand crept up my neck to fiddle with my hair and I ducked my gaze to the floor. When I glanced up again, Travis watched me with a narrow-eyed smile. I could almost feel his renewed interest when he looked from Robyn's flushed face to my own. Interesting. Travis wasn't angry. He looked intrigued. Like I was a challenge he didn't expect. His eyes brightened with predator-like anticipation.

I was back in the game. Besting him made me a challenge. I lifted my chin and walked toward the couple. Kevin hurried to catch up with me. I kept my gaze, bright with challenge, firmly on Travis. Maybe this evening wouldn't be so bad after all.

"Hi, you two. You look great." I hooked my arm through Kevin's.

"Hey, Travis, hey, Robyn," Kevin greeted. "Next year everybody will be matching, you think?" He smiled. "We're trendsetters."

"You wish," Robyn said, lips tight with anger. Her gaze took Kevin in from head to toe. "So, greenie, want to dance?"

She took his arm without waiting for an answer and tugged him toward the dance floor. I had to let go or risk stumbling along beside them. I watched Robyn take my date, wrap her arms around his neck and press herself against him in a slow dance. Kevin glanced at me, eyebrows raised in question and confusion. They were soon lost in a sea of swaying bodies.

Travis slid his arm around my waist and pulled me close. "Dance?"

An hour later, I hurried to keep up with Kevin as we left the gym and headed to the parking lot. Kevin reached up to undo his tie and unbutton the top button of his shirt. He yanked his tie off and jammed it in a pocket. He didn't say a word and he wouldn't look at me. I finally grabbed his arm and tried to slow him down. "Kev, wait."

"I'm not waiting, Sara. I just want to get you home." We reached the car. Out of breath, I slumped against the car door and turned to face Kevin's grim face.

"What?" Even I could hear the assumed innocence in my tone.

Kevin shook his head. "You have really changed. Or maybe I don't know you as well as I thought. I guess you and Travis will make a good pair. You're a lot more like him than I realized. Do you get what you want no matter what it does to somebody else, too?"

"What do you mean?" My voice sounded shrill in my ears. "What did I do?"

"Did you notice how early Robyn and Travis left the dance? You totally embarrassed her. That's not like you. And why weren't you honest with me? You could've told me you asked Travis first and he changed his mind to ask Robyn. That doesn't surprise me at all. He always does stuff like that. But you?" He shook his head. "I know not to trust Travis. Didn't know I can't trust you. I don't know about you, but I'm apologizing to Robyn on Monday. She's brand new at school. How could you do that to her?"

The injustice of it infuriated me. "What about what she did to me? She asked Travis and I had already asked him. And you agreed to dress alike. It wasn't all me," I reminded him.

"Do you think I would've agreed if you had told me the whole story up front? And how do you know Robyn knew you had already asked Travis? She's new, remember?" He shook his head and kicked at the stones in the parking lot. "No, this is about you and Travis."

I didn't answer. He was right, but I couldn't back down now. Kevin rubbed the back of his neck and blew out a frustrated raspberry. One hand on his hip and the other curled with his finger pointed straight at me, he held my gaze with his own. "I think you didn't tell me about Travis and your whole plan with him because you knew I wouldn't go for it. Oh, I would've gone to the dance with you, but I wouldn't have set out to embarrass Robyn, which is exactly what you did. From now on, Sara, leave me out of your schemes with your boyfriend. And I'd appreciate it if you didn't lie to me anymore either. Get in," he yanked the door open. "I'll take you home."

Silence sat between us like a third passenger on the drive home. When Kevin stopped in front of my house, I quickly opened the door and jumped out before he could get out to open the door for me. "Thanks," I threw over my shoulder as I hurried away. "See you."

Once inside, my parents looked up in surprise. Mom put down her knitting and Dad his Kindle. "You're home early. Are you all right? Have fun?"

"Yeah, I'm fine. The dance was pretty lame is all. 'Night." I turned to head up the stairs.

"Wait a minute," Dad called. "Did you have fun?"

I stopped on the stairs, but didn't turn around. "It was okay. Crowded. I felt tired so we came home."

"Come and sit for a minute," Dad suggested.

I turned with dragging feet and sagged onto a chair.

"You and Kevin looked really great tonight. It was nice of Mrs. Richards to make sure he matched your outfit. What did the other kids think?" Mom resumed her knitting but glanced up at me.

"Nobody really talks about stuff like that, Mom. Tawny liked it though."

Dad leaned forward from his seat on the couch. "I have to admit your mother and I were relieved Travis wasn't able to go to the dance with you. We're much more comfortable with you spending time with Kevin. You won't forget what we told you about seeing Travis, will you?"

Not willing to meet his gaze, I stared at the small glittery black purse in my lap. "No, Dad. I won't forget. Can I go now? I'm really tired."

"Sure, honey. Go on up to bed." Dad picked up his Kindle and Mom smiled a good night.

In my room, I undressed, tossing the dress and the rest of my outfit around the room. I grabbed sweats then sat on the bed and began taking down my hair. My fingers tugged impatiently at clips and I winced when I pulled too hard. I had to calm down, but I felt jittery and restless. I had accomplished my plan. Why did it feel so rotten?

I finger-combed my hair and shook it out. My glance caught my image in the mirror on the closet door. I stared. I didn't like whiners. When had I become one? It seemed all I did lately was complain. About everything. Who am I? The mirror image looked uncertain. Memory dissected my thoughts. I remembered my determination to go after what I wanted for a change. My posture straightened. The mirror image shifted and resolve replaced uncertainty.

I didn't care what Kevin thought. Robyn deserved everything that happened. She and Travis both. And what if I decided to fight for what I wanted for a change? There was nothing wrong with that. Everybody deserved some happiness and right now I got to have fun with Travis if I could. My parents just didn't understand relationships these days, and they for sure didn't understand guys like Travis. Besides, Mom and Dad weren't being honest with me—I heard them in the doctor's office agreeing they shouldn't tell me everything. I decided I didn't have to tell them everything either. I'd text Travis in the morning and ask him to meet me before school in the gym.

Results of the dance? Not a total bust. I could probably mend fences with Kevin, but even if I couldn't at least I had salvaged some part of the evening. Travis was back in my sights. If it cost me Kevin, I guessed I could live with that.

Chapter 15

Clue. Less. That's me in a nutshell.
Sara's Diary

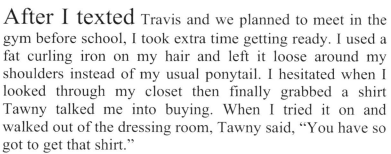

After I texted Travis and we planned to meet in the gym before school, I took extra time getting ready. I used a fat curling iron on my hair and left it loose around my shoulders instead of my usual ponytail. I hesitated when I looked through my closet then finally grabbed a shirt Tawny talked me into buying. When I tried it on and walked out of the dressing room, Tawny said, "You have so got to get that shirt."

"It's too tight. And too low in the front." I protested while I pulled at the shirt to stretch it out. "I'm not getting this."

Tawny walked up to me and tugged the shirt back in place. "It's not too tight. It fits. You always wear such lame stuff. Get something sassy for a change. It's cute. I understand the whole horse show, Star thing, but there are times you can sass it up a little."

I pulled the shirt over my head and had to admit with my hair down, the shirt did look pretty good. What had Tawny said? Sassy. I look sassy, I assured myself. For a change.

At school, I waited for Travis in the gym. Every time one of the doors banged, I looked around to see if it was him. He didn't show. I finally left the gym just minutes before the bell rang. I knew I wouldn't see him before lunch because of our schedules, so I settled myself to pay attention in class. My mind sifted through possible explanations for the no show.

At lunch I scanned the cafeteria for Travis. When I finally spotted him at a table with a bunch of football players and cheerleaders, I started through the maze of tables and students. Then the group at the table shifted and I saw Robyn. Dread stiffened my shoulders. I paused. Even with a new shirt I was no match for her ice-blonde beauty. I turned to go just as Travis caught sight of me. He motioned for me to come. Like an obedient pet, I obeyed the summons. When I approached the group, Travis scooted over on the bench and nodded toward the space. I squeezed in next to him and he draped an arm around my shoulders.

"Hey, there arm candy." He cupped my chin and angled my face toward him. His intended kiss missed its mark when Robyn, walking behind us, bumped Travis' arm.

"Hey," I complained. "Watch it."

"Or what, saint-girl?" Robyn challenged.

"Uh-oh, ladies putting the smack down," one of the football players snickered.

Travis reached for Robyn's hand. "Hey, little bird. How about you fly away and we'll perch later?" He winked at her and turned back to me. The super-charged awkward moment stretched while Robyn glowered at Travis. He stared her down. Chin high she pivoted toward the boy next to her and hooked her arm through his.

"Maybe. Maybe not. Come on, Logan. Let's bail." She pressed against Logan and they walked toward the door. Logan curled his arm around Robyn, his hand resting in the back pocket of her jeans.

Travis laughed. "So the little bird is going to settle." He shrugged. "Her loss." His arm draped around my shoulders again. He leaned forward until his forehead touched mine. "You understand a man can't be limited to one chica, right?" He cupped my chin again, but just before our lips connected there was a loud, "Excuse me, Mr. Baker."

Mr. Salz, the principal, towered over us, arms crossed over his chest. "You know the rules about personal displays of affection in the cafeteria. We've had this discussion before."

"Aw, Mr. S. You think this is out of bounds? A friendly little kiss?"

I edged away from Travis's encircling arm. The principal's eyebrows raised when he saw me.

"Sara? Sara Mitchell?"

"Hi, Mr. Salz." Heat chased up my cheeks and into my hairline. The principal's face looked confused. I could relate.

"I certainly didn't expect to see you at this table."

I shrugged. "We're just having lunch." My voice sounded lame even to me.

Mr. Salz shook his head. "Is that what you're calling it now? I can't keep up with all the slang."

You and me, both, I agreed silently.

The principal turned to go. "Whatever you call it, just make sure you follow the rules." He directed a stern look at Travis. "At least while you're in the school building."

Travis shook his head and laughed. "What a suit." He turned back to me. "Now where were we..."

I jumped when the bell rang for class and pushed up from the table. "Uh, guess I better go. See you after school? Parking lot?"

Travis looked at me like I was a geometry problem to be solved, eyes calculating. He shrugged. "Why not?"

"Okay. See you then." I hurried toward the door, but turned at the last minute to wave. Travis had already rotated back on the seat and was laughing with his friends. They didn't seem in any hurry to leave the cafeteria.

After school, I rushed to the parking lot and looked for Travis's car. His dad owned a car dealership in town so Travis pretty much had his pick of cars and changed often. I looked for the red Mustang he'd been driving lately and spotted it immediately. So different from the old Jeep Kevin drove.

Travis had parked the Mustang across two parking spaces to keep anyone from parking close. He leaned against the car checking his phone. Suddenly, he shoved away from the car and stood; all his attention focused on the small screen of his phone. He didn't notice me walk up and startled when I said hi.

"Uh, oh, hi, babe." He stared at his phone. "Ah, I've got to jet. Something came up." He shoved the phone in his pocket and retrieved his car keys in the same motion. He grabbed me around the waist and pulled me close to give me a quick kiss. "Hey," he squeezed the extra flesh at the waistband of my jeans, "you're still packing it on, huh?" He wagged a finger back and forth in front of my face. "Not cool," he scolded. "I'm not down with that. I'll check you later."

"But, Travis," I objected. "I just got here. When later?"

The only answer was the roar of the car engine and screeching tires when the Mustang fish-tailed out of the parking lot. I jumped out of the way and watched him go.

After dinner, I tried texting Travis and finally got an answer after I had all my homework done and was getting ready for bed.

Give it a rest, saint-girl.

What do you mean? I thought we were going to get together.

Sorry, chica. Don't think you have WIT. Peace out.

Saint-girl. That's what Robyn called me at lunch. A catchy remake of my Sara-the-Saint nickname. And what was WIT again? I'm witty, I protested indignantly. A vague memory disappeared like fog in the sun and I ground my teeth in frustration. I almost had it. Then I remembered what the principal said at lunch about keeping up with slang. Quickly I texted Tawny.

What does WIT mean, and do I have it?

LOL. How should I know if you have it? Means, "whatever it takes." Seriously, you need a dictionary. Y?

Just saw it in a text and wondered.

What text? Who u talking to?

Travis.

A winking face emoji appeared on my screen. **Does he think you have WIT?** Then a heart emoji.

I hesitated so long another text chimed in.

S? What's up?

He thinks I don't have WIT.

Now it was my turn to stare at the inactive screen and blinking three dots.

Probably for the best. Ry says T's just a PB.

Peanut butter? A confused face emoji was my answer.

Within a few seconds Tawny's Taylor Swift ringtone sounded and I thumbed the little green answer button and pushed speaker in the same motion.

"Are you kidding me right now?"

"About what"

"Sara. For reals? You are so from another planet. PB means playboy. Travis is a playboy. Maybe it's for the best if you guys aren't together. He's probably not the best guy for you. I know you hoped you could change him, but maybe he'll always be a player. Hey, I have to catch some z's, but meet me after school tomorrow?"

"Sure. Right now, I think you're the only person still talking to me."

Tawny laughed and teased, "AGYB."

I smiled. This one I knew because it was the code we made up when we were twelve. "Always got your back," I agreed. "See you tomorrow."

Dad dropped me off at school the next morning with a wave. I walked up the sidewalk, eyes scanning for familiar faces. I felt a hand on my shoulder and turned to see Tawny practically vibrating with energy.

"You are not going to believe this. This is so legend, I even have trouble believing it. Guess."

I opened my mouth to answer, but Tawny interrupted me.

"Never mind. You'll never guess. Ryan was in the locker room this morning and he heard a bunch of guys talking. He said he heard Travis laughing and heard him say, 'Brothers, my bird just moved from a dime to an eleven.' So, Ryan waited and you are not going to believe this." Tawny could hardly keep her words straight she was talking so fast.

I put a hand on her arm. "Wait a minute. I'm already lost. Eleven from a dime? Following your train of thought is like trying to track a squirrel on meth."

Tawny rolled her eyes. "I'm pretty sure when he talks about his bird he's talking about Robyn, and eleven from a dime means an eleven on a scale of one to ten."

I must've looked blank because Tawny continued, "How can you be so smart and so clueless at the same time? You need to get out of the barn. A dime...ten...you know? A dime is ten. If someone is a dime that means they're a ten on a one-to-ten scale. An eleven means they're better than the best. Get it?" Tawny practically bounced in frustration and excitement.

"Got it. Travis basically said Robyn is an eleven on a scale of one to ten. You think. Or Ryan thinks."

Tawny picked up her story. "Then Ryan hears Travis say his bird sent him some pics and there aren't many feathers. Then Ryan said everything got quiet so he peeked around the corner and all the guys were looking at Travis's phone. They started high-fiving and fist-bumping and laughing and calling Travis dude and stuff." Tawny gulped in a deep breath. "Ry says he's pretty sure Robyn must have texted Travis some action pics." She peered at me. "Do you know what that means?"

It was my turn to roll my eyes at my friend. "Tawny. Even I know what action means. Do you really think Robyn would send pictures of…you know…like, suggestive stuff?"

"Ryan's sure she did because of the reaction of the guys. He's pretty disgusted that Travis would show everybody his phone. Hey, I've gotta go. If I'm late to English again, I'm going to get detention. See you later."

Trance-like, I shuffled toward the school building. Travis's actions yesterday and his message to me last night suddenly made sense. He must've gotten Robyn's pictures while he was waiting for me after school. I didn't understand any of this. How could Robyn do what Tawny thinks she did? And how could Travis do what Tawny thinks *he* did? Pretty disgusting. Was Ryan right about what he saw and heard?

Stacking my books in my arms from my locker, I headed for my first class. By third period I knew Ryan's suspicion of what happened in the locker room was right on. One of the football players was in my third period class. When I walked in the room, I noticed several boys gathered around the athlete's desk pushing at each other to get a closer look at his phone. I took my seat, but could tell from the snatches of conversation that not only had Travis shown his friends Robyn's pictures, he had shared the photos. That meant they were on countless phone screens. The boys stared at the phone with such concentration they didn't see our teacher enter the room. Their first clue was when the teacher calmly reached through the group and grasped the phone.

My dislike of Robyn shifted. Sympathy washed over me. She had no idea what was just about to break wide open.

The teacher instructed us to take our seats and review the next chapter in our textbook. Then he ushered the group of boys who had been gawking at the cell phone through the door. After about five minutes, he came back by himself and calmly began our lesson. As soon as the bell rang, every student snatched their things and rushed out the door. I heard bits of conversations and knew everyone was talking about the phone and disappearance of the boys. I headed to my next class knowing I would find out what was happening during lunch after my next period.

Fifty minutes later I hurried to the lunchroom and looked for a familiar face. I didn't see Tawny or Ryan. My frown of disappointment turned into a grimace of resignation when I spied the cheerleaders at a table in the middle of the room. From somewhere I summoned the energy to deal with them and headed their way. Courtney and the girl next to her slid apart to make room for me.

"Hey. Did you guys hear about what happened in third period?" I kept my voice as casual as possible.

"Of course we've heard," Alyssa answered with a toss of her head. "Did you know the police are on campus?"

"The police? What are they doing here? What happened?" My hands froze around my sandwich poised halfway to my mouth.

Courtney turned to look at me, her mouth pinched into a frown. "Why should we tell you, saint-girl? It doesn't have anything to do with you. Butt out." She made a show of turning her back to me. The rest of the girls shifted uneasily, but they had all learned the hard way not to go against Courtney. She always got even.

Sandwich still arrested in midair, I felt every slight I'd swallowed overflow and spill out in resentment. "What is it with you? You're rude to me every chance you get, you complain about everything I do and you never miss an opportunity to make fun of me. It's really getting old. What did I ever do to you? We used to be friends." My shrill tone turned quite a few heads our way.

"Right. Friends." Courtney's voice mocked. "What friend would tell everyone my mom and dad split up because my mom cheated. That's not true and you know it."

My body froze in shock. Eyes wide I tried to speak coherently. "I didn't...I never said...you were my friend I would never...who told you I said that?"

A tell-tale glance at Alyssa told me everything.

My gaze switched to Alyssa who took her time facing me. "Why would you say that? It's not true. I never said that and you know it."

"Pretty sure I heard you talking about it and saying that's why Courtney was so messed up." Alyssa gave me the stink-eye then examined her nails.

My attention switched to Courtney who had an uncertain look on her face. "Courtney, I promise I never said anything about you or your mom and dad to anybody. I wouldn't do that. We were friends."

Courtney looked to Alyssa. Alyssa shrugged. "Who are you going to believe? Me or saint-girl here?"

Which, ironic, right? If I'm a saint, wouldn't that automatically make me the more honest one?

Courtney's gaze shifted between Alyssa and me. I understood her dilemma. I'm just a regular person at school. All I had to offer was friendship. Alyssa was a force to be reckoned with and nobody contradicted her without huge consequences.

Courtney's subtle shift away from me and downcast gaze told me all I needed to know. She chose Alyssa.

I faced Alyssa again. Her victory smirk flipped a switch in me. Faced with fight or flight, this time I chose fight.

"And why do you have it in for me? We don't even know each other that well. You take every opportunity you can to put me down? Why? What did I ever do to you?"

Her fury-narrowed gaze caused an involuntary swallow. "You want to know what it is with me?" Her tone was menacing and low. She slapped her hand down hard on the table. "I'll tell you what gets me about you. You're one of the most uncool losers in this school. I have no idea why you tried out for cheer in the first place, but I know the *only* reason you were voted in was that Travis seemed to like you. And the only reason Travis liked you was because your picture was in the local paper on that stupid horse of yours and he thought it made you kind of cool." Alyssa leaned close to me, eyes narrowed into a sneer. "Puh-leese. Horses? We all left horses behind with our dolls in elementary school. The horse makes you a loser, not cool. So lame." She turned her back again, dismissing me like I was invisible.

Tears stung my eyes. "But...but." I had no words. I left my lunch and lunged away from the table. Through blurry vision I located an exit and pushed through the door. I recognized the stairway to the music room and rushed up the stairs to the sanctuary of the deserted room. I sat on a windowsill and leaned my hot cheek against the cool glass. Now I knew. Alyssa made it crystal clear why I felt like such an outsider. I *was* an outsider. They didn't accept me and never would. My getting voted in at the tryouts was a matter of timing and Travis's momentary interest. How could I have been so stupid as to think people at school were finally accepting me? A movement outside the window caught my attention. I wiped the tears from my eyes with the sleeve of my hoodie and squinted to see better.

Two police officers walked down the sidewalk deep in conversation with the principal. They spoke for a few minutes at the squad car parked by the curb, then the officers got in the car and drove away.

The warning bell for fifth period rang and I hurried to my next class. Only two classes left until the end of school when I would be able to find out from Tawny what was going on. Time dragged until the final bell.

In my hurry to find my friend, my fingers fumbled the lock on my locker, but finally I had book-free hands and could text Tawny.

Location?

Football field.

Can I meet u?

Can't wait.

I fumbled stuffing my phone in my pocket, dropped it and had to stop to pick it up. Successfully tucking it into my back pocket, I hurried to the football field. Tawny waved and I scrambled up the bleacher steps to join her.

"I saw the police here at lunch. What happened?" Out of breath from rushing, my chest heaved while I tried to talk and breathe at the same time.

"You. Are. Not. Going to believe this." Tawny's eyes widened with excitement.

"What?"

"Travis, Robyn and every boy who got the pictures of Robyn were taken to the office at lunch time. The suits used the phones to figure out who the pics were forwarded to. It took them both lunch periods to get everybody involved." Tawny clutched my arm and leaned close. "And then—wait for it—the police came!"

"I know. I saw them."

"Oh." Disappointed and deflated, Tawny slumped back against the bleachers. Then she brightened and sat up. "But do you know why?"

I laughed. "No. You can tell me."

"Well," Tawny paused to get every ounce of drama she could out of the story. "The black and whites were here because those pics and sharing them on phones is illegal. Who knew? I heard the office secretary telling a teacher that depending on the guys' ages they'll get charged either as adults or juveniles. The cops are coming back after school to meet with all the kids and their parents to sort it out. And, your dream boy, Trav? He's probably at least suspended and maybe expelled. He's so out of here. His evil ways finally caught up with him." Tawny sat back with satisfaction written all over her face.

"No way! It's illegal to share pictures?"

"Well, depends on the photo shoot, doesn't it? The police took all the phones to the station to check out how bad it is. That's why the meeting after school. It sounds to me like the law might be pretty new." Tawny spread her hands on her knees and regarded her vibrant pink fingernails. I noticed she had little black plus signs painted on the pink and wondered what it meant. I didn't want to interrupt the story so put my curiosity on hold. "Is Travis in the most trouble?"

"Yep." Tawny's voice was saturated with approval. "He's not going to be able to charm his way out of this."

"Why are you so glad he's going to get in trouble?" Tawny was usually so easy going. I couldn't figure out where the payback tone was coming from.

Tawny turned to me with a serious expression on her face. "Because he always slides out of stuff. He does awful things to people and totally gets off. I've tried to tell you, to warn you he's just not a great guy. He's a bully and a liar and doesn't care who he hurts. I've been worried about how you seemed to be going for him, but it seems lately like you're backing off. I'm glad. I like a good time as much as the next person, but Travis is just plain mean and I am not down for him hurting you or anyone else."

Remembering his smile and how easily I had been

pulled in by his attention I felt myself stiffen defensively. "What happened to him possibly being my BAE? Why is that so hard to imagine?"

Tawny put her hands on my shoulders. "You have been my bestie a long time and I love you. AGYB, remember? You've always been there for me when I've needed you and I'll always be there for you. Yes?"

My throat tightened with emotion. All I could do was nod and choke out, "AGYB."

"You're a good person. Inside, I mean. I worried a little when you got voted on the squad because those girls are piranhas, but I knew you wanted a way to join in and, besides, you really are good. But I didn't want you to become like the rest of them. Know what I mean?" Tawny let her hands drop from my shoulders and clasped them loosely in her lap.

"No, not really," I admitted. "And what about you? You're a nice person, too. Why aren't you like the rest of the cheerleaders?"

"You're kidding me, right? Ryan would smack me upside the head if I started acting like them. Ryan is the straightest person I know, though Kevin has his head on right, too. Anyway, Travis had something to do with every one of those girls. It's like he infected them or something. Oh, I can't explain it. I just don't want you to be hurt."

We sat quietly for a minute. I fiddled with the backpack on my lap and said without looking up. "I know why I got voted to be a cheerleader."

"What do you mean? You tried out, were great and got voted on the squad. What's to figure out?"

I shook my head. "Nope. I've wondered how I made it and if I was finally going to be popular, but Alyssa told me today how I made it."

Tawny's eyes widened with disbelief. "And you believe that...that...shark?" She answered her own question. "Of course you do. All right. Give. What did she say?"

"She said it was because the tryouts were right after my picture was in the paper with Star. Right before school started. That's when Travis started to pay attention to me and that's why people voted for me."

Tawny shook her head. "That girl deserves somebody like Travis. She's poison, too. It's not true, you know. It's just what I said. Poison. But I can tell you don't believe me." She stood up and brushed the dust from the bleachers off her jeans. "Ry's coming." She nodded toward her slowly jogging boyfriend. "Want to come hang with us?" Then she peered at me closely. "What? You look like you're just about to say something."

The news about my diagnosis was on the tip of my tongue, but I felt relieved at the interruption. I would tell Tawny another time. I shook my head. "Nothing. Really. You go on with Ryan. I'll come another time."

I gave a little wave when I greeted Ryan as he jogged up. "Hi, Ryan."

"Hey, Sara." He made as if to fist-bump me, but ducked his hand when I put mine up to bump his. "Ha! Gotcha."

"Oh, you," I couldn't help but grin. "You get me every time."

He put his hand to his chin and stroked an imaginary goatee. "Why, yes, I do," he intoned, sounding like the principal. "You should consider this, young lady, and decide how it will affect you in the future."

He dropped his pose, fist-bumped me for real then glanced up at Tawny. "Ready, T?"

"Yep." Tawny put her hands on Ryan's shoulders and he grabbed her by the waist to easily lift her down off the bleachers.

"Thanks, TDH," Tawny laughed. "Tall, dark and handsome," she added over her shoulder to me. She took Ryan's hand and they walked off.

I watched them wistfully then remembered my hungry horse at home. I hurried to catch the last bus.

Star kicked up his heels and bucked when I turned him loose in the corral. I leaned against the fence and watched him. Not being able to ride left me with a sad emptiness that nothing filled. He trotted up to the fence and nudged my arm. I scratched under his forelock. He pushed into my hand and his upper lip twitched in ecstasy. Star apparently agreed with Tawny that I was a good person. Did I agree with them? I wasn't sure anymore.

Chapter 16

Evidently, I'm school-smart and relationship dumb.
Sara's Diary

The next day after school, I changed my clothes and hurried to the barn. I'd been rushing Star's care and needed to give his stall a good turnout. I gave him fresh hay and water, then filled his grain bucket. The bucket handle slipped from my hand and I barely caught it before it spilled all over. It felt like everything took longer because my hands were swollen and clumsy. Star nosed his grain then lipped in a huge mouthful. As always, he chewed with occasional grunts of ecstasy. His steady munching gave me a rhythm to toss soiled straw into the wheelbarrow. Every so often, I paused to catch my breath and rest. Soon, the stall looked immaculate.

"I wish it wasn't so hard to do things," I grumbled. "I can't believe how out of shape I am. Cleaning your stall used to take me ten minutes tops, and now I'm lucky if I'm done in twenty or thirty. And at school? Boy, you should see what happens when I have to get from the first floor to the third. Those stairs get harder every day. I know I was really mad when the doctor wrote me a note saying I had to stop cheerleading, but the truth is I can't even get my outfit on let alone kick my legs or do a cartwheel. All my joints just ache. But the worst thing," I leaned the pitchfork against the stall door and walked over to Star.

"The worst thing is I still can't ride you. It's even hard to feed and groom you." I slipped both arms up and over Star's back and leaned my cheek against his side. "Feed you, groom you, take care of you. Everything I love is harder to do." I leaned into him, comforted by his warm solid presence. "I can let go of other stuff, but if I lose you, I don't know what I'll do. Would I even want to live, Star? What would be the point if I can't ride or take care of you? Even Travis said how much he misses time with horses."

"You're kidding me. Travis said something about horses? What'd he say?"

I turned so fast at the sound of Ben's skeptical voice I lost my balance and almost fell. Clutching at Star's mane, I regained my balance and glared at Ben. "You have to stop doing that. You can't just sneak in here and listen to my private conversations. It's so rude."

Ben leaned over the stall wall. "First of all, a conversation is an informal exchange of ideas or thoughts between two or more people. You, dear sis, are talking to a horse. It might be a monologue, maybe even a soliloquy, but it's not a conversation. Second, the barn belongs to all of us. I can come in here when I want. Besides, Mom wants you to come in for dinner."

Too tired to argue, I pushed off of Star and grabbed the pitchfork. "I don't care what you call it, I was talking and it was private."

"Then think it next time. Star doesn't understand what you're saying anyway. Though I admit sometimes it seems like he does. You guys fit together like Legos."

I hung the pitchfork on a rack and closed the tack room door. "I know he doesn't understand language, exactly, but I know he listens. And he does seem to understand sometimes." I could tell Ben was ready to object so added, "Not the words. I know. But he gets the feelings or something. He understands me. Like we have our own language that doesn't involve words. It's like a, a heart language or something."

"Heart language."

I could practically see wheels turning in Ben's brain while he considered my explanation.

"Yeah. I get that. That's actually very interesting. When I'm a veterinarian I might study that. Maybe I can do my dissertation on it."

"You're going to be a vet? What happened to the CIA? And clown college?"

"Keeping my options open, Sis." He jumped up and slapped the door frame. "Come on. Mom says dinner."

While we walked toward the house Ben repeated his question. "What did Travis say about horses?"

"It was when we were first getting to know each other. He told me how much he loves horses…" I stopped when I realized Ben was no longer by my side. I turned to find him staring at me, an interesting look on his face.

"He said what?"

"He was telling me how much he loves horses," I repeated. I placed my hands on my hips and cocked my head at him. "Why?"

"Travis Baker. Football star, all-around jock and who I heard Alyssa call, 'stud muffin'? No way." Ben shook his head and resumed walking.

"What do you mean, it can't be true? Why not? Why would he lie to me about loving horses?"

My brother stopped again and stared at me. "How can you even be my sister? One of us has to be adopted. There's no way we're from the same gene pool." He stepped close to me and looked me in the eye. He explained patiently, as if to a child. "He lied to get the girl. Duh. It's classic."

My brain cycled through possible comebacks and came up empty. All the occasions Travis had been around Star replayed in my mind. Travis didn't have a clue how to act around a horse. And he never came to horse shows. And once he realized Star had no interest in him, Travis never came around again.

My jaw dropped. I lifted my gaze to Ben's. "You're right. It's irritating, but you're right." We started toward the house again.

I slapped both my palms against my forehead. "Stupid, stupid, stupid. I can't believe how stupid I am. Even my brother knows more about guys than I do."

Ben interrupted my tirade. "Well. I *am* a guy. Of course I know more about guys than you do."

Frustrated and embarrassed by another example of how clueless I had been about Travis, I burst into tears and rushed into the house. I pounded up the stairs to my room, ignoring Mom's concerned, "Sara?"

I curled myself around a pillow on my bed while waves of humiliation washed over me. No wonder everybody thought I was a loser. Probably everybody I knew understood how completely Travis had fooled me. My stomach clenched when I remembered how I ran after him in the hall at school. I punched my pillow in frustration. I even believed I could be the one to change him. How sad is that?

But...he left the flower at my locker. And he visited me in the hospital. What if...what if deep down he did have feelings for me? I mean, it's not impossible he could get tired of the airhead cheerleaders.

Then the memory of the boys clustered around a cell phone gawking at the photos forwarded from Travis intruded into my hopeful theories. What kind of guy did something like that with private photos?

I jammed my hand into my mouth to smother my cry of frustration. Human relationships baffled me. Give me horses any day.

A soft knock on the door interrupted my inner rant. I sat up and took a deep breath. "Yeah?"

"It's me. May I come in?" Mom made it a question, but I knew she'd eventually come in no matter what.

"Sure, Mom. Come in."

Mom slipped through the door and joined me on the bed. "Are you all right? Why the tears?"

"I'm just tired. And I hurt. I didn't think lupus would be so achy all the time. Everything I do makes me hurt. Even taking care of Star is hard. And I don't feel hungry. Can I just get a snack later?"

"I'd rather you come down for dinner. You know we believe it's important for us to eat together as a family."

"I know. I'm just so tired, and I have homework to do before I go to bed. Where I won't be able to sleep anyway, but at least I can lie down. I'm exhausted and I can't sleep. Just another perk of the medications," I added sarcastically. "Please let me skip dinner tonight."

Mom smoothed the hair away from my forehead. "It will get better. The doctor said it takes time for your body to adjust. We have to be patient."

I jerked away from Mom's hand against my face. "Not we, Mom. Me. I'm the one who has the disease and has to take the pills. Me. You, Dad and Ben, you're just going ahead with your lives as usual." My mouth crumpled and tears welled in my eyes again. I dashed one from my cheek and gritted my teeth. Can't Mom see I'm dying inside? What will it take for my family to notice how absolutely miserable I am?

"That's not true, honey," Mom protested. "Your illness affects all of us. We all care about you and worry about how you're doing. If you'd let us, we might even be able to help. You seem to be more and more closed off."

"That's because I'm the one who has to watch my life fall apart. And there's nothing I can do, and there's nothing you can do. It just is. Can I please get going on my homework now?" I got up from the bed and sat down at my desk, back turned toward my mom in rude dismissal.

"Sara," Mom objected. "I know you don't feel well, but that doesn't mean it's suddenly okay to be impolite."

I hesitated, then twisted partway toward Mom. "I'm sorry. I know. I just feel really lousy."

"Okay. Go ahead with your homework. If you get hungry, we can fix you a snack before bed." Mom got up, started toward the door then paused. "Oh, one more thing. Your dad and I got an email from the school about a parent's meeting tomorrow afternoon. Something about cell phone usage. Pictures and social media. Do you know what that's about?"

I bent over my books and picked up a pen. "Oh, there was some drama today about photos on some guy's phone. I don't know. Probably no big deal."

"Does this have anything to do with Travis?"

I slammed my pen down on my notebook. "Really? Seriously? Why do you assume it's Travis's fault because they're calling a meeting? You and Dad are so prejudiced against him." My anger at Travis just minutes ago evaporated and defensive Sara roared to life.

Mom closed the door and turned to face me; arms crossed across her chest. "Sara! You cannot talk to me like this. I know you don't feel well, but that's no excuse for your attitude and tone. It was just a question, and it's a legitimate one. Travis has been in trouble before. Your dad and I don't live in a bubble and we talk with other parents and keep track of what's happening at both yours and Ben's schools. Now, what do you know about this cell phone problem?"

Thinking feverishly, I answered. "Actually, it does involve Travis, but it's not his fault. Some girl sent him some photos to his phone. He didn't even ask for them. She just did it. It's her fault. Not his. That's all it is. You and

Dad don't need to bother going to the meeting. Waste of time." I turned back to my homework. I could feel Mom's gaze, but kept my focus on my books.

"Like I said, your dad and I like to stay informed," Mom answered quietly. "There'll be leftovers in the fridge if you need a snack later." She stepped into the hallway and closed the door.

"Great," I muttered to my notebook. "Now they'll have even more against Travis and they'll never accept him." It didn't take much to get him back in my sights.

By the next day at school, everything had changed again. Tawny met me before school and filled me in. She talked so fast; I could barely understand her.

Turns out the police and principal acted quickly. Travis and several of his friends were suspended for two weeks, which meant they were off the football team. They had also received a legal citation in the form of a warning. The warning would stay on their juvenile record until they were eighteen; then at that time, if there were no more violations their records would be wiped clean as adults.

"What about Robyn? And how do you know all this? Are you bugging the principal's phone or what?"

Tawny rolled her eyes. "Yeah, like I know how to do that. No, it's just basic. You know the teacher's lounge?" I nodded. "So, you know how I have serious FOMO?"

Predicting my question she supplied, "Fear of missing out. Anyway, the teachers don't always close the door, especially in the morning when they're in a hurry. If you happen to be standing by the door, you can hear everything. I just listen." Tawny studied her nails, which I noticed were still bright pink with black plus signs.

I held up a finger to put her on pause. "I gotta ask. What do your nails mean?"

Tawny glanced at her nails. "Oh, this? I'm trying it out. It might be a new logo for the shop. You know, like Nails Plus. Snaps, huh?"

"Brilliant," I agreed. "Okay, now what about Robyn? She's the one that started this whole thing by sending those photos in the first place."

Tawny's steady gaze rested on my face. "You think this is all Robyn's fault?"

"Well, yeah. She sent the pictures. If she hadn't, none of this would have happened."

"You have a point, I guess." Doubt edged Tawny's voice. "But the police don't agree. Evidently Trav's bird is a baby. She's only fifteen so she gets a warning both from the law and from the school."

"You're kidding! How can she be only fifteen and be a junior?"

"It's when her birthday is or something. She's always been a year ahead because she was allowed to start school early, I guess."

"She's fifteen going on twenty-five," I grumbled. "It's so unfair that nothing happens to her."

Tawny's gaze rested on me again. Her eyebrows drew together in a slight frown. Why was she looking at me that way?

"What?"

"I don't know. You just seem kind of harsh. Robyn has private pictures of herself circulating who knows where. Don't you think that's pretty unfair? How would you feel?"

"Number one, I wouldn't take pictures like that of myself and, number two, even if I did, I wouldn't send them to anybody. She shouldn't have sent them to Travis in the first place," I argued.

Tawny's attention returned to her nails.

"What? What now? You're on Robyn's side? Really?"

"I didn't know there were sides," Tawny answered quietly. "I don't know, Sara. I guess…I don't know…I guess I always thought you were nicer than this. I'm just surprised is all."

I stared at my friend. "Nice never got me anywhere," I

finally muttered. I pushed past Tawny toward the school.

Chapter 17

The ocean cleans the shore every day—all the garbage gone. I need a wave to wash over me.
Sara's Diary

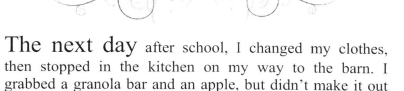

The next day after school, I changed my clothes, then stopped in the kitchen on my way to the barn. I grabbed a granola bar and an apple, but didn't make it out the door before Mom's voice stopped me.

"Sara, I forgot to tell you that Mr. King called. He wondered where you've been and why you haven't been coming to the stable for training. Have you told him about your diagnosis?"

My hand grasped the back door handle. So close to escaping. I answered without turning around. "No. I haven't really told anybody much of anything. Nobody cares anyway."

"Could you please turn around when you're talking to me?"

I turned to face Mom.

"Thank you. Your friends don't know about the SLE? Why?"

"Number one, I don't have any friends anymore, and number two, there's no point. Nobody can do anything and it just makes me feel more of a freak. I've always been different from everybody and now it's just worse. Like I said, nobody cares. You don't get it, Mom. I'm not important to people." I hoped Mom couldn't tell how close I was to crying. I swallowed the lump in my throat and blinked my eyes like crazy.

"That's not true," Mom protested. "Kevin and Tawny, your friends at the stable and at Big Sky—they all care about you. Your brother, I know he can be a pest, but he loves you. And Dad and I, oh honey, if you only knew how hard this diagnosis is for us."

Mom's voice broke and I guessed the lump I just swallowed was contagious. "We'd give anything to be able to make it go away. We hate seeing you suffer. If you would let us, we could help you get through this. We know it's not easy and we're devastated by the turn your life has taken, but there are still a lot of good things in your life. Is it possible for you to see any of the blessings you still have?"

My tight control on the feelings caused by loneliness and misery wobbled. My eyes flooded with tears so that the sight of Mom walking toward me with outstretched arms blurred. My arms stayed tight by my sides; my hands clenched into fists. But when Mom gathered me close, instinct loosened my arms and I found myself gripping her and resting my head against her shoulder. The emotions I tried so hard to control burst through the wall I'd built and all the fear, pain and misery seeped away with the spilling tears.

Mom's soft flannel shirt was soon damp. One hand clasped me tightly against her while the other stroked my hair and back. After a few minutes, she moved slightly away to fumble with the tissue box on the counter. She grabbed a handful of tissues, gave a wad to me then used the rest to blot tears gently off my cheeks. With an arm around my shoulder, she guided me to the kitchen table and onto a chair.

"Why haven't you told your friends about what's going on with your health?"

I blew my nose. "I told Kevin. And I mentioned a little bit to Tawny. Everybody else just thinks I had an accident at cheer practice, got hurt and had to quit. People have noticed I'm gaining weight, but that's pretty much it. It's all negative. It's just so depressing on top of feeling tired and in pain all the time." A sudden moment of clarity revealed the truth that Travis was the only one who had actually made negative remarks. Everybody else was pretty much the same. Even Alyssa was just her same snippy rude self. Nothing new.

Could it be that all the negative feelings originated within myself? Could Mom be right and people might actually care if they knew I was sick? Is that what it took to find out I mattered? Maybe that could be true for some people, but I'd bet my best saddle most people couldn't care less. Another flash of insight blazed across my thoughts and I realized I'm not much good at letting people know I care about them either.

"Mom, how do you know if you matter to people?" I used the last of the tissues to mop my eyes and blow my nose.

"Hmmm. Haven't really thought about it before." A tiny frown of concentration wrinkled her forehead while she thought about her answer. "I guess I know I matter to people when they spend time with me. Your dad is good about making sure he checks in with me to find out about my day and tell me about his. I like that. And I like when people mention something they appreciate about me. Like when you and Ben actually say dinner is good." She laughed. "I can always tell, especially with your brother because the food disappears, but when any of you say you liked something in particular, I feel like you've noticed and appreciate me. Is that what you mean about 'do I matter'?"

"Yeah. Sort of."

"Then let me ask you why you think you *don't* matter to anybody? What would make you feel like you mattered?"

Mom's question stunned me. I had no idea. All I knew was it felt like I didn't matter and I believed that. It was easy to believe nobody cared. Maybe I was wrong?

"I guess," I struggled to put feelings into words. "I'm the same as you. I like it when somebody wants to spend time with me. Tawny's really good about that. She makes me feel like I'm important to her. But mostly I just feel like I don't matter. Except to Star," I admitted with a smile.

Mom laughed. "Star is definitely not shy about letting everybody know how he feels about things—good or bad. And it's clear as a sunny day you are his human priority. Tell you what, why don't you figure out how you know you matter to Star and maybe you can figure out what it is you're missing from people. And when you do?" Mom cupped my face between her hands. "Please let me know because I want more than anything for you to know how very much you matter to me." Mom's eyes glistened with tears when she leaned forward to hug me tightly.

When I returned Mom's hug, I remembered there was something I know about myself, but before I could tell Mom, Ben burst through the door.

"Mom! I really need…" His request cut off abruptly when he caught sight of our tear-stained faces. "Oh, ah. Sorry. Didn't mean to interrupt. Is, ah, everything okay?" He eyed us warily, poised to vanish like smoke.

"We're fine," I assured him. "We're not going to pull you in for a group hug."

His obvious relief made Mom and me laugh.

Knowing the mood was broken, I smiled at Mom and got up from the table. "Thanks, Mom. I'll think about what you said. Is it okay if I take the car and go over to talk to Mr. King? And maybe I'll stop by Big Sky, too."

"Sure, honey. Go ahead." She turned to Ben. "Now, what do you need, Ben?"

I grabbed the car keys off the hook and headed out the door. Star lifted his head over the corral fence and nickered when he saw me. "Be back in a bit, big guy. Hold tight."

Within twenty minutes I pulled into a stable yard and saw Mr. King, my friend and trainer, coming out of the tack room that doubled as an office. When he recognized the car, he waved, waited for me to park then walked to meet me.

"Hey, stranger," he called when he was several feet away. I got out of the car and walked up to him. I met him with a half hug and asked if he was busy.

"Just going to check on a beginner class. Want to come?"

I nodded and we walked over to a training ring where six children were circling the ring on patiently plodding horses. We watched silently for a few minutes, then I said, "Mr. King, I can't train for a while because I'm having some health problems."

"Shoot, Sara. I'm sorry to hear that." Mr. King pushed his hat back on his head and fastened all his attention on me. "Anything I can do to help? Need me to exercise that big spotted guy of yours?"

I laughed and answered, "No, but thanks. I turn him out in the field so he can run, and Ben helps, too. I just can't train or jump for now. I hope next season I can come back."

"I surely hope so. You and Star make a great team and that horse was born to jump. Are you going to be okay?" I saw genuine concern in his gaze and knew Mom was right. At least about Mr. King.

"I'm doing what the doctor says and I hope I'll be feeling better soon. I have SLE." I looked at him with a question in my gaze wondering if he knew the disease.

"Now that's a real shame. I have a niece who has lupus and I know it's not easy to deal with. She goes through long stretches where she's symptom-free though. I hope that happens for you. And when you feel like it, you can always come around just to visit or supervise a class. You know you're always welcome. Over at Big Sky, too." He nodded his head across the road. "Justine was just saying the other day she could use more spotters with her students when they're riding. That's something you could do, I reckon."

"Thanks, Mr. King. I was going to stop over there next. I'll talk to her. See you."

Leaving the car where it was, I walked across the road to Big Sky Hoofbeats, a riding center for disabled children and young adults. It had only been open a couple of years. The director, Justine, was a friend of Mr. King's and I knew they helped each other out whenever possible.

I've been interested in Big Sky ever since it opened. I followed the sound of voices to a small corral. Justine leaned against the top rail while she watched a volunteer spot a little girl wrapped in a riding harness on top of a splashy pinto.

The volunteer paid close attention to the little girl, ready to offer a quick helping hand for balance or security. I had watched Justine train volunteers before and knew spotters were key to the success of the program. I was pretty sure I'd enjoy being a volunteer and it seemed like something I could do in spite of my diagnosis.

Justine turned when my movement caught her eye. She waved me over to the fence. "Hey, Sara. Good to see you. You haven't been around in a while."

"Hi, Justine. No, I haven't been training lately. Haven't been feeling very good." I didn't know Justine as well as I knew Mr. King so wasn't comfortable explaining the whole story. "How are things at Big Sky? How's my friend, Alex?"

Justine laughed. "That boy. He's not going to be happy until he's jumping like you and Star. You have an admirer, that's for sure. I'm trying to work out a way that he could go over a small jump or two, but I want to make sure he won't get hurt. Any chance you have some time to volunteer now that you're not training? I could really use more experienced help."

While I watched the volunteer spotting, the young girl in the ring reached up a hand to steady the rider in the cradle-like saddle created for disabled riders. The rider laughed and grabbed the pinto's mane. "I've been thinking about it," I admitted to Justine.

"Why don't I give you an application to take home and we can take it from there? You'd be a big help around here and it would totally make Alex's day." The woman pushed away from the fence and turned toward the larger barn. "Come on to the office. I'll give you the paperwork."

Driving home, for the first time in a long time, I looked forward to dinner. I knew my family would be excited to hear about the possibility of volunteering at Big Sky. When Ben had been going through a phase of wanting to be a physical therapist, he had checked into volunteering at the therapy ranch. When he got the news that he needed to be sixteen to volunteer, he had shrugged philosophically and announced he could wait.

When I drove into our driveway, I could see Star chasing a big soccer ball around the corral. He'd kick the ball then chase after it, his tail flying like a flag. Sometimes he even bucked a step or two. I smiled when the ball hit the fence and bounced back. Star shied like a yearling.

I slid out of the car and walked over to the corral. "You big goof," I called. "That ball can't hurt you. C'mon, let's get you in and fed. It's my dinner time, too."

After dinner and helping with dishes, I texted Tawny.
Busy?

Yep. Talking with JLo. She wants me for her makeup team. U?

Olympic coach on other line. Wants to know when I can join the team. Put JLo on hold and come over?

For sure. In a flash.

Twenty minutes later I heard a knock at the back door and a murmur of voices. Tawny was everybody's favorite. It wasn't long before she burst through my bedroom door and threw herself dramatically across the bed.

"I am seriously in danger of a food coma every time I come here. Your mom makes the best cinnamon rolls." She licked her fingers and rolled onto her back. "Well," she announced cheerfully. "So much for JLo. She wants me to relo. How could I possibly leave my peeps here? All y'all would wither and die without me. What's up anyway? You haven't asked me over since the dance."

I rolled my desk chair over by the bed. Indecision put me briefly on hold while I tried to figure out how to begin. I had a lot to explain and some apologies to make. Tawny made it easy.

"Sara. Just say it. It's only me. If it helps at all, I know something's wrong. And I want to know how I can help."

"T, I haven't been much of a friend. Remember when I had trouble with that horse show a couple months ago? Well…" I told my friend all that had happened. I recalled all the doctor said, how afraid and angry I was, the dishonest, dumb and cruel things I'd done. I took a deep breath and even repeated the conversation I'd overheard between my parents and the doctor—the one where he said I might die. Tawny's eyes filled with tears. I finished with the conversation I had with Mom that afternoon. I paused for a second then concluded, "I feel like that guy in that Greek story we studied. Remember the one who had to push the rock up the hill, but then it would just roll back down and he had to do it all over? That's how my life feels right now."

"Whoa. That's heavy." Tawny dead-panned.

"Ahhhh." I groaned. "That's so bad."

"I know, right?" She grinned. "I couldn't resist. Seriously, how could you not tell me this? I would so help you push the rock up the hill. And we could decorate it with graffiti while we did it. I could literally rock spray paint."

Tawny patted the bed by her side. I got up, pushed my chair back to the desk and sat beside her. Tawny's hands cupped my face and turned me so I faced her directly. "I don't care if it's a rock or your boyfriend or a bad bod, tell me." She patted my cheek, not completely gently. "You tell me so I can help. Yes?"

I leaned my forehead to touch Tawny's. "Yes."

Could I tell Tawny about the dark fog that threatened to overwhelm me? Would it help to have someone help me push back the darkness? My moment was lost when Tawny spoke.

"So, that's what's up. I knew there was something. How could you not tell me about this? Wait, never mind. I get it. I'd be freaked out, too. Okay, let's sort the trash from the treasure and figure this out."

"Trash from the treasure?" I felt confused. I often felt confused around Tawny,

"Yeah. It's something Ry and I do when we fight."

"You and Ryan argue? No. Way."

"Way." Tawny rolled her eyes dramatically. "We've just learned how to fight. It's Ry's idea. He is *so* not like any other guy I know. Basically, it means we look for anything good that can come out of our argument. One time the only good thing Ryan could find was that we would eventually kiss and make up. Is that not the most dope thing a boyfriend could say?"

"If dope means good, yes."

Tawny nodded. "It means seriously good. Anyway, you have this whole scuz bod thing going on…"

"Scuz bod?" I interrupted. "You're joking."

"SLE sounds boring. Revolting-ish. So…old person. Scuz bod it is. Okay, so number one. You have to promise me you will do what the doctor says."

"Tawny." My eyes filled with tears and stopped my words.

"I know, SJ, I know. It stinks. But you have to."

I drew in a deep breath then nodded. "Okay, I will. But not SJ," I protested. "You know I hate my middle name."

"Why Sara Jane, how you talk." Tawny put on a heavy southern accent and we both laughed. Then we were heavily quiet.

"I really hate it." I looked at my friend and she took my hand and held it tightly. "I feel so cruddy all the time and I can't ride. And I'm so tired. The medicine really does a number on me. And I never knew I could ache in so many places. Even when I used to fall off Star when I was learning to ride, I never hurt like this. I really don't see any treasure," I admitted.

Tawny scooted close to me on the bed. "I know. I mean, I don't know because I'm not sick, but I will try to understand and help. Just don't stop talking to me, okay? I guess we have to believe what the white suit says, that eventually the medicine will help and you can stop taking it. That will be the treasure we'll count on."

"Yeah, but what about the whole fatal thing? It's bad enough not having kids, but the fatal thing is scary. I can't believe Mom and Dad are lying to me about that."

Tawny's expression sobered. "You know, I can't believe it either. I know what you think you heard, but your mom and dad rock the whole parenting gig. Are you sure they're lying to you?"

I stood and wandered over to a display of horse show ribbons on my wall. I smoothed the silky fabric with my fingers and shrugged. "I was there. In the restroom. I told you."

"I know. It just seems weird. Hey," with a lightning quick change of mood, Tawny asked, "would it help if I came over and did your nails for you every few days? Check it out." She held her bright-tipped nails out for inspection.

I walked back to the bed and took her hand in mine. Each nail was divided into four squares with thin black polish lines. Then each small square was a different color. I couldn't see any repeat colors. "How did you do that? It must've taken hours." I shook my head and laughed. "I can't imagine you sitting still that long."

"I know, right?" Tawny inspected her nails. "Ry and Dad were watching some stupid game so I did my nails. It took an hour and a half. I'm pretty sure I'll never do this pattern again. It was a major grind. Hey, I've got to jet. Mom said I couldn't stay late so I better go. Is it okay if I tell Ryan about what's going on?"

"Sure. I know he won't say anything."

"Nope. Silent as a mime is my Ry. And I won't say anything either, but I'm so glad you told me." Tawny wrapped me in a giant bear hug. "We'll make it through this. AGYB, right?" Tawny stepped back and smiled at me.

"AGYB," I agreed. "Thanks, Tawn. I'll see you tomorrow."

I finished my homework then got ready for bed. I read my Kindle for a while, then turned off the light. The conversation I had with Mom that afternoon replayed in my mind. I realized I knew one thing for sure that helped me know I mattered to someone. It's when they're honest with me. Are Mom and Dad lying to me? From what I remember, they are. I wish I knew. I rolled over on my side and punched my pillow into the right shape. Tawny's right. It's not like them. Maybe I should ask? Sighing into sleep I knew I wasn't ready for that.

Chapter 18

*When the hurtful things are on the inside, no one
knows or cares. Maybe I could speak up?*
Sara's Diary

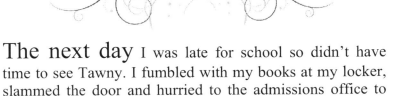

The next day I was late for school so didn't have
time to see Tawny. I fumbled with my books at my locker,
slammed the door and hurried to the admissions office to
get a late pass.

The principal glanced at me while he wrote on a slip of
paper. "It's not like you to be late. Everything okay?"

"Sorry, Mr. Salz. Everything's okay. I just overslept."

"It happens." He smiled. "Here's your pass."

It doesn't happen to me, I muttered as I banged
through the office door and hurried down the deserted
hallway. I don't understand how I can feel so tired and
can't sleep. I slipped into the door of my first class and the
day began.

By lunchtime I noticed four or five empty seats in
every class. And the snatches of conversation I heard
between classes confirmed that fifteen boys, including
Travis, had been suspended. I wondered what happened to
Robyn, but didn't have anybody to ask. Tawny was sure to

know. I just needed to be patient until lunchtime.

For a change, Tawny didn't know anything about Robyn. "But Travis' bird isn't in school so something's going on."

I scowled at my friend. "I wish you'd quit calling her that. She's not his bird."

"Get over yourself," Tawny advised. "That's what everybody's calling her." She smashed her sandwich bag, napkin and other wrappers up in a ball and pushed up from the table. "I gotta go. I told Ryan I'd meet him in the weight room. He says I need resistance training to be healthy, but mostly I just watch him mansplain what he thinks I should do. Like I'm going to lift sweaty weights." She shuddered. "Not happening."

I gathered up my trash when I felt the presence of someone stop by my side. I stopped and glanced up to see Kevin.

"Hi."

"Hi, Kev. Haven't seen you in a while."

"Oh, I've been around. You've just been busy." His half-smile, half-grimace let me know he was referring to all the time I'd spent chasing Travis.

I fake-smiled and fought my impulse to flee. All I could manage was a lame, "Yeah."

A strained silence stretched between us. Finally, Kevin shrugged and said, "Well, I guess I'll see you around." He turned to leave.

A wave of loneliness swept over me. "Kevin? Wait..."

He stopped and looked back at me.

"I've been meaning to talk to you about the dance."

He kept his gaze on me.

My heel started to tap against the floor and I fiddled with my lunch. "Could you sit down? My neck's getting stiff." I tried a laugh, but it fell flat.

He sat across from me. "What did you want to talk about?"

I looked at the ceiling for inspiration. Nothing. I plunged in. "I'm really sorry. I know not telling you and ambushing Robyn and Travis like that wasn't a nice thing to do. I just…I just…I don't know. I guess I wanted to get back at her. But I shouldn't have used you to do it and I'm sorry."

"Shouldn't have used me, or shouldn't have done it at all?"

Why is he being so tough about this? I'm apologizing! "Shouldn't have done it at all, I guess." He made a move to get up and I rushed to add, "I mean, I know I shouldn't have done it at all. It was a mean thing to do." I waited, my hands clenched in my lap, then looked directly at him. "Friends again?"

His face relaxed into a smile. "Friends," he agreed.

I tried a return smile. "I have been busy lately, but that's going to change. I mean, I'm going to have more time now so maybe…maybe you could come over and we could go for a walk or something?" I held my breath while I waited for his answer.

After way too long, he asked, "When?"

I let go of tension I didn't know I was holding in my chest. "How about…this afternoon?"

He kept a steady gaze on me. I felt the rest of the tension and misery I'd been feeling melt away when I met his friendly brown-eyed gaze. He smiled. "That'd be great. I'll meet you on the beach after school."

"Okay. See you." My answering smile felt good. It had been a while.

He slid off the bench and gathered his books. When he looked down at me his lips curved into a grin. "Nice to see you've still got your smile."

His grin warmed me all afternoon and I was still in a happy glow when I got home. I found Dad in his study, tapped at the door and entered without waiting for an answer. He looked up from grading papers. "Hey, Snapper, what's up? Have a seat."

My favorite cushy leather chair called my name and I sprawled into its comfy hug. "Dad, I've been taking my medication for a while and I wondered if I could ride Star to the beach to meet Kevin for a walk. I won't go far and I'll be careful, I promise."

Dad put down his pen and leaned back in his chair. "How are your hands doing? Any Raynaud's?"

"Sometimes. Usually when it's cold. But it's nice out today and they're fine. See?" I spread my hands out for his inspection.

"Looking good. How about an hour of riding and we'll go from there?"

"Thanks, Dad. I think I'm well enough. I'll be fine."

"All right, honey. Have fun."

I changed and went out to the barn to bridle Star. I didn't want to bother with the saddle since lifting it over his back might be more than I could manage. Bareback was fine. As long as I got to ride.

We took our favorite path to the beach. Relief loosened the knot in my stomach when I realized the dizziness that had plagued me was gone. I guess the medication really was doing its job. I spied Kevin by the rocks and rode in that direction.

"Hey," Kevin greeted when I pulled Star to a stop.

"Hey, Kev." I looked down at him from my perch on Star's back. "Shall I come down or do you want to come up?"

"Come up? To ride? Really?" His voice sounded nervous and excited all at once. "Won't that be too heavy for him?"

I laughed. "Nope. He can carry both of us easy. C'mon. Let's find a rock and you can jump on."

I nudged Star to a big rock with a sheer side. Kevin moved slowly and carefully around Star which I really appreciated. He even talked softly to him while we walked over to the rock.

"You're pretty good around Star. Where did you learn how to act around a horse?" I asked while I maneuvered Star closer to the rock.

"I watch you. Whenever you let me help you with him, I pay attention to what you do. I think you're almost close enough. Can he move just a little more this way?"

"Sure." I pressed Star's right side with my heel and pulled softly on the left rein. Star side-stepped to the left until I said, "Whoa," then he stopped and waited, his ears cocked back to track what was going on.

"Okay," I directed Kevin, "put your hands on my shoulders while you put your leg over his back. As long as you don't bounce, you won't hurt him."

Kevin eased himself onto Star's back using my shoulders to steady himself. Once he settled in behind me, he dropped his hands to his thighs. I caught a whiff of a tangy citrus scent. Whether it was from his mom's aromatherapy oils or the popular deodorant most guys used, I didn't know. Either way he smelled great. And his solid presence behind me felt good, too. Gave a whole new meaning to the idea of someone having my back. Comforting and exciting at the same time.

I touched my heels to Star's sides and he walked away from the rocks down the beach. I let him choose his own path and he wandered in and out of the gently curling wave foam. He seemed to enjoy bringing down a big hoof in the middle of foamy patches and I wondered if he had invented his own game.

Kevin let out a deep breath against my back.

"You okay back there?"

"Yeah. It's just really different bareback than on a saddle. That time I rode him home from the fairgrounds I was glad I had the saddle to hang onto. This is cool, though. I can feel his muscles."

"You said you're doing a project for Biology using the

tide pools. What's that all about?"

Kevin talked about his project while we plodded down the beach, but after about fifteen minutes I knew we had to head back. I could feel cramps starting in my calves and knew it would only get worse. I turned Star and explained, "Sorry, Kev. We have to head back now."

"Oh, sure. No problem. Sorry about all my blabbing." He sounded embarrassed.

I rushed to reassure him. "Oh no, that's not it. I like hearing about your project. It's just that I can't ride as long as I used to."

"Is it because of the SLE?"

I stretched my head around to look at him. "How do you know what it's called? Did I tell you?" I had a hard time remembering the emotion-filled conversation I had with him a few months ago.

"You told me it was called lupus. I looked it up and read about it."

My mind blanked and I went completely still. I must've pulled on the reins because Star abruptly stopped. I turned my head to look at Kevin. "You did? Why?"

Kevin's neck and cheeks blushed and he rubbed the back of his neck. "For a smart girl, you sure can be dumb. How can you not know how I feel about you? I really like you, Sara. I wanted to know about the lupus in case there's something I can do to help."

"You're basically saying I matter to you?" I clarified.

"Of course, you matter to me!" He kind of sounded angry. "Gosh. How can you even ask that? I'm sorry you feel so bad. When you had to quit cheer, I figured it had to really bother you and I know you weren't at the last horse show because I was there to watch you. How are you, anyway? What's going on now?"

I faced forward again and pressed my heels against Star's sides to urge him on. I brought Kevin up to speed on my current symptoms. When I told him I couldn't ride much anymore and today was a brief reprieve, his arms went around me in a sympathetic hug. It felt good. Safe. I relaxed against him while I finished my story. It didn't take long to return to the rocks. I pulled Star to a stop. "And now, as Tawny would say, you've got all the deets."

He dropped his arms from my waist and carefully lifted his right leg over Star's rump to jump down. He reached up to cover my hands where they rested against Star's neck with his own. He looked up at me and all I saw was compassion in his gaze. "I know this has to be hard. If you ever need to talk, let me know, okay?"

He took his hands away and stuffed them in the pockets of his jacket. He looked startled. "I'm such an idiot. I completely forgot." He drew a small brown bottle out of his pocket. "You mentioned you were having trouble sleeping so I asked Mom if she had anything that would help. She told me to give you this oil blend. It has lavender and some other stuff in it. She said it might help you sleep. You're supposed to massage it onto the bottom of your feet before you go to bed." He shrugged. "She's pretty good at this. Maybe it will help."

"Thanks, Kev. And thank your mom. This is really nice." I smiled while I stowed the tiny bottle in my pocket.

"It's really nice to see you smile again. And thanks for letting me ride with you. It was fun."

"Welcome. Thanks for meeting me. See you."

"Hey, wait a sec." Kevin reached for a rein. "I'm going to help chaperone the junior youth group for roller skating tomorrow morning. Want to come? Please? Don't strand me alone with those kids," he begged with a laugh.

"I don't know, Kev. I haven't skated in I don't remember when."

"Please? It'll be fun. Just two hours and we're done."

Remembering Saturday mornings were full of nothing now that I couldn't train, I decided to go for it. "Sure. Why not? What time?"

"I'll pick you up at 9:30. See you then." He turned with a wave and walked back toward the rocks.

I rode home deep in thought about Kevin. "So," I said to Star. "I guess I understand something else that helps me know if I matter to somebody. If they care enough to try to understand what I'm going through." Star's ears flicked back and forward as he listened to the sound of my voice. "I mean can you believe he even looked up what lupus is? And brought me aromatherapy oil? I guess that's something else that shows me I matter. When somebody gives me something thoughtful. That makes me feel cared about."

Star caught sight of the barn and quickened his pace. I clutched at his mane. "Hey!" Startled out of my thoughts I realized where we were and that Star's attention was on the hay and oats he knew were coming.

"Okay, okay. Dinner's coming right up." We hurried up the path that led to home.

Chapter 19

Maybe I can learn to see myself through Kevin's eyes?
Does he know me better than I know myself?
Sara's Diary

Kevin picked me up the next morning and we drove to the church where thirty kids milled around the parking lot. Some were already on the bus, hanging out the windows shouting to their friends. Kevin got a clipboard from the youth pastor and began checking off the kids already on the bus, then organized the others into a line at the bus door. He motioned me to stand by him. Once everyone was on board, we rolled out of the parking lot and headed for the skating rink. Kevin and I sat in the front seats behind the driver. A few other chaperones were scattered throughout the length of the bus.

My hands lay clenched in my lap. "I'm sorry I said yes to this," I muttered to Kevin. "I haven't skated in a long time and even then, I didn't do much. I've always been so into horses I just never did anything else. I know I'll make a fool of myself, especially because my feet get numb sometimes. I wish I hadn't let you talk me into coming." I kept my voice low so nobody else could hear.

"Relax. This is no big deal. Listen, you have good balance and coordination or you wouldn't be able to ride Star like you do; you'll be a natural at roller-skating. And anyhow, anybody can fall. Nobody will even notice if you do. This is a pretty good group. I've had a lot of fun since I agreed to be a mentor."

"But you know them all. I've seen a few of them at church, but I don't know anybody here but you." Whining or protesting? I wasn't sure.

Just then someone tapped my shoulder. I turned to see a younger girl who looked vaguely familiar.

"Do you, oh, this sounds so stupid, do you have a horse named Star?"

"Yes, I do. Why? How do you know that?"

The girl blushed and looked at her feet. "I've seen you ride at the horse shows. He's the coolest horse I've ever seen! Except Tucker, of course. Tucker's my horse. This is my first year of showing. I'd give anything if I could ride like you." Her face turned even pinker.

My apprehension disappeared. I squirmed around in my seat to face the girl. "Oh, you will. You just have to keep practicing. What kind of horse do you have?"

"He's a Quarter Horse. I've only had him about six months. At first my parents didn't want to let me show him, but I convinced them it's safe. We haven't done very well so far. It's not Tucker's fault," she rushed to explain. "I just haven't ridden much. Did it take you very long to get as good as you are?"

"I'm not that great. Mostly I have a great horse. And we practice, like, a lot."

"Sorry you guys," Kevin broke in. "We're here. Horse talk later. Right now, it's time to skate."

"Oh darn," I complained. I was just getting interested. "At least tell me your name. I'll look for you at the next show, okay?"

"That'd be great. I'd like you to meet Tucker. My

name's Cassie Andrews. See you," Cassie called as she hurried to catch up with her friends.

The two hours of skating flew by. Much to my surprise, I did have a good time. And I only fell once. Maybe the pills were helping?

Back on the bus, Kevin put his arm lightly around my shoulders. "See? There is life outside of horses and barns," he teased.

"What else have I been missing?" I laughed, but then reached down to rub my aching legs.

Kevin's eyebrows drew together and his voice deepened in concern. "Are you hurt?"

"Not really. My feet and legs ache most of the time now. No big deal." I continued massaging my calf.

"I'm sorry. I should've remembered and checked to see how you were doing. Will you be okay?"

"Yeah, I will. Anyway, it was worth it." The frown on his face seemed set in stone so I rushed to reassure him. "Really. It was fun and the kids were nice. Don't worry. I'm really okay."

"Sure?"

"Absolutely. Hey! We're back already."

Kevin put his hand on my arm. "Is it okay if I come over for a while? I don't have to help Mom this afternoon."

I bit my lip and glanced out the window. Kevin noticed my hesitation and removed his hand from my arm.

"No problem. I'll just see you later."

"No, Kev," I protested. "I'd like for you to come, really. It's just that Saturday afternoon is when I clean the barn. It takes quite a while now since I'm so slow. Probably wouldn't be much fun."

Kevin grinned. "You'd be surprised what I consider fun. I'd like to come. Maybe I can even help."

"Okay, but don't say I didn't warn you." I shook my finger at him. Kevin laughed and grabbed my hand. Fingers lightly entwined, we turned and walked toward the Jeep. It didn't take long to get back to my house.

I called through the back door to let my parents know I was home. Mom asked a question I couldn't quite hear so I followed her voice into the kitchen. She wanted to know how the roller-skating went and laughed when I described my first wobbly times around the ring. Then Mom noticed Kevin and invited us in for a snack.

"Thanks, Mom, but Kevin's going to help me clean the barn."

"That will help the work go faster. Thanks, Kevin, and, oh, I almost forgot. Tawny wants you to call her."

"Shoot. She's probably been texting me and I've had my phone off. I'll give her a call," I assured Mom as we headed out the door.

Once we were inside the barn, I slid the main door closed and opened Star's stall so he could wander around the wide walkway. Then Kevin and I tackled the dirty straw. With both of us working, it didn't take long and I was glad of the help.

"You're kidding. He eats that much?" Kevin sat in the hay manger and watched me fill the grain bucket.

"Yep. He gets even more when we're doing all those horse shows."

"Wow. I thought horses just ate grass. I didn't know you had to feed them oats and corn and all that other stuff. Here, let me do that for you. You sit down." Kevin took the pitchfork from my hands and stabbed a section of fresh hay to fill the manger.

I leaned against the manger and rubbed my hands. "Thanks. Sometimes my hands are so sore I can't hold the pitchfork very well. Look how swollen and ugly they are." I held out my hands in disgust.

Kevin kept fluffing out the straw around the stall. "Your hands aren't ugly."

"Oh, come on, Kev. Look at me. Fat hands, fat face, fat body. I'm ugly, ugly, ugly. I hate what the medication is doing to me."

Kevin leaned the pitchfork against the wall and walked over to me. Taking both my hands in his, he studied them for a moment. "Your hands handle Star so gently it's like you're managing clouds. Your hands aren't ugly. Your face lights up when you smile and your hair reminds me of the color in the last few minutes of the sunset. You're not ugly. You're a little heavier than you used to be, but so what? You said yourself the doctor says you'll lose weight as soon as he can decrease that one pill you have to take. You just have to be patient. Okay?"

I looked up at him through my lashes. What was that fluttering feeling in my chest? And why did I want to touch his face? I loosened a hand from his grasp and reached up. Kevin watched me, smiling gently, when suddenly a loud, "Uff!" exploded from him. He lurched forward tipping me into the hay manger.

"Oh gosh. Are you okay? Here, let me pull you up." He helped me out of the manger, then turned to see Star standing behind us with a bright, inquisitive look on his face. Star nudged Kevin's shoulder, knocking him into me again. Kevin grabbed me, but not in time to keep me from falling back into the manger and pulling him with me.

I giggled. Then laughed. Soon we were both breathless with laughter. I caught my breath while I picked pieces of hay out of my hair. "Not sure how you can put up with me. All I do is complain." We struggled out of the manger. "Moan and complain, that's me."

"Oh, you're not so bad. And if you really want to know, I put up with you only because I'm hoping you'll teach me how to ride Star."

"That's the way it is, huh? I get it. Love me, love my horse? Or should I say, love my horse, love me?" I teased.

He moved a step closer. "I think so, Sara. I think you've hit the nail right on the head."

He sounded bashful instead of arrogant. I liked it. I

placed my hand against his chest. He curled his hand around mine and leaned forward. Star stepped forward to get to his hay and nudged us both out of the way. Spell broken.

Kevin stepped back and tucked his hands in his pockets. "Guess I better get going. See you in church tomorrow?"

"Yeah. Probably." I grabbed the pitchforks and stowed them in the tack room.

"Want to meet me for Sunday school?"

"I don't think so. I feel funny when I go. And I usually don't understand what everybody's talking about. I never did understand really, but Mom and Dad always made me go. Now that I'm supposed to get more rest, they let me sleep in if I want." I snorted. "I guess that's one good thing that's come from this stupid disease."

"I wish you'd come. I think if you understood more about God, you wouldn't worry so much about being sick. By the way, I've been meaning to apologize for how pushy I was when you told me about your diagnosis. You were right, I shouldn't have come on so strong about God and faith. All I did was push you further away."

"Yeah, well. I wasn't in the best shape that day."

"Exactly. Instead of preaching, I should have just listened and been your friend. Anyway, sorry."

"Apology accepted. And as far as church tomorrow, what else is there to know? I know who God is. I have read the Bible, you know." I dug my toe into the dirt and squirmed. "I just don't know if I believe everything I've been told. I'm not saying I don't, I just don't know. And I don't know about you, but when someone doesn't answer me, I eventually quit talking. God stopped answering me a long time ago. Plus, how can I believe He loves me when I'm so miserable? Remember when I said I could tell I mattered to you?"

"Yeah. I was glad you told me that. You do matter to

me."

"Well, I can't tell if I matter to God. I can tell with you, Tawny and my family by what you all do and how you care about me, but God's a big unknown. I think if anything, I'm kind of mad at Him."

Kevin shifted his weight and looked at the ceiling. His lips pursed in thought. Then his gaze sought mine again.

"How would you know God cared about you?"

I pulled a piece of hay out of a handy bale and stuck it in my mouth. Chewing thoughtfully, I finally answered, "Mom asked me the same thing the other day about people. God seems a bit different than people though."

Kevin smiled. "You think?"

I munched on my piece of hay, then frowned. "You know, I guess I don't know how I would know I matter to God. I know it's supposed to be about believing and having faith, but that feels pretty empty. And a lot of work. How can I believe in someone who doesn't seem real? Any suggestions?"

He took my hands in his. "Why don't you just ask Him?"

"What? You mean like pray?"

Kevin nodded and shrugged. "Praying is just talking to God. Try talking to Him and see what happens. Can't hurt."

I considered his suggestion. "I guess. Feels weird though."

"Most things feel weird when you first try them. Your skates felt weird this morning until you went around the ring a couple of times and got your balance. Get your balance with God. I know from my own experience He's willing to meet you more than halfway if you try at all."

My emotions roller-coastered from confusion to doubt to hope to determination. Apparently, Kevin could read my face because he smiled at me. I couldn't help but smile back and his breath caught.

"I do not understand how you can possibly think

you're ugly. When you smile...I don't know...you sort of light up. You are so not ugly." He bent toward me and I moved my hands up to rest on his shoulders. His hands clasped my waist and embarrassment about my extra weight dissolved when Kevin's lips met mine. His lips were soft, not demanding. One hand moved up so his palm gently cradled my cheek. I felt connected and transfixed all at once. A perfect kiss. It was, however, short because the barn door rattled and Ben's voice called, "Hey! You guys in there? I see Kevin's Jeep. You in there, Kev? I want to talk to you about your project."

Kevin and I stepped apart, linked by our gaze on each other. Still looking at me, Kevin answered, "Yeah, Ben. I'm here. Just a sec."

My hands skimmed slowly down Kevin's chest while he reluctantly removed his hand from my cheek. "Guess we better let your brother in?"

I snorted. "I know for a fact he won't go away so, yeah, we'd better."

The door rattled again to punctuate my remarks. "C'mon you guys. Open the door."

"Hold on. I'm coming," I called. The latch clunked loudly when I unfastened it and Ben burst through the door.

"What's going on in here? Why's the door locked? What are you guys doing?"

"Not that it's any of your business, but we're cleaning Star's stall. Just got done. I locked the door so he couldn't open it. You know he's figured out the latch. Relax, would you?"

"Yeah, right. I bet that's what you were doing," Ben challenged suspiciously. He peered into the stall. He took in the pristine straw and Star calmly munching new hay. Kevin stood at Star's shoulder smoothing his mane.

"Oh." Ben calmed down. As soon as he spotted Kevin, he walked into the stall already talking with his hands as he went. "So, Kev. About the tide pool project. I was thinking..."

Kevin interrupted Ben with a final pat on Star's shoulder. "Sorry, Ben. I've gotta get going. I have homework and chores to finish. We'll have to talk about my project later."

Kevin walked out of the stall toward the door, but stopped when he got to me and held out his hand. "Walk me to the car?"

"Sure." I took his hand and we walked out of the barn toward the worn Jeep. Ben followed protesting loudly. "But I have a great idea and I really think you'll like it. Hey, how about if I come with you? I can help with your chores." He hurried to catch up with us.

Kevin looked past me to Ben. "If you want to come and help, that's fine with me. Go ask your mom first though."

"Oh. Yeah. Good idea. Just a sec." Ben hurried toward the house calling back over his shoulder, "Don't leave without me."

We arrived at the car. Kevin turned to lean against the driver's door and took both my hands in his. I responded with a light squeeze. "You're a saint to put up with him."

"No. You're the saint. I'm a greenie, remember?"

Surprised he could joke about our nicknames, I asked, "You don't mind what they call you?"

"Naw. Why should I? They don't know me. They just need to label everybody so they feel better about themselves."

"I don't like my nickname," I admitted. "It bugs me. That's not who I am."

"That's the whole point. They don't know you. I'm going to start calling you Sunny because your hair reminds me of a sunset. How's that for a nickname?" he teased.

"Better than saint, that's for sure."

The back door slammed. I warned, "He's back," in a singsong tone. We laughed.

Kevin let go of my hands and turned to get in the car. "See you tomorrow at church." he confirmed.

"Yeah. Want to sit with us?"

"As Tawny would say, absofreakinlutely."

I laughed and he climbed in the car just as Ben skidded to a stop on the passenger side. He was talking before he was even inside the car. I waved as the car backed up and drove away.

While I walked toward the house, I retrieved my phone from my pocket to text Tawny. I couldn't stop thinking about what happened in the barn with Kevin. Did I want to tell Tawny about it or not? Not, I decided. I hugged the memory of his kiss to myself. I knew he had to have felt the fat roll around the waist of my jeans, but he didn't seem at all bothered. It felt good to experience acceptance and love. Love. Did he love me? He seemed to be saying so, but I wasn't sure. I sat down on the back steps. Drawn like a magnet, Abby glided onto my lap. She circled a few times then settled down purring and kneading my thigh lightly with her paws. As usual, Spot strolled up and demanded his share of attention. The cat put out a paw to push against the dog's nose, but she didn't stop purring. Spot laid down by my feet, his head covering one foot.

Idly stroking the cat, I wondered how I could know if Kevin loved me. Tawny would have an answer. Tawny had an answer for everything. And more experience with guys.

"If I was going to describe Kevin's kiss to Tawny, I would say it was kind. If that's even possible," I informed Abby. She looked at me through half-closed eyes as if to say, "Interesting. Tell me more." I smiled at my own imagination, but decided the little calico was a good listener.

"I don't know. His kiss was like he is. Kind. Generous. He gives but doesn't take," I advised the cat. Abby's purr deepened as if she approved. "Oh, don't get me wrong," I hurried to clarify. "It wasn't boring. Not. At.

All. So does that mean he loves me?"

I couldn't help but compare kisses between Kevin and Travis. They were such different guys. Different kisses. Different feelings. I stared unseeing at the barn. "I've gone from wondering if I matter to how much I matter. Feelings are sure hard to figure out." My phone sounded the opening chords to Taylor Swift's "Shake It Off," signaling Tawny's answering text. The chords startled the cat who jumped from my lap, gaining traction by digging in with her claws.

"Ow! Hey." I rubbed my thighs to take out the sting and muttered, "See if I tell you any more secrets." I picked up my phone and settled in for an electronic talk with my friend.

Chapter 20

Pain is the wind under despair's black wings.
Sara's Diary

Now that I had talked Dad into letting me do some light riding, the next day after church I asked Ben to lift my saddle onto Star's back so I could ride down to the beach. Star's ears pricked forward and he tossed his head when he saw the long stretch of sand.

"Sorry, boy. It hurts too much for me to do more than just sit here. You'll have to do your running by yourself in the pasture. I miss it as much as you do, believe me." I stroked the muscular shoulder under his mane.

We walked up to the rocks. I pulled Star to a stop and dismounted with the grace of a drunken sailor. I leaned against the solid bulk of my horse for support. Face buried in his mane, I breathed in the familiar scent of warm horse and musky leather. My own personal aromatherapy never failed to relax me. I sat down against a boulder, warmed from the sun and turned my face toward the ocean breeze. Star nibbled at the toe of my boot.

Everything had changed in such a short time. I couldn't ride Star because of my physical condition. In fact,

I couldn't do most of the stuff I enjoyed anymore. Like cheerleading…and babysitting…dating Travis. Wait. Where did that come from? I have a boyfriend now and it's Kevin, I reminded myself. One of the biggest changes is Mom and Dad lying to me. They still haven't talked to me about my disease being fatal. You'd think they'd know I'm old enough for them to tell me the truth. I stared at the waves. "I wonder what it's like to die," I murmured to Star.

During the last bone marrow test I thought about dying. The test was just so painful. At least when I died, I wouldn't have to worry about the tests anymore. I'd had two more since the first one in the hospital. Each had been worse than the last because I knew what to expect now. Anticipation, or dread, made everything more difficult. During the last procedure, I gripped the nurse's hand so tightly I wondered if I might break her fingers. That was the first time I actually thought about death. Besides not having to experience the tests again, I wouldn't have to wonder who my friends were anymore. I wouldn't have to try so hard to fit in. Maybe dying could be a relief, who knew?

A startled snort from Star interrupted my dark thoughts. A scuba diver walked out from the other side of the rocks. I laughed at the astonished look on Star's face. His ears perked up and he threw his head high, nostrils flaring. He had never seen a human in black rubber skin before. We watched while the diver put fins on his feet, shrugged into his air tanks and fastened the straps. That done, he positioned the mouthpiece and pulled his mask over his face. Star stamped a front hoof and backed up a step. I laughed out loud. The diver heard me, turned and waved. He adjusted his mask then duck-walked into the incoming tide.

Gradually, the water reached the man's chest then before my fascinated gaze his sleek black head slipped beneath the water without a ripple. He was gone. It was as if he never existed.

Struggling to my feet, I stared at the spot where the diver disappeared. "It must be so peaceful down there," I whispered. "He leaves all his problems on the surface. It's hard to believe the water's so calm when sometimes it's chaos from the riptide. You know, my life is kind of like a rip current. I don't move forward and I can't go back. I'm stuck." I kept staring at the water until Star nudged my arm.

"Huh? Oh. Star. You bored, boy? Okay, let's go."

I led him to a rock and scrambled into the saddle. "Not my usual graceful self, huh, Star? How does it feel to have someone climb you like you're a tree?" I turned his head and we walked slowly home.

"Hi, sweetheart." Dad waved when I rode into the yard.

I lifted my hand briefly, then urged Star into the barn. Dad followed us. His cheerful comment died on his lips when he saw how gingerly I dismounted. He hurried forward to catch me when I stumbled as my feet touched the ground.

"It's still this bad?" Emotion made his voice sharp.

"What, Dad?"

"Come on, Sara. You know what I mean. You lower yourself out of the saddle an inch at a time, put your feet on the ground like you're stepping on hot coals, then collapse? And breathing like you've run a marathon? Why did you tell me riding was no problem now?"

My shoulders lifted toward my ears, "It's not that bad, really. I can handle it."

"I don't want you to handle it!"

Star shuffled his feet and tossed his head at the emotional tension.

Dad ran a hand through his hair and grasped the back of his neck. Then he let his hand drop and he shook his head. His tone notched down. "What I mean is, I don't want you to do things that obviously hurt. I think it would be better to put off riding again until you feel better."

It felt like the ground shifted beneath my feet. "Dad, you can't do that. Riding is the only thing I have left. Star is the only thing I have left. Please..."

"I'm sorry, Sara. I can't let you ride while it causes so much pain. You have tears on your cheeks just from dismounting."

"Please don't make me stop again. I don't care if it hurts. Really. I just want to be able to..."

"I care. I'm not going to let you do something that hurts you like that. It's for your own good, honey, don't you see? It's just until your medicine starts working better. It won't be long."

Desperation fueled my voice. "Dad. Please. I'll be really careful. And I'll only ride a few times a week. Please don't make me stop again."

I ran smack into the brick wall of Dad's decision. "No. Come up to the house with me now. I'll send your brother down to settle Star for the night."

"No! He's mine. He's all I have left. Don't..." My cries faded when he grasped me firmly but gently by the shoulders and pressed me along with him toward the house.

I turned my head and could see Star through my tears standing in the open door of the barn. His ears shifted forward, then back. One black hoof lifted and pawed the ground nervously. He didn't understand but he could read my emotion like I read a book.

"Ben," Dad yelled when we got to the house. "Go put Star up, will you?"

Dad steered me toward the couch and helped me sit. I heard the back door slam and imagined Ben reaching the barn and leading Star into his stall. Star would submit to a clumsy grooming, let Ben pet him briefly and then be left in the dark with his feed and water.

I tossed and turned that night. I'd developed a new, sharp source of pain in my index finger. It burned constantly and was so sensitive to touch I kept a band-aid around it for protection. I turned one way in bed and faced pain. Turning the other way was no better. There I faced grief and a life without Star. My head knew Star was still my horse and always would be, but my heart knew the special connection we enjoyed would diminish if all I could do was sit in the barn or groom him. That was better than nothing, but riding was our ticket to freedom and the key to our bond. Prison loomed without that connection. Imprisoned with illness. What a life.

Sleeping late in the morning didn't seem to matter and stopping by the office for a late pass became routine. It barely registered that the boys from the football team were back in their seats. I saw Robyn in the lunchroom sitting by herself and remembered Tawny said Robyn received the same suspension as the boys, but with the added requirement by the judge that Robyn see a counselor. I wondered idly what it would be like to talk to someone who could help, but it was a passing thought. I had a brief impulse to sit down and join Robyn, but that passed also. I made my way to an empty table and sat with my back to the room.

I made myself eat lunch and tried to read a book, but my mind was busy wondering about Robyn. Why had the girl taken pictures of herself and texted them to Travis? Maybe the pictures were Robyn's shot at trying to matter to Travis? Did it work? I hadn't seen Travis so had no idea if he and Robyn were together or not. Why did I care? Travis obviously didn't care about me. Did Robyn matter to Travis?

If I was honest with myself, I knew that if Robyn mattered to Travis, he wouldn't have shared those photos with the other guys. That wasn't caring, I decided. Then a thought from nowhere invaded my mind. Did what happen to Robyn matter to me?

The subject of my thoughts plunked a stack of books

down on the table and straddled the bench next to me. I looked up from my musings and regarded Robyn cautiously, not sure what to expect.

"What's shakin', Saint-girl?"

I propped my elbows on the table and rested my head on my clasped hands. "I really hate that nickname." I turned to look at Robyn. "Can you please just use my name?"

Robyn stared back at me. "Sure, Saaarrraaa." She drew it out mockingly. "I heard you might be sick."

Where had that come from? Ben, maybe, at his school? Surely not Tawny or Kevin. I stared at the wall, irritation tightening my chest. "Yeah? Well, I heard you were naked."

Robyn gasped. I turned to look at her. Her eyes narrowed to slits. "So. The good girl isn't all that good after all." She stood and grabbed her books. Then bent down and hissed in my ear, "And everybody says you're such a nice girl. Yeah, right." She turned to go. "Later, Saaarrraa."

Eyes lowered; I could see a pit of shame opening beneath my feet. I called toward Robyn's retreating back. "Wait, Robyn. I'm sorry. I didn't mean it. Please come back."

Robyn's hand raised in a one-finger salute was the only answer.

I dropped my head back onto my hands. What was wrong with me? That was such an awful thing to say. And now it was out there and I couldn't take it back. Regret piled into my dark cloud.

The rest of the day dragged. A deep sigh escaped when the last bell rang and I trudged toward my locker. I squinted when I thought I saw something on my locker handle. I hurried forward and saw a single golden rose stuck in the handle. There was no note. Just a single lovely bud.

"Boy, you have all the luck."

Startled, I looked up to see Tawny.

"Most guys in this school are such clods. They'd never think to give a girl a rose. And this is the second time. 'Course it helps that his cousin owns the florist shop I guess."

"What do you mean?"

"Travis, of course. His cousin owns the florist shop. And he gave you a carnation before. He's back in school today and he's brown nosing everybody. Trying to get in good with you, too, I guess. Talk later? Ry's waiting for me." Tawny sniffed the rose then walked down the hall.

The rose held carefully in one hand; I closed my locker. Was Tawny right? Was Travis trying to get in good with me? Maybe this was his way of saying he was sorry. Maybe I was the first girl he really cared about. I wandered out the front door to wait for Kevin on the steps.

"Hey, Sara."

I shaded my eyes with my hand when I looked up to see Travis standing on the top step. I smiled. "Thank you for the rose. It's really pretty. Looks like a sunset."

His blank look vanished so fast I figured I'd imagined it. "Rose?"

"Yeah. I found it on my locker. It was nice of you to leave it for me." I looked down and lifted the rose to my nose.

"Oh. Oh, yeah. The rose."

I looked up to see a fleeting sly look in his eyes, instantly gone. Did I imagine it?

"You put it on my locker, right?"

Travis hesitated. "Sure. Glad you like it."

"I love it." I sniffed the rose again and smiled at him.

"Ah," he said with a grin. "There's that sexy smile. When're you and me going out again?"

"Uh, I don't know. Aren't you with Robyn?"

Travis shrugged. "Sometimes. But what she doesn't know can't hurt her. I haven't seen much of you lately. How about the two of us hanging out?"

"I'm not sure I, oh, hi, Kev."

"Hey, it's the Killer." Travis punched Kevin on the arm and laughed. "How's it going, Killer?"

I looked uncertainly between the two. Travis turned his gaze on me. "What's this? This greenie helping you with your homework or something? That's cray."

My neck and cheeks flushed. "Uh, well, yeah. Sometimes," I answered. My gaze avoided Kevin.

"Well, when you get done with the boring stuff, let me know and I'll add the excitement for you. See ya around."

Ignoring Kevin completely, Travis finger brushed my cheek then continued down the stairs playing catch with his car keys.

Silence.

I stood and brushed off my jeans with one hand while I clutched my books and the rose in my other. "Well, guess we better go." The brightness in my tone sounded fake even to me.

Kevin didn't move.

"Kevin? Aren't you coming"

"You didn't tell him you're dating me?" Kevin's voice sounded tight.

"No. He didn't ask." My voice sounded shrill.

"You could have told him."

"Why should I tell him? It's none of his business." Now soprano shrill.

Kevin searched my face. "You still like him, don't you?"

I hesitated just a moment too long to answer.

Kevin shook his head and looked out across the football field. "I don't believe it. After how he treated you. Not to mention Robyn. I thought I knew you. How dumb can I be?"

He glanced at the rose in my hand. "Guess the rose makes a goodbye gift."

My hand choked the rose stem and bent it. "*You* gave

me the rose?"

"Yeah. I thought you'd like it. It kind of goes with your hair. Who did you think…oh, I get it. You thought Travis gave it to you. You have a one-track mind where he's concerned. I don't stand a chance. See you, Sara. I won't bother you anymore. Even with your homework." The sarcasm wasn't like him.

"But, Kev…" I protested.

He turned to face me full on. "Can you honestly tell me you wouldn't go out with him if he asked you?"

My lowered glance was answer enough.

"That's what I thought. Bye, Sara."

I watched him go with mixed feelings. If Travis was interested in me…but Kevin was good to me…but Travis was so exciting…but Kevin was there when I needed him. Except Kevin was walking away from me now.

"Fine," I muttered. "If he can't take a little competition, he can't like me very much." I ignored how empty I felt walking home alone.

That night my phone buzzed. It was Travis.

"So, pretty lady. When are we going to hang?"

Trying to control the eagerness in my voice, I answered, "I don't know. As soon as you ask me, I guess."

"Sure you can handle that greenie? He really gave me the stink-eye, you know."

"He's just a friend."

"Great. How about tomorrow night? I'll meet you at the library at 7:00. S'okay?"

I wavered. Tomorrow was a school night. I knew my parents preferred I didn't go out on week nights, let alone with Travis. My heart beat loudly in my ears. I couldn't lose him again. "Sure. I'll be there."

My lie to Mom and Dad worked, a study group at the library, and I pulled into the parking lot of the brick building a little before 7:00. I sat on the steps where I'd be sure to see Travis when he pulled up. Finally, at 7:30 he showed up.

"C'mon, sexy Sara! Let's get going," he yelled, leaning through the passenger window.

I wished he would keep his voice down. I hurried to the car so he wouldn't shout again.

He fish-tailed the car away from the curb leaving a stain of rubber. He headed out of town toward my house and the beach. The car weaved through traffic. More than once, he drove straight through stop signs. My heart raced and my hands slicked with sweat. Travis remained deaf to my pleas to slow down. To be careful. My hand clasped the door handle with a death-grip and every once in a while, a quiet moan escaped my lips.

He skidded around the corner of a small dirt road, drove a short way until he reached a clearing then stopped the car so abruptly, I was thrown against the seat belt. He unbuckled the belt, grabbed my arm and yanked me over to his side of the seat. I struggled against him, but he kept me imprisoned tight at his side.

"You're hurting me. Let me go." I squirmed beneath the weight of his arm. "Come on, Travis. I can't breathe. You're scaring me," I panted.

"Come off it, Sara. Knock off the Miss Innocent act. I know you're not really Sara the Saint. I know what you're all about. You want some of the magic to rub off, you gotta be closer for that. Here, try some of this. Even if you're not a saint, this'll make you feel heavenly."

He cackled at his poor joke then released me. I scooched away while he pulled a small bag out of his pocket. He poured some white powder on the back of his hand. Holding one nostril closed he sniffed the powder up his nose. Then he poured out another small pile and held his hand towards me. "Here, my lady. Heaven awaits."

My heart hammered like a trapped sparrow's. "Uh, no thank you. I don't want any. And I really think I should be getting home."

"Home? No way. You've been teasing me and leading me on. No way are you going home yet. Now come here."

He reached for me, but his movements were clumsy. I dodged him. I scrambled toward my door, clawed for the handle and jerked it up.

"Oh, no you don't. You come back here." Travis laughed.

He sounded like the villain in the TV show I watched last night. Cruel and hardhearted. Fear notched up to dread.

Travis grabbed my sleeve and held on. Terrified, I jerked my arm away and my sleeve tore from his grasp. I yanked the handle, rammed my body against the door and stumbled out of the car. I ran toward the beach, sobbing in fright. Heavy footsteps pounded after me. I panted and prayed under my breath.

"God, help me. Please, help me!" I chanted the plea until two strong arms caught me and held tight. I screamed and struggled to get free. A calm voice pierced my distress. "Take it easy. It's me. Kevin. You're all right now."

I stopped struggling just as Travis burst into view. Adrenaline tremors shook my body.

"Hey!" Travis snarled. "What are you doing here?"

"Taking a walk," Kevin snapped. "Last I heard this is a free country."

"Well, you can just walk somewhere else. And take your hands off my dimepiece."

Kevin glanced down at me, huddled against him and holding on for dear life. "Want me to leave?"

I shook my head and clutched his jacket even tighter. Too bad I didn't understand until now how good it felt to hold onto something solid.

"I guess she's had enough of your company. Maybe you're the one who needs to leave." Kevin's voice was quiet, but firm. And not afraid.

"Why you dumb greenie…you can't tell me what to do. I'll tear you apart, you Bible thumping sissy."

Travis lunged for Kevin who anticipated the move and stepped away from me, nudging me gently out of the way. He backed up and Travis lost his balance and sprawled in the dirt. Travis scrambled up and dived again towards Kevin, who easily moved out of reach. Travis fell, breathing heavily.

"We'll be going now," Kevin said quietly. Taking my arm, he led me a few feet away then turned to assess the other boy. "How about letting me call you an Uber, Trav? Pretty sure you shouldn't be driving."

A curse, a slammed door and gravel kicked up from squealing tires were the only answer.

Kevin settled me down on a log and sat next to me. "You okay?"

Too shaken to talk, I nodded. My body shivered.

"Your sleeve's torn. Here, take my jacket. It'll cover up your shirt and you can tell your folks you borrowed it. Want me to walk you home?"

I nodded while I shrugged into his jean jacket and pulled it close. It smelled like peppermint. We stood and started toward my house. After a few minutes I looked up at him and asked, "Don't you want to know what happened?"

His jaw tightened and he ran a hand impatiently through his hair. His gaze looked ice-cold. "I may be a Bible-thumping sissy, but I'm not stupid. I know what happened. Though to be fair, Travis might not remember. He was pretty high. He's probably in a haze right now."

I stopped and stared at him. "You're defending him. I don't believe it."

"Don't be an idiot. Of course, I'm not defending him. He's a moron for taking drugs in the first place, but you're not much better for going along with him. What did you expect?"

Kevin's unfamiliar harshness landed on me like Thor's hammer. "I don't know." My voice trembled. "I didn't think…I didn't know…I thought he liked me," I cried.

Kevin stared at me. Gradually his jaw loosened and his gaze turned kind. Or was it pity? "You mean you didn't know he's been using coke? You didn't see how everybody's avoiding him?"

I shook my head.

He blew out a breath. "I'm sorry. I thought you knew and were going out with him anyway. I'm sorry for what I said."

Crying in earnest now, I shook my head and clutched at the jacket around my shoulders. "That's okay. You're right. I'm an idiot for thinking he really liked me. I'm just a plain, stupid idiot. Oh," my throat caught on a sob, "I wish I was dead."

Chapter 21

I wanted him to love me. Instead, he destroyed me.
Sara's Diary

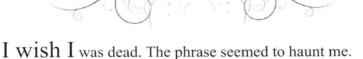

I wish I was dead. The phrase seemed to haunt me.

I assumed people were laughing at me because of what happened with Travis, so I began to avoid everyone. Including my friends. Tawny tried to reason with me.

"I haven't heard anybody say anything about you and Travis. I think Kevin's right. Travis was stoned and doesn't remember. His crowd is not about stealth, you know that. They blab everything."

My feelings were so strong they felt like the truth. And I believed my emotions. I shook my head at Tawny and walked away. Tawny hurried after me and placed a gentle hand on my arm.

"Hey."

"Yeah?"

"Do you want to go to that new movie with me tomorrow night? It's supposed to be good and my mom said you can spend the night afterwards if you want. I totally have not talked to you in so long." Tawny's voice faltered and trailed off.

I stared at the books in my arms. "I don't think so. I, ah, I have some stuff to do at home. But thanks anyway." I hurried away before Tawny could answer.

That became my habit. I turned down the few invitations I got. I quit going to games and ate my lunch alone in a corner of the cafeteria. Gradually, my only companion became Star. I spent long hours ambling down the beach with him on a long lead. Or sometimes I just sat in his stall and read a book while he munched his hay. He was the only one who truly understood and cared about me.

My parents tiptoed around me so they must have sensed something was wrong. I passed by their bedroom one afternoon and heard a whispered conversation that depression and fatigue could be due to medication. They agreed not to confront me about continued disobedience with chores and homework.

Finally, I congratulated myself. Finally, they figured out I could, and would, make my own decisions.

One night after we finished dinner, I got up from the table and headed to the family room. Dad looked up. "Sara? Aren't you going to help your mother with the dishes? I think it's your week."

"Oh, Dad. Not tonight. I'm too tired," I moaned. I kept walking.

"Sara," Dad insisted. "This week it's your turn to help your mother after dinner. She's tired, too. Now please go out in the kitchen and give her a hand."

"But, Dad," I grumbled. "I don't feel good. Can't I go sit down?"

"No, honey. You can't. Come here a minute."

I returned to the table dragging my feet. I sagged into a chair.

"I know this is hard for you," Dad began. "And I know you don't feel well a lot of the time. But you need to keep going and try to keep your life as normal as possible. You'll be much happier if you keep up with your regular chores and make an effort to help other people. If you just concentrate on how bad you feel, you'll only feel worse. I know it's hard, but you're just going to have to find a way to live with SLE. You have no choice."

He actually patted my hand. I snatched it away, pushed back my chair and stomped to the kitchen. He was wrong. I didn't have to live with it. I could end this garbage once and for all any time I wanted.

I focused more and more on all my problems. I skipped classes and ignored most of my homework assignments. A silent, burning anger began to gnaw at me. The intermittent dark thoughts became a permanent dreary cloud that enveloped me like a heavy cape. How could God let this happen to me? What about how much He was supposed to love me? The Bible on the table next to my bed caught my eye and I grabbed it and threw it across the room. It slid under my bed. Good riddance.

The next Sunday while everybody got ready for church, I approached Mom. "I don't feel up to going to church today. I'd like to stay home and rest."

"Sure, honey. You do look tired. You'll be fine next Sunday."

But the next Sunday was the same story. And the next.

"Sara, this is the third Sunday in a row you've missed church," Mom protested. "Are you sure you don't feel well enough to go?"

"I really don't," I moaned. "I feel exhausted."

It became an established pattern for me to stay home on Sunday and rest. Sometimes, I hated to admit, I missed the service. It felt safe and peaceful at church. When I used to sit with Kevin, I felt a part of everything. Now I mostly felt alone and miserable. Much easier to stay home where I didn't have to be reminded of all my mistakes.

One Sunday afternoon I walked along the beach leading Star for company when I saw Kevin coming toward me. He waved. I hesitated, but waved back. I fought the urge to wait until he came up to me so we could talk. I hadn't talked to anybody in a long time, but in the end, I turned Star and walked toward home. Alone. Seems like I'm always fighting my feelings.

"Why don't I know what I want anymore?" I asked Star as we dodged foamy water on the beach. "All I know is I'm miserable and nobody cares. Nobody but you, Star. You're all I have."

We reached the barn and I followed him into his stall. "You're all I have," I repeated as I brushed and wiped him dry. The brush slipped out of my hand.

"Clumsy," I muttered and bent to pick it up. When my hand reached for the brush, I noticed my index finger was almost completely white. It felt cold and I wondered why just one finger would feel cold. I shrugged and finished brushing Star.

By the time I got back to the house, my finger looked almost normal. I forgot about it.

The next day at school I had trouble holding my pen. The same finger was white and cold again; I couldn't control it. I looked closely and noticed a small sore. I didn't remember cutting myself and wondered where it came from. Within a couple of days, it spread and covered the whole tip of my finger. As the wound grew, it became sort of a grayish color and was sensitive and easily hurt. I decided to ask the doctor about it and called for an appointment. I got in that day on a cancellation.

"Your finger hurts?" Doctor Adams said, amusement in his tone. "Well, maybe you have a sliver or something. Here, let me take a look."

He reached over his desk and took my hand. "Good Lord, your finger's freezing. How long has it been this way?" He poked at the sore. Tears flooded my eyes. My finger really hurt. At last, he let go of my hand and I sat back in the chair.

"What's wrong with my finger? Where did the sore

come from?" I cradled my finger carefully in my other hand to protect and warm it.

He looked serious when he answered, "I'm afraid your circulation has gotten so bad your finger isn't getting any blood at the end. The sore is gangrene. Now, I can…"

"Gangrene!" I froze. That was when flesh died for lack of blood supply. My history class had been studying the Civil War. I gagged when I remembered the horrible descriptions of soldiers who had gangrene. Most of the time they had to have the gangrenous parts amputated.

The bottled-up stress of the last months and increasingly dark thoughts kindled sparks of fear when I imagined what gangrene in my finger could mean. Panic ignited my imagination: amputation, disfigurement, pain, more ridicule. My lungs tightened and I couldn't breathe. My brain felt like a volcano ready to erupt and my hands began to tingle. I grabbed my forehead with both hands and pressed to contain the building pressure. I gulped at air, but couldn't take a breath.

A vague memory of Dad describing a panic attack coincided with the doctor's voice. "Sara, you're okay. Think about breathing and inhale as deeply as you can then exhale slowly. Do it again. Inhale and exhale slowly."

The doctor kept up his instructions while he moved to the chair next to me. I felt hands on my shoulders and heard the rustle of a nurse's scrubs. The nurse took up the doctor's calming dialogue while she gently rubbed my back in a slow circle.

"Sara, continue to breathe slowly and deeply. Concentrate on letting your muscles relax. Inhale like you're smelling your favorite soup, then slowly exhale to cool the soup. You're in a safe place and can relax. Inhale and smell the soup, exhale and cool it off."

The nurse continued her soothing directions. I felt the pressure in my brain ease. I could breathe again. My doctor took my hand and pressed his fingers to the inside of my wrist. His hand holding mine felt warm and comforting. The small warm sensation made me realize I was freezing. The nurse must have felt shivers because she patted my shoulder and said she'd be right back.

The nurse returned quickly and wrapped a warm blanket around my shoulders. The doctor returned to his chair behind the desk so the nurse could sit in the chair next to me. She smiled at me and pushed the hair off my forehead. "Feeling better?"

I nodded. "Thank you," came out a scratchy whisper. I cleared my throat.

The nurse squeezed my hand. "Let me get you some water. Are you okay now? Panic attacks are scary."

The kindness in her voice thickened my throat with emotion. "Yes, thank you. I'm fine."

"Okay. I'll be right back."

I looked at the doctor. "You won't cut my finger off?"

"No. We don't have to be that drastic. What's happening with your finger is because of the Raynaud's. It's a lack of circulation to extremities and can become dangerous, but, smart girl that you are, you came to see me in plenty of time. A new prescription will help your circulation and I want you to soak you hand in warm water and Epsom salts as many times a day as possible. I see no reason why this small area of gangrene won't disappear within a week or so."

"More medicine?" My whole body drooped. "I'm so tired of pills."

Doctor Adams nodded. "This one won't make you feel sick or tired. It's just a boost for your circulation. You'll take it for a couple weeks as a precaution, then you can stop. Now that you know what to watch for, you'll be able to monitor when you need it and can start again if necessary. The gangrene is unusual. Have you been under a lot of stress lately? That could contribute. How are you feeling?"

"I'm okay," I lied.

"This diagnosis can be scary and I know while we get your medications stable your symptoms can feel alarming. It's understandable that you could feel more stress than usual. I'd like to recommend a counselor. I think it would be helpful for you to have someone to talk to and support you through this process. What do you think?"

"I don't need a counselor, Dr. Adams. I have Star. I talk to him all the time. He understands when I'm upset. I don't need a counselor."

"I've seen you ride and I agree Star is a great horse, but he is just a horse. I'd feel better if I knew you were talking about how you feel to another human. Do you talk to your parents or your friends about how you're feeling?"

I shook my head. My lips pressed into a stubborn line. "I don't need to talk to anybody. Star is the one who understands and accepts me just like I am. It was only the idea of gangrene that freaked me out."

The doctor handed me a piece of paper. "All right then. If you decide you'd like to talk to a counselor, just call my office and the receptionist will give you the information. For now, take this prescription downstairs and have it filled at the pharmacy. Take it for two weeks, soak your finger, then come back to see me. All right?"

I sighed. "Okay."

While I waited outside the clinic for Mom to pick me up, I was surprised to hear Travis's voice at my side. My kryptonite.

"Well, well. If it isn't sexy Sara. Where've you been hiding yourself? I never see you around anymore." It was as if the last time we were together had never happened.

I slipped my hand into the pocket of my jacket to hide my finger. "Oh. Hi, Travis. Just been busy, I guess."

"Too busy to go to a party with me at Robyn's tomorrow night?" He brushed the carelessly arranged curls off his forehead and gave me a wicked smile.

I hesitated, but realized he really didn't remember the last date we had. That made me feel safe. Oh, why not? Nobody else was interested in me. Even if it was for wrong reasons, at least he wanted to be with me. Evidently, even Robyn still wanted to be with him and Travis had treated her way worse than he'd treated me. Maybe this is normal relationship stuff? Maybe I was finally getting the hang of being like other girls.

"Sure, Travis. That'd be fun."

"Robyn's dad is gone for the weekend. She's invited the whole gang over. Should be great. I'll pick you up at eight."

Thinking fast I said, "Uh, no. Why don't I meet you at school? Outside the gym?"

"Sure. No prob. Gonna exercise the bod, huh? See you then." He walked away just as Mom drove up.

"Was that Travis?"

"Yeah. He was just passing by. Uh, Mom? Tomorrow night the cheerleading squad is going to practice in the gym. Okay if I go and watch for a while?"

"That'll be fine, honey. I'm glad you feel like doing something with your friends. I'll drop you off and you can just call when you're ready to come home. How did it go with the doctor? Why did you have to stop by his office?"

"Uh, oh, fine. Just checking on one of my medications. You know." I shrugged while I kept my finger hidden under my backpack. "And, actually, we'll probably go out for pizza or something after practice. One of the girls can give me a ride home."

"All right. Don't be too late. Remember how easily you tire."

How can I forget? I wondered without answering Mom.

I shivered while I waited for Travis in front of the gym. The school grounds were deserted and it felt uncomfortable standing there alone. I hoped Travis wouldn't be as late as he was the last time he took me out. The shadows around the parking lot shifted. I twisted the ring on my finger.

Fortunately, Travis was just a few minutes late. I had just about decided this was a really bad idea when he drove up.

"Hey, there, baby doll. Need a ride?" He called from his car.

I gave him a half-hearted smile while I walked over to the car. He seemed normal, not high, that is, and I breathed a sigh of relief. Maybe I will have a good time. It could happen. Clearly in a good mood, Travis teased me until we pulled up to Robyn's house. Sudden nerves made my mouth dry and I had an urge to flee. Would Robyn let me apologize?

Travis pulled in and stopped at the curb in front of a house. Music blared before I'd even opened the car door and boosted myself out. Travis grabbed my hand and yelled, "C'mon. Let's go!" I winced when his grip crushed my sore finger.

He hurried me up the steps and opened the door to mass confusion. A crush of kids danced to the pulse of rap music. Their friends shouted encouragement. A keg, beer bottles and even a few wine bottles crowded the dining room table. I didn't see any soft drinks anywhere. The scent of marijuana wafted through the odors of perfume, vaping and sweat.

Scattered throughout all the confusion were couples clinging to each other, kissing and touching. I turned my head in embarrassment when I saw Alyssa with a guy, but it didn't do me any good. Everywhere I looked couples were making out. It could have been the set of an R rated movie scene. I wanted more than anything to go home.

Travis yanked on my hand. "Let's dance!"

The sore finger was squashed by Travis' grip. I let out a sharp cry of pain and tugged my hand out of his grasp. I cradled my injured hand in my good hand and hugged them to my stomach.

Travis looked back. "What are you waiting for? Let's party!"

Then he caught sight of my finger.

"Gross!" He backed away from me. "What's wrong with you? You got leprosy or something? Am I gonna get it? I touched that! Forget it, Sara. You're diseased or something and I sure don't want to get it. Our date's off."

Embarrassment burned on my cheeks while I watched Travis hurry away. I tracked his disappearance through the dancing crowd. He headed straight for his target. Robyn.

I backed up a few steps then turned and hurried toward the door. People pushed and shoved against me, but nobody tried to stop me. Nobody said anything to me. It felt like I didn't exist. At the edge of my vision, I glimpsed Travis talking to Robyn. He waved his arms then pointed to his index finger. He and Robyn scanned the room. Pretty sure they were looking for me, I ducked behind the living room door frame. Embarrassment turned to fear. I felt clammy with sweat in the small of my back and under my arms. I had almost inched my way to the front door when the music stopped. I froze.

"Hey. Saint-girl." Robyn's voice rang out in the room gone silent. I felt the gaze of everyone, like lasers focused on a target. Fear-based nausea lurched in my stomach. Robyn's revenge was inevitable. I braced myself and turned around.

"I hear you're the walking plague." Robyn stepped through the obstacle course of party-goers and stopped in front of me. She held out her hand. "Let's see," she demanded.

I tucked my hand behind me and backed away. Trembling, I looked uselessly around for help. A couple guys surged forward, grabbed my hand and forced it out and toward Robyn. I cried out in pain.

Robyn gripped my hand and examined the infected finger. Travis came up and peered over her shoulder. Robyn gave an exaggerated shudder. "Ewww. That's disgusting." She dropped my hand with a throwing away motion.

Robyn turned toward Travis and put her arm through his, drawing him up beside her. Her gaze locked on mine, she warned Travis, "You better go disinfect, baby, you don't want to end up with a revolting sickness. You actually touched her, you know."

Travis turned and belted toward the bathroom. The crowd around me backed away, dread on their faces.

My throat tightened with pain, I croaked, "It's not contagious. Really, you guys, it's just a sore." My eyes burned with tears of shame.

"Right. And I'm just a naked bird." Robyn's words slashed at me. "It's gross and repulsive. I think you better leave." Robyn turned in dismissal, but as she walked away, she nailed me with one final shot. "Sucks to be you, Saint-girl."

I stood frozen to the spot as the pack of kids melted uneasily away. I turned and stumbled toward the door unhindered. Everybody shied away from me in silence. Some smirked as I sidled by. Someone laughed. Within seconds the thump of music pulsed from the house.

Once outside, I realized I was about a mile from home. Like a sleepwalker, I started in that direction. My thoughts bounced back and forth between two ideas. I had to get home to Star where I'd be safe, and I wished I was dead.

By the time I got home, I was chilled to the bone and ached everywhere. My feet had swollen so badly I had to take my shoes off to walk the last quarter mile in just my socks. My infamous finger throbbed in pain. I stumbled into the barn and headed blindly for my only source of comfort.

SUSAN M. THODE

Chapter 22

Nobody knows, or cares, about pain on the inside.
Sara's Diary

School became a living hell. Travis and Robyn told everyone about my gangrenous finger and the rumors grew. People actively avoided me in the classrooms and moved their desks as far away from me as possible. Students pointed at me in the hall. I caught whispers about AIDS and leprosy. I died a thousand deaths every time I walked into a room.

I stared after Tawny as she hurried past. Even my best friend won't talk to me? AGYB. Right. I lashed out at a candy wrapper and kicked it against the row of lockers. Out of the corner of my eye I saw Ryan waving at Tawny. Was that why she hurried past? Didn't matter. I booted the candy wrapper again then stomped it underfoot. Tawny could have at least paused to say hi.

Sometimes I wondered if I had driven Tawny away. I could still faintly hear my reasonable inner voice remind that the last time Tawny invited me for a nail session, I had a lame excuse why I couldn't go. I mostly had lame excuses to avoid hanging out with her. My reasonable inner voice suggested the truth that Tawny knew I was miserable about my situation and would support and stand by me. But the deceptive loud voice of anger quickly drowned out the weaker voice. I had a momentary impulse to text my friend and check in, but despair settled more heavily on me and the urge faded.

I began to cut full days of school instead of just a class here and there. My grades plummeted from A's and B's to D's and F's. Detention became my second home, when I actually went.

The principal eventually called me out of class to his office. I froze at the office door when I saw my parents chatting to Mr. Salz. I swallowed hard and felt a hard knot of dread in my stomach.

Mr. Salz ushered all of us into his office and motioned toward chairs. Once Mom and Dad sat next to each other and I grabbed a chair by the door, the principal leaned forward, clasped his hands in front of him and cleared his throat.

"Hello, Mr. and Mrs. Mitchell. Thank you for taking time to come for a conference with Sara today. Sara, I thought it would be a good idea to include your parents in a discussion about where you currently are in your studies. We're always concerned when our best students suddenly begin to cut attendance and their grades fall. I think it's important for all of us to agree on a plan to get you back on track."

I scowled, but didn't answer.

"What do you mean, Mr. Salz?" asked Mom.

The principal leaned back in his chair. "You mean you don't know why I've asked you to come in to see me?"

Mom and Dad looked at each other, then their twin gazes lasered onto me. I shifted in my seat.

Dad answered, "No, I'm afraid we don't."

"Did you see Sara's quarterly grade summary?"

"No. We haven't checked online in quite a while.

She's always diligent to keep her grades up."

Mr. Salz picked up his phone and talked briefly with his secretary. Soon, she came, handed him a piece of paper and left the room. Silently the principal handed the paper to my parents.

Mom looked up in confusion. "An F in algebra, a D in history, a D in chemistry…this can't be Sara's. There must be some mistake. She's an honor student," she protested.

"There's no mistake, I'm afraid. That's her latest report. This is why I've asked you to come in and asked Sara to join us. Sara has been truant three to four days a week from most of her classes. She's not turning in homework and doesn't participate in class. I hoped to have a conversation with the three of you to find out why this change of behavior, and how the school can help. Has anything happened at home that might be the problem?"

In unison, Mom and Dad shifted in their chairs to focus on me. I slumped further into my seat. Dad spoke first. "You've been skipping school? Where have you been? What do you do when you're not here?"

I crossed my arms over my chest. My fingernails dug into my skin. "I'd rather not talk about it."

"Sara," Mom protested. Dad placed a soothing hand on her arm. He addressed the principal.

"No, Mr. Salz. It's not a family problem. I'm sure this is somehow related to the news we gave you a few months ago when we found out Sara has SLE. She's taking medication for the symptoms and doesn't feel well a lot of the time, but we had no idea she's been reacting like this. We knew she was having a hard time adjusting, but we thought it was just at home."

Gaze glued to the floor, I remained silent. The conversation flowed around me like water around a rock. I knew my parents were embarrassed. I didn't care.

"Well, I'm glad there's a logical explanation at least. Too often we find out character changes like this point to drug involvement. I'm glad that's apparently not the case with Sara. Maybe she needs extra support from her teachers and from you as well." Principal Salz suggested.

He turned to bring me into the conversation. "I remember now about your illness. Is there something either your parents or the school staff can do to help you through this difficult time?"

"There's nothing anyone can do," I muttered to the floor.

"Excuse me, I couldn't hear you, Sara. What did you say?"

"I said there is nothing you can do," I forced out through gritted teeth. "I'm going to die, there's nothing anyone can do. Why can't you just leave me alone?"

"Sara!" Dad's voice sounded shocked and hurt. "Honey, don't talk like that."

My gaze whipped over to him. "Why not, Dad? It's true, isn't it? Why should I waste time coming to school and doing stupid homework? I'm never going to be able to do anything with what I learn. It's a stupid waste of time."

"You don't know that," he protested. "You can't just throw your life away."

"Why not? It's my life, isn't it? What's left of it anyway. It's my life," I insisted, "and I'm going to do whatever I want with it."

I jumped up from my chair and yanked the door open. I bolted out the front door of the school and hurried down the road toward home. A car soon slowed and stopped beside me. A glance confirmed our family car. The back door opened in invitation. Or maybe command. It was a silent ride home. Once inside, Dad guided me to the kitchen table where the three of us took seats.

The uncomfortable silence was broken by Dad. "Sara, Mr. Salz suggested we talk about how to get you back on track with your schoolwork. He's willing to work with you, but honey, you have to want to make an effort. We can't help you unless you tell us what's going on. You've been skipping classes. That's not like you. What's happened, Sara? Your mother and I would like to understand."

Defiance and anger melted by the warmth of Dad's genuine concern. I couldn't look at them, but I told them the story. "The kids point at me and whisper. They see my finger and think I have AIDS or something. I don't have any friends anymore. Nobody likes me because I've gotten so fat and ugly. I can't wear most of my clothes, and my face is all broken out. It's awful. I just can't stand to go." The dam of tears broke and flooded down my cheeks.

Mom handed me a box of tissues and put her hand on my arm. "We've noticed you've been withdrawn. We've tried to talk, but you always say you're too tired. We thought it best to let you come to us when you were ready. Why didn't you tell us?"

I shrugged.

Dad took one of my hands in his. "You have to go to school. But now that we know how things are, we can talk with Mr. Salz and make some changes. I know this is hard for you, but if you can just be patient things will get better. The doctor says it takes a few months for the medication to settle into your system, but once it does most of your unpleasant symptoms will go away. It will get better, Sara, I know it will. Can you hang on just a little longer?"

My lips trembled and I lost it. "How can you say that, Dad? How can you and Mom keep lying to me?"

Mom and Dad looked at each other. Their faces mirrored confusion. "Lying to you? We haven't, as far as I know." Dad looked at Mom for confirmation. She shrugged and gave a slight shake of her head. "This is why we need to talk. We..."

Anger rushed back. "Forget it, Dad. I know the truth. I heard the doctor talking to you and Mom that day in his office. I know I'm not going to get better. Why didn't you tell me there's no cure? You haven't told me the truth," I accused. "Why should I talk to you?"

"What are you talking about? Do you mean the day Dr. Adams gave us the results of the tests?"

Mom interrupted Dad. "What do you think Dr. Adams said that we're keeping from you? We wouldn't lie to you. And neither would Dr. Adams." She was good. She sounded so sincere.

I looked out the window and fought to control my emotions.

"Sara?" Mom coaxed.

"All right," my tone was edgy and loud and I took a deep breath. "All right. I was in the bathroom while the doctor was talking, I heard him say SLE is life threatening and fatal. I heard both of you agree not to tell me about," I held up both hands and mimed quotation marks, "the nature of my disease. I heard the doctor and I heard you say it would be better not to tell me. You haven't been telling me the truth, why should I tell you the truth?"

My parents looked at each other and had a whole conversation with their eyes to figure out who should talk and what should be said. Dad won.

"I remember that day in the doctor's office and I'm sure you think you heard and understood what he said, but I also remember there was a lot of background noise and you were in the restroom with the door partly closed. You didn't hear everything," he assured me, "and some of your conclusions are way off."

I wasn't convinced. "Like what?" I challenged.

"Dr. Adams did use the terms life-threatening and fatal. He also said it's possible, but not likely. SLE is treatable with medication and life-style changes. And, yes, your mother and I did say, at first, that we shouldn't tell you." He shrugged his shoulders and held out a hand in an unspoken plea. "We wanted to protect you. That was our first reaction. You're our daughter and we love…" His voice broke and he put a hand to his forehead while he struggled to contain his emotions. "We love you and it killed us that you were going to have to go through the treatment." His gaze sought mine. "But Dr. Adams also explained about the ethics of disclosure, which means he had to let you know the full results of the tests. Did you hear his explanation when you came out of the restroom? Actually, now that I think about it, you did seem pretty dazed. Maybe some of what he said just didn't sink in. Anyway, I wish you had talked to us before this, but can we talk about it now? There are some things it might help you to know."

"Like what?" My gaze narrowed and my voice was sharp.

"Like they're making progress in the treatment of lupus all the time. It's true there's no cure now, but hopefully there will be. And they know a lot about how to treat the symptoms. Once the medication kicks in completely, you won't feel the way you do now. Plus, there will likely be long periods when you won't even remember you're sick. We have to hope, honey. Please trust us. Things will get better. Can you try?"

Not convinced, but worn out, I nodded.

"That's my girl. I knew you weren't a quitter. I'll talk to Mr. Salz and see what he suggests. You have to complete your detention, but if you stop skipping, at least you won't have anymore. I'll go call him." He stood and pulled his phone out of his shirt pocket. He touched my cheek as he pressed numbers, "Let us know when things get hard, okay?"

Skepticism had a chokehold on me, but I nodded anyway.

The next day at school, Mr. Salz explained his solution. He would make sure all the teachers knew about the lupus. He also suggested telling some of the upperclassmen so word would get around the school grapevine that I didn't have AIDS or leprosy.

I stiffened. Did he not understand teenagers at all? The rumors were way more interesting than the truth. My classmates weren't interested in truth. They were interested in drama. The situation wouldn't change. Unless it was for the worse.

Things did get worse. It was great the teachers gave me a break. But the students? They continued to make my life a living hell.

During one of the detention periods, I made up my mind. After all, the lupus was probably going to kill me anyway. The doctor and my parents both used words like probably, hopefully, maybe. My recovery wasn't written in stone, that was for sure.

No more. I grimaced at the clock on the wall. I'm not letting them poke me anymore. No more pills that make me dizzy and tired. No more not riding Star. No more gossip.

I watched the second-hand tick down another minute. This would be my last detention. In fact, this would be the last time I'd be at school for anything. My breath caught. I considered my involuntary reaction. Was that regret? Nope, I decided. Not going there.

Going over my plan helped me make it through the remainder of detention. I had thought it out carefully. I knew I didn't matter to anybody. I knew that before I even got sick and now it was worse. And now that I couldn't even ride Star, life was pretty miserable. I did have a little bit of regret when I thought about Star. He definitely wouldn't understand that I was gone.

Star was actually a key part of my plan. There was always somebody home so I couldn't carry out my idea there. Plus, I didn't want to make even my stupid brother feel bad by being the one to find me. Better to just cleanly disappear. That way nobody could blame anybody else.

I remembered how cleanly the scuba diver disappeared. If they found me at all, it would be too late and I'd be free of my miserable life.

I was still considering my plan and thinking through any indecision when the teacher finally excused the class. I gathered my books and went to my locker. Uncertainty made me move in slow motion in the process of retrieving my books. Steps down the hall caught my attention and I turned to see Courtney and a friend coming my way. They saw me, froze then deliberately turned to go back the way they came. They glanced back once, then hurried away whispering to each other as they went.

I heaved my books into my locker, slammed the door and rushed out of the building. My mind was made up.

No more homework, no more chores, no more feeling sick, *no more medicine*! I smiled with grim pleasure. No more Mom and Dad telling me what to do, no more waiting for Travis to ask me out. No more worrying about my grades, no more worrying about anything. I slammed my hand against the front door and it crashed open.

When I reached home, I went directly to the stable and tossed my backpack on a bale of hay.

"Hi, Star. Ready to go?"

My tall guy whinnied at the sound of my voice and lifted his head over the stall door. I talked to him while I quickly brushed off hay and dust.

"Something important you need to help me with this afternoon, boy. You won't mind getting a little wet, will you? Just like when we go swimming in the summer only you have to come home by yourself. Dad will take care of you, so don't worry."

Grimacing with pain, I lumbered my way up onto Star's back with the help of a hay bale. Lips pressed into a thin line of agony, I pulled myself into a seated position and sucked in a deep breath. A smile tugged at my lips. I made it.

"More fun this way isn't it, Star? Just you and me." I caressed his shoulder and urged him through the door.

We walked down the path to the beach and onto the

sand. Star's head bobbed eagerly and he lengthened his stride. When we rounded the rocks, I pulled Star to a stop and watched the waves. Nobody could see us here and the breeze from the ocean smelled and felt great after the stuffy classroom.

"We've had some good times here, haven't we? Just us, but also with Kevin. He seems to think life is a gift." I combed my fingers through Star's mane. "Could he be right? Doesn't feel like much of a gift to me. Mostly feels miserable. He also thinks I shouldn't worry about death because of heaven. I don't know what I think about heaven. I just know I can't stand how my life is right now." I took a deep breath and nudged Star forward. A wisp of doubt crossed my mind. Is this the right thing to do? Could Kevin be right? I closed my mind to that thought and recalled again how cleanly and peacefully the scuba diver entered the water and disappeared. I prodded Star with my heels.

Star willingly entered the water in spite of the chilly air. The waves splashed against his legs and I shuddered. Soon the water reached Star's chest. My feet were soaked as the water crept up his shoulders. I felt his muscles tense as he fought the current and knew I had to get off and free him to go back to shore. The current would catch me and sweep me out past the breakwater. The last thing I wanted was to endanger him.

I tied the reins over his neck so they wouldn't tangle in his legs. Then, I leaned over and hugged his strong neck one more time, whispered, "Bye, boy," and slipped off his back.

Never in my wildest dreams did I imagine Star would not let me go. When I slipped down his side, he dipped in the water and pushed against me, forcing me back up on his back. I tried the other side and he moved with me. He wasn't going to let me off his back.

The Appaloosa lost his footing and floundered in the pulling tide.

"No, Star, no! Leave me and go back to shore. You'll drown!"

Desperation strengthened me and I shoved against him when I leaned toward the water. He scrambled for footing and dipped under me again. Sobbing in frustration, I tried again. This time I was helped by a receding wave that swept me off Star's back before he could react. I put my hand against his cheek and pushed his head toward shore. The current wrenched me away from him.

The powerful undertow tugged at my legs, and I knew my plan would work. I let myself go limp so the current could take me easily. But I heard a determined neigh and lifted my head above the water. Star fought his way after me. He wasn't going to let me go.

Furiously I splashed at him and he jerked his head in surprise. I yelled, "Go back, Star. I don't want you. I want to die. Don't you understand? Go back, Star."

He hesitated and a wave swept over his head. He surfaced and blew water out flaring nostrils as he struggled for breath. I thought the wave had finally scared him enough to make him turn back, but no. He tried to reach me again.

A wave broke over my head, submerging me. The powerful undertow forced me deeper. All would be over quickly now. Nothing to worry about anymore. No more pain. No more heartache. No more sickness.

But it wasn't quiet and peaceful. Fear closed my throat. If I die, there's no second chance. What about Mom and Dad? Ben? The salt water burned my eyes. I panicked when I submerged. I couldn't breathe. The waves smashed me down, then tossed me up in a soggy wrestling match. My lungs burned painfully.

Lack of oxygen made me dizzy. Terror buzzed in my brain. This wasn't what I expected at all. I imagined a peaceful and quiet descent into nothingness. Instead, freezing water and darkness engulfed me. My body craved air. My body wanted life.

Suddenly, my will craved life, too. Panic flooded my senses, but my mind burst with clarity. Air, I needed air. Can't breathe, can't breathe, can't breathe. I tried desperately to think, but suffocation clouded my thoughts. I can't breathe!

Then a quiet voice spoke to my exhausted brain. A familiar voice. *Yes, you can. Just take a breath.*

Incredibly, I could. My face broke the surface long enough to gasp in a breath. I began to sink again, but fought my way to the surface, thoughts crowding my head.

Thoughts of warm chocolate chip cookies. Crisp fall days. Happy Christmas mornings with my family all together. Special hugs from Dad after a horse show. The memory of Dad prompted a picture of my parents together. For the first time since I made my plan, I considered my family. They loved me—I knew that. What I was doing would bring them terrible pain.

Then, as if a light switched on in my mind and banished the darkness, I knew I couldn't do it. Kevin was right. Life is a gift. I couldn't just throw it away.

"I don't want to die! Star, where are you?" I screamed when my head broke through the surface again. I heard a loud snort and turned to see Star still fighting his way toward me. His eyes were white-rimmed with panic. My heart sank when I noticed his labored breathing. He was exhausted.

My will to live renewed, I fought the current and finally reached Star. I might not be able to beat my salt-water opponent, but Star could. Knowing the safest place for me was on his back, I avoided his thrashing legs and used his mane to pull myself up.

I heard my father's instructions clearly in my mind. "If you're ever caught in a riptide, don't try to fight it straight in. Choose an angle toward the beach, parallel for a while if you have to, then gradually work your way in. Above all, don't panic. Reserve your energy. Take it slow and you'll make it."

I turned Star's head and began a low pep talk in his ear. "Come on, Star. We can do it," I encouraged. "You're the biggest and strongest horse in the world. You can do it. Come on, boy, just a little longer. Keep it up. You're the best horse in the world, Star. I know you can do it."

Dangerously tired, Star's strong legs struck at the water more and more slowly. His head bobbed, periodically going under. He coughed and snorted water out of his nostrils. Again and again, he struggled to the surface.

"Please, Star," I begged. "Keep going, boy."

I had almost given up when I glanced up and saw we really were closer to shore. Dad was right! Hope renewed I leaned forward on Star's neck. "Look, boy. We're getting there. Just a little longer."

Star's ears briefly cocked forward. His head stopped bobbing and with renewed effort his legs churned the water. Impulsively I cried, "Please, God. Help us make it. Don't let us die."

Closer and closer to the beach. Star's legs touched solid ground once, twice, then he was walking. As soon as I knew we were in shallow water I slipped from his back and stumbled by his side through the tide. The sand was wet when I finally dropped to my hands and knees. Star's head hung low. His legs trembled and his sides heaved as he coughed and gulped air into his lungs.

I slumped to the sand and rolled to my back. My breathing matched Star's while we both fought to get air into our oxygen-starved bodies. Eventually I felt cold and wet. And I had sand all over my clothes. My hair clung like limp spaghetti to my face. And my body was one giant ache. But I was alive.

"I'm alive," I whispered.

Then more loudly. "I'm alive."

Then an exultant shout. "I'm alive!"

I struggled to my feet to hug my exhausted horse. "Thank you, Star. Thank you for not giving up on me. You helped me see. I'm so sorry I did this to you, boy."

I dropped to my knees and with one hand on Star's stringy mane prayed, "Thank you, God. Thank you for helping me understand. Thank you for helping us get through the surf. Thank you for life, and for all the good things I forgot about. And especially, God, thank you for Star."

We stumbled home together, my life-saving horse and me. Star's feet dragged through the sand and his head hung low, nodding with each step. We both shivered by the time we got inside the barn. I made sure Star was dry and warm though my motions were hampered by stiff hands and arms. I fed him then closed the barn door. I walked slowly toward the house. Mom ran out and met me halfway there.

Chapter 23

*I found out I can survive truth. It's the lies I believe
that will destroy me.*
Sara's Diary

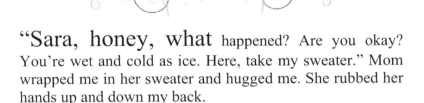

"Sara, honey, what happened? Are you okay?
You're wet and cold as ice. Here, take my sweater." Mom
wrapped me in her sweater and hugged me. She rubbed her
hands up and down my back.

"You're shivering so hard. What happened? Did you
fall off Star into the water?

The worry in her tone broke me. I began to sob, great
gasping sobs that released the despair and loneliness
consuming me. While sobs racked my body, Mom's hug
strengthened until there wasn't any space between us.

"Sara, did somebody hurt you? Attack you? Answer
me, honey. Tell me what it is."

That's what my mom always said. From skinned knees
to broken toys, Mom's instant response to tears has always
been, "Tell me what it is."

I laughed through my sobs, which turned into a
coughing fit. When I could croak it out, I said, "Oh, Mom. I
love you so much."

"I love you, too, sweetie, but tell me what happened."

"It's a long story. Can we talk?"

"Absolutely, but let's get you warm and dry first."

An hour later, dry and holding a cup of tea, I faced my parents. I took a deep breath and let it out slowly. "I tried to kill myself this afternoon."

The shock on Dad's face and Mom's sharp intake of breath were all the prompting I needed to rush on. "I don't know what got into me. I've been so miserable lately and feeling so awful. It just seemed like I didn't have anything to live for. I felt hopeless. I just wanted to die."

An uneasy silence brooded in the air. I looked at Mom. "Remember when I talked to you about if I matter or not?"

"Yes. I asked you to figure out how you would know when you matter to people."

"Yeah," I confirmed. "And I've been trying to do that. Lately all I can think about was how it seemed like I didn't matter to anybody. I really believed that was true."

My gaze turned to Dad. "It pretty much seemed nobody at school cared about me and then when I got so sick, I figured I didn't matter to God either because He let me get lupus. I started to wonder more and more why I would want to live if nobody cared if I was around or not. And overhearing what the doctor said about lupus didn't help. Then I thought you guys were lying to me, that made me feel like I didn't matter to you either."

"But, Sara," Mom protested. "We talked about that. I thought you understood. We went over what the doctor said and our response. Besides, you have so many good things in your life, even with the lupus."

A deep sigh escaped and I looked at the ceiling. When I gathered my thoughts, I continued. "I know, Mom. I just forgot about them for a while. All the bad stuff felt bigger. It seemed like I was in a dark pit with a concrete belt around my waist. But then, when I was out in the water with Star, I started thinking about you and Dad, the things I like about our family, the things I like about life, and suddenly I realized how much I have to live for. Even if I am sick. I was so mad at God for letting me get sick I forgot about all the good things He's given me. I believed death would be a friend." My voice tapered off and I stared at my lap. A hush settled between us until I lifted my gaze to peer at them. "Do you forgive me?"

Dad rushed to gather me into his arms. Fortunately, my tea was gone because my cup went flying. "Of course, we do." His voice thickened with emotion. "Sara, we love you so much. Our lives would have such an empty place if you left us."

Dad's tears were wet against my cheek. I hugged him with all my strength. His strong arms enveloped me and the familiar scent of his after-shave added to the comfort. The whiskers on his cheek scratched my neck.

After a long silence, I said against his neck, "I wouldn't have made it if Star hadn't been there."

Mom's voice cracked. She cleared her throat. "Maybe not, honey. I think God must've used him as a miracle horse. Or at least He used Star to give us a miracle today."

Dad released me and wiped his hand across his cheeks. "You must be exhausted. I know we still have a lot of things to figure out, but why don't you go rest for now? We'll call the doctor in the morning and have him check you over."

"Okay. I am pretty tired and sore. It feels like the ocean beat me up. And, Mom...Dad? I'm really sorry. I didn't mean to hurt you. I just...things got to be too much and I couldn't handle it anymore."

"We know," Dad answered. He gave me a quick side hug. "Will you let us help you handle it from now on?"

"Yeah, Dad. I'd like some help. And one thing I need to get straight are my ideas about God. I don't know if I believe everything you do, but I know I want to keep living even if I don't always feel good."

"You know your situation hasn't changed, and may not for a while," he warned.

"I know. My situation hasn't changed, but I have. When I was in the water with Star, I suddenly realized no matter how bad I thought my life was, there are still a lot of good things, too. I've been selfish. I know if I had died it would've been really hard on you both. I never even thought about you when I planned to kill myself."

Dad's voice trembled. "Oh, Sara, if you only knew. We love you so much. Even when it seems like we're irritated with you, we never stop loving you. If you were gone..." Words failed and he crushed me against him.

Dad and I held onto each other until Mom softly touched my shoulder. "Why don't you go on and rest? We'll have dinner and I think an early bedtime for all of us. It's been quite an afternoon."

"Okay, Mom. But first I have to go out and..."

"...check on Star," my parents finished my sentence for me. "All right. Go make sure he's settled for the night, but don't stay out too long," Mom warned.

"I won't." I flashed a smile at Mom and gave her a lingering hug before I hurried outside.

Star seemed tired, even more than after a horse show. But, I reasoned, what he had to do in the water was a lot harder than competition. His body gave a convulsive shudder occasionally, so I got out his horse blanket and buckled it on. I made sure he had plenty of straw, gave him a final pat then headed in to my own bed.

Later that night, Mom's urgent voice and insistent prodding made me struggle awake. "Wake up. Come on, Sara. Wake up."

"What?" I grumbled. "What is it? I'm so tired. Let me sleep." I grabbed the covers and tried to turn away from Mom. She pulled me back.

"You have to get up. There's something wrong with Star. I think he's sick."

Mom's anxious tone finally cut through my sleep-clogged brain. I sat up. "Star? What's wrong?" I swung out of bed and reached for my sweats. "What's the matter with him?"

"I couldn't sleep so I got a carrot for Star to thank him for getting you safely out of the surf." She grabbed my hoodie and helped me shrug into it. "He wouldn't come to the door to get the carrot so I went into the stall. When he turned to look at me, I offered him the carrot, but he just turned away. I set the carrot in his feed bucket then tried to hug him, but he coughed so hard I couldn't get near him. He's damp and coughing. Something is really wrong. Dad's calling the vet."

We hurried to the barn and I rushed into the stall. Star's big body was caught by spasm after spasm of deep coughing. I watched helplessly as he fought to take a normal breath. Panic welled up when I heard the dreadful rattle in his throat each time he tried to take a breath.

"Oh no. Dear God, please, not Star." Mom's voice begged.

We watched in horror as Star's legs folded and he crumpled to the ground like a puppet whose strings had been cut.

Chapter 24

Living with regret is like a splinter under my skin.
Sara's Diary

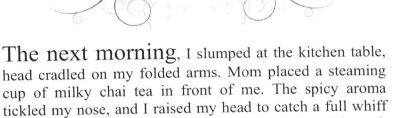

The next morning, I slumped at the kitchen table, head cradled on my folded arms. Mom placed a steaming cup of milky chai tea in front of me. The spicy aroma tickled my nose, and I raised my head to catch a full whiff of the tea. Mom sat down beside me while I sipped through the foam.

I licked the froth off my lips. "I'm glad Ben and Dad could help us with Star last night. And I really appreciate your spending the night in the barn with me, Mom. The vet said propping Star up with the hay bales was the best thing we could've done until he could get here."

Mom patted my shoulder. The toaster popped up two browned slices and Mom got up to butter them. I watched her sprinkle cinnamon sugar on top, lick her fingers then she placed the plate in front of me. "Thanks, Mom. My fave."

The crunchy sweetness revived me. I paused between bites when a memory hit me hard. "Mom? I was thinking in the barn last night that Star saved my life. What will I do if that means he loses his? I don't know how I'll live without him. How much longer do you think they'll be out there?"

Mom busied herself at the sink, but answered over her shoulder. "Dr. Heins said to give them a half hour. It's been about twenty minutes."

She dried her hands and returned to the chair by my side. She pressed me back in my chair when I tried to stand. "We have to wait. Dr. Heins knows what he's doing and he needs your dad and Ben's help. We'll just be in the way. Ben will come and get us."

"But I should be out there," I protested. "Star will be calmer if I'm there."

Mom squeezed my shoulder. "Honey, the doctor said there's nothing you can do. Star doesn't know who's there and who isn't. He has a pretty high fever."

I jumped to my feet, knocking over my chair. "I need to go out there. Star needs me. I'll help him get well. I'll…"

Mom gently grasped my arm and drew me back onto my chair. Her voice was gentle, but firm. "The doctor said we should stay out of the barn. He knows Star has bronchitis, and maybe pneumonia. He and his tech, plus your dad and Ben, are rigging up a sling contraption to help Star stand." Mom repeated what I already knew. She was doing her best to calm my fear, but I knew how seriously ill Star was.

"I hope they get him set up pretty soon. It kills me that he's too weak to stand on his own." My voice broke. Vivid memories of last night and Star struggling unsuccessfully to get to his feet broke my heart all over again. My big strong horse never had to struggle at anything. Until now.

Mom tried to reassure me. "Once they get him settled in the sling, you can go check on him."

She placed a gentle hand on my arm again and used her other hand to turn my face toward her. "Sara, Dr. Heins asked me to warn you that Star may not make it."

My wail of protest drowned out the rest of Mom's statement. "Noooooo! He can't die, he can't. I did it. I did it to him. Oh, Star, I'm sorry. I'm sorry!" My upper body collapsed onto the table and I buried my head in my arms and sobbed.

"Sara. Sara, listen to me. The doctor also said Star has a chance. He's a fine strong animal and he's fighting for his life with everything in him. Don't lose hope. Star needs your strength to encourage him."

The back door opened and Dad came into the kitchen. I jumped up from the chair and stared at him. I wiped my sweaty hands on my jeans and my heart pounded while I searched Dad's expression for a clue. He stepped forward and pulled me into a tight hug, reaching out an arm to include Mom. He spoke into my hair. "Gingersnap, we got him into the sling and he's resting. He's very sick, but the doctor is doing everything possible for him."

I stepped back from Dad and wiped my eyes with my sleeve. "Can I go out there now? I want to see him."

"Finish your tea and breakfast first. Star is resting and he's fine for now. He's sedated, but even without that he's so weak he can't hurt himself. The doctor just left and I have his instructions for you. Sit down and I'll fill you in while I eat breakfast."

I could tell by Dad's tone it wouldn't do any good to argue. I sat beside him and choked down my toast while Dad explained the doctor's instructions. I asked questions, then fell silent. I stared at the last of the foam in the bottom of my cup. I raised my gaze to Dad.

"Did Dr. Heins say," my voice thickened and I cleared my throat. "Did he say what Star's chances are?"

Dad paused with a spoonful of cereal halfway to his mouth. He lowered the spoon back to the bowl and turned to look at me. "He said Star is very sick. Bronchitis and pneumonia are dangerous for horses. Either one on its own would be bad, but he's developed both. The infection and fluid in his lungs are the most dangerous problems right now, but he's up off the floor and that will help him breathe."

Dad's hand covered mine and he stared intently into my eyes. "Why don't we pray for him? That's the best thing we can do."

"I don't think God hears me." I was a perfect mix of certain and uncertain about this. "Don't you think I tried praying about being sick? About being so fat and ugly? I don't think God hears me because He doesn't love me. As far as I'm concerned, I don't matter to God."

Or do I? My first panic attack played like a movie in my mind and the soundtrack of the quiet voice that broke through the chaos to calm me down, calmed me just remembering it. Then a flashback of my so-called date with Travis dredged up the danger I'd been in and how Kevin turned up just when I needed him. Was that God taking care of me? Another crystal-clear memory surfaced from yesterday when I was in the ocean and it felt like Star and I were not going to make it. I had been literally under the surface with a mouthful of water, not able to breathe, and the quiet voice was there again. Then I had asked for God's help and Star's feet struck sand instead of water. Was that God?

A microscopic thread of faith began to weave its way through doubt.

"Sara, that's not true," Dad protested. "God loves you so much. Even more than your mother and I."

The thread frayed and uncertainty returned. "Oh sure, that's what Kevin tried to tell me. I don't buy it. Look at all that's happened to me and now Star is sick, too." I shook my head. "You know who actually does love me unconditionally and would do anything for me? Star. Star was ready to die for me yesterday, and that's because he loves me and knows I love him. He has never done or been anything but good to me."

Dad dropped his gaze and shook his head. "I feel like Mom and I have completely let you down by not making sure you understand about God's love."

"This doesn't have anything to do with you and Mom. I'm my own person and old enough to think for myself, you know. You taught me the truth as you see it, I just don't see it that way."

"What do you mean? Why?"

"What you've taught me doesn't hold up. My life totally sucks. How can God care about me and let all this crummy stuff happen to me? I've been going to church because I figure showing up can't hurt."

Dad shook his head. "Sorry, honey, just going to church doesn't do it. There's a lot more to knowing and trusting God."

"Every once in a while, I wonder if God notices me, but I'm still not sure. Here's the thing, Mom said I should figure out how I know if I matter to somebody so I started to pay attention. I don't think I have it completely figured out, but I know I feel like I matter when someone pays attention and tells me I've done something well. Like encouragement or a compliment, but not just empty words."

I shook my head in frustration. "I don't know how to explain it. It's like when I work hard at school and you both notice and appreciate my good grades. Another way I feel like I matter is when somebody gives me something meaningful. Like Mom knows my favorite is cinnamon toast." I smiled at her. "Or when Kevin brought me that aromatherapy oil to help me sleep? That made me feel special because I knew he paid attention to what I said." I shrugged. "I know it wasn't expensive or anything, but that's not the point. It was thoughtful."

My ears burned and I looked down at my hands so my hair hid my face. I sucked in a deep breath and returned my gaze to Mom and Dad. "So those are two ways I know I matter to somebody. Well, I don't hear God noticing anything good about what I'm doing or how I'm doing. And all I see He's given me is this stupid disease."

Dad thought for a minute. "I don't know about God telling you things so I can only tell you what happens with me, okay?"

I nodded.

"I don't hear an actual voice, but I get ideas or thoughts in my mind that I know aren't mine and I believe that's God telling me things. And sometimes I just feel a sense He's near—like if I could just see better, I'd see Him because it feels like He's right there. And it always feels calm when that happens. Another way I believe He talks to me is through the Bible. Maybe you could start to read your Bible and see if any of the words feel alive to you or like they're highlighted on the page. That happens to me all the time. And you can pray. You say God doesn't talk to you or care about you, well, maybe you need to try talking to Him. Praying is just talking to God. You can ask questions and see what happens."

"Like praying for Star?"

"Yes, like Star. But, Sara?"

"Yeah."

"Believing in God doesn't mean you automatically get everything you want. God doesn't promise things won't get hard; He just promises to be with us whatever happens. We're never alone."

"Star could still die?"

"Star could still die."

"Because of what I did?"

Dad hesitated. "Because of natural causes. He's got bronchitis and pneumonia. That's serious."

"If he dies it'll be because he saved me."

"Then," Mom got up and put her hands on my shoulders. "I suggest we start to pray right now."

I nodded, and, for the first time ever, really actually

prayed for something with my parents.

After we finished my first time ever real prayer, I made a quick stop in my room before heading to the barn. I wasn't convinced about Dad's ideas about faith, but figured my own hadn't turned out great so I thought I'd give his a try. I dug around in my room until I found my Bible under my bed. Grabbing it, I pounded down the stairs and hurried to the barn. I entered quietly, and found my horse, head drooping low, in a drugged sleep.

Remembering the instructions about how much rest Star needed, I quietly backed out of the stall so I could stack a few bales of hay to create a chair and plopped down with the Bible in my lap. Randomly opening the book was probably not the most intelligent way to study the Bible, but I had no idea how to start. I opened it and turned to a page that said Romans 12 at the top. I scanned until I saw the words, "If it is possible, as far as it depends on you, live at peace with everyone." Well. That certainly got my attention.

"Wow," I breathed. "How cool is that?" Just like Dad said. The words seemed like a personal message meant just for me. I knew I had to talk to Tawny and Kevin. Apologize, at least, and hopefully get their friendship back. Without the darkness of despair, I could see how I misjudged my friends. Somehow, Tawny seemed easier than Kevin, so I started with my oldest friend. I began with a text.

Busy?

Totally slammed. T Swift on consult call. Wants me to do hair. U?

Miss my friend.

Three little dots floated for a second then disappeared. After a minute they returned.

Want to come over?

Can't. S sick. U come 2 barn?

I'm there.

I gripped my phone tightly, trusting…hoping Tawny's response meant she was still my friend.

While I waited, I got up and peeked into Star's stall. His eyes were open so I walked up beside him. He shifted his weight slightly and tried to lift his head. It must have felt like it weighed a hundred pounds because he lowered it right away.

I sat on my heels so I was eye-level to him. "Hi, boy." I stroked his nose and under his forelock. He closed his eyes and tried to take a breath, but a coarse cough erupted out of his lungs. I finger-combed straw out of his mane and talked softly to him. The coughing fit subsided. He closed his eyes and groaned. I stood and fussed with his blanket. I checked the canvas straps of the sling and smoothed the hair underneath them.

The sling looked like a hammock turned sideways. The wide canvas hammock fit under his belly and attached over his back at heavy metal support bars. The metal bars attached to an adjustable metal base. The vet told me they'd had to extend the vertical supports almost to their maximum height.

The contraption kept Star upright. He could stand if he wanted and was able, but if he slumped, the sling kept him from falling. I saw the hammock stretched tight and knew my horse wasn't strong enough to stand on his own. His head continued to hang down and deep ragged coughs sometimes shuddered his whole body. I brushed his shoulder with my hand and talked softly to him until I heard Tawny's car door slam.

I gave Star a final pat then walked to the barn door to greet my friend. I had no idea how to begin, but Tawny rammed right through my awkwardness by grabbing me in a fierce hug. My arms returned the hug and we stood, rocking slightly, until I drew back and demanded with a laugh, "Let me see your nails." I knew Tawny's nails were a reflection of her feelings.

Tawny spread out her fingers. On one hand the nails had a blue background with silver raindrops. On the other hand, each nail was covered by a black background with a gold lightning bolt down the center. My eyebrows arched in question.

Tawny lifted the raindrop hand and turned it so the nails faced me. "This is how I've felt the past few weeks when I couldn't talk to you no matter how hard I tried." Tawny spoke sternly. "I can't handle when you ignore me. Don't do it anymore."

"I won't," I promised meekly.

"See that you don't." Tawny could have been a queen talking to her subject. Then she held up the lightning bolt hand. "This is how I feel when I hear what the kids at school say about you. I am a total rageaholic. I mean, really? Seriously? AIDS? They think you have AIDS? Morons."

She flipped the lightning nail hand to the side as if flinging off the entire student body. Then she pointed at me. "We are absolutely going to talk. I am so not down with you just ghosting me, but first, what's this about the big S being sick?"

I drew Tawny's arm through mine and guided her into the barn. I explained as we went. We peered over the stall door at Star still suspended by his hammock, then I gestured toward my hay bale seat. Taking a deep breath, I plunged into the details of what happened since my fall on the football field and trip to the emergency room, right up to the part where I rode Star into the tide. I didn't hold anything back. Tears sparkled in Tawny's eyes when she turned to give me a crushing hug.

The hug ended abruptly when she drew back and grabbed my upper arms so she could hold me captive.

"Why didn't you tell me?" Tawny demanded. "You should know you could tell me. What happened to AGYB, huh? You are so going to have to help me leave this hurt behind because I am about to blow a fuse. What were you thinking?"

Tawny squeezed my arms and shook me. "You. Tell. Me. When things get too much. Okay?" She shook me again less passionately.

I nodded.

"So, when you rode into the ocean is that how Star got sick?"

I continued my story. When I got to the part where Star swam after me and wouldn't leave, tears sparkled again and Tawny turned her gaze toward Star's stall. Afraid she was going to jump up and give Star a repeat of the bear hug I got, I put a restraining hand on her leg just in case. I quickly told her the rest of the story. Silence filled the barn.

Finally, Tawny looked at me and held up her rain-tipped nails. "Want me to give you rainy-day nails?"

"No, thanks. Though they're really awesome," I hurried to add.

"Is Star going to be okay?"

"The doctor says he's strong and that's in his favor, but he exhausted himself in the water and got quite a bit of ocean in his lungs. Saltwater, bacteria—I'm sure Kevin and Ben could tell us how polluted the water is, but I don't think I want to know."

Tawny grew uncharacteristically quiet. Then, "Are you going to be all right?"

"Yeah. I cleared some things up with my parents. You were right, they weren't lying to me. I totally zoned out in the doctor's office and didn't hear some of the things he said. I filled in with my own assumptions. Not my most shining hour," I admitted. "I also assumed you didn't want to see me. I'm beginning to understand how often I saw myself by what I assumed other people thought of me. Bad idea. Assuming I know what people are thinking."

"You definitely should not assume about me." Tawny bumped my shoulder with her own. "AGYB, remember?

You must've felt totally solo." She held up her lightning-tipped nails. "I'm not kidding. I have been volcano-angry about all those creeps at school. Listen up; we are going to trash file that whole crowd. Ry and I will help you. You are not going solo when you go back to school. And this time I expect you to believe me." Tawny's voice was fierce.

I returned her shoulder bump. "Thanks. I'm sorry I misjudged you. I should've trusted you."

"Yes. You totally should have. But I get how this all landed on you like a pile of bricks. What happens now?"

"My parents think it would be good for me to talk to a counselor." I shrugged. "I'm not sure if that will do any good, but I'm okay giving it a try. I'm going to ask Justine out at Big Sky if she can recommend somebody. I know some of the kids in her program have counselors."

"That is a stellar idea. Justine's cool. Listen, I have to get going because Mom needs the car, but call me, okay? Let me know how Star's doing."

Tawny stood and brushed hay off her jeans. She put her hand on my shoulder. "I will be seriously bent if you don't talk to me when you feel bad, okay?"

I smiled at my friend. "Thanks. I won't—how would you say-- be quiet?"

"Go underground?"

"I promise not to go underground again."

Tawny saluted me, did a soldier-pivot and walked toward the door. She paused, then turned back. "Just FYI, nobody's seen Travis all this last week. Word is his dad sent him off to some drug rehab. Could be true, could be buzz." She shrugged. "Who knows?"

"Who cares," I retorted.

Tawny laughed, waved and closed the barn door behind her.

I got up and checked the straps under Star's belly. Good. No rubbing, no sores. I patted his rump and returned to the hay bale. My Bible caught my eye. I picked it up and ran my hand across the smooth surface. I opened it to the Romans 12 passage again. Did being at peace with everyone to the best of my ability include Courtney and Alyssa? Robyn? I frowned at the ceiling and drew in a deep breath. I leaned back in my hay chair and crossed my ankles. Quickly, before I could change my mind, I drew my phone out of my pocket. I thumbed my contacts.

"Going to bite off the part I think I can chew." I jabbed at my phone until I got a blank screen for Courtney. My fingers waited for my mind to catch up. Mind or courage. Either one. Finally, my fingers moved.

I didn't do what Alyssa accused me of. I don't want to be your enemy. Can we be friends? It's up to you.

My thumb hovered over the send arrow then took the plunge. Quickly, I typed a similar message to Alyssa.

My phone chimed. Courtney.

Whatevs, Saint. I guess we'll see.

I waited. A second chime sounded.

In your dreams. Friends are overrated.

All-righty then. I had my answers. Alyssa seemed like a dead end. That was okay. Courtney could be a maybe. I'd think about how to take another step. However it worked out, I wasn't going to lose any sleep over it. I would do the best I could. I didn't care anymore what they thought about me. Awesome. I'd never not cared what they thought about me. My shoulders relaxed muscles I didn't even know were tense.

And Robyn? My hands clutched my phone. I paused. Nope. Robyn was going to have to wait.

Chapter 25

*My glass has been half empty and leaking for so long
it's hard to believe it's filling up again.*
Sara's Diary

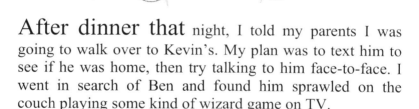

After dinner that night, I told my parents I was going to walk over to Kevin's. My plan was to text him to see if he was home, then try talking to him face-to-face. I went in search of Ben and found him sprawled on the couch playing some kind of wizard game on TV.

"Hey. Do me a favor?" I nudged his foot.

"Yeah. Sure." Clearly focused completely on the game, he barely acknowledged me. I moved in front of him to block his view of the TV screen.

"Hey!" he protested, trying to look around me.

"Just pause it a sec, okay?"

"Okay," he grumbled. "What?"

"I need to go see Kev, but I don't want to leave Star alone. Stay with him until I get back? I promise I won't be long."

"Really? You want me to babysit Star? You actually trust me to competently sit there with an incapacitated horse and make sure he's safe?"

I nudged his foot again. "Enough with the sarcasm. Will you? Just while I'm gone."

"Sure. Just messing with you. Let me finish this level first, okay?"

"Yeah. I'll be in the barn." I turned to go, but called back over my shoulder, "And thanks. I appreciate it."

Eyes on the action, Ben murmured, "Sure. No problem," while feverishly jabbing at the game controller in his hands.

Spot joined me when I walked out the back door to head back to the barn. His solid presence felt comforting. He followed me into Star's stall, turned a few circles, then curled up in a corner.

I checked Star's water, the straps of the sling and rested a hand under his mane at his withers. He wasn't sweating. A good sign. The level in his water bucket had gone down a bit. Another encouraging sign.

My hay bale couch needed maintenance so I pushed the bales tightly together and sat down. I thumbed through my phone until I found an old text thread with Kevin. I touched the new message box and stared at the blinking cursor. I tried a few messages, but backspaced each one. Maybe I could just walk over to see if he was around? I sure had no idea what to say by text. The worst that could happen would be that he was home, but refused to talk to me.

While I waited for Ben, I returned to Star. I smoothed his forelock, stroked his neck and then reached a hand behind each ear and gently massaged. He still felt hot to my touch and his hide felt rough. I leaned my forehead against his and whispered, "You have to get better, boy. You're not just a shooting star. You're not even a constellation. You're my whole galaxy, Star. Please. Please, fight hard to get better."

I traced a hand down his neck and walked slowly

around him. His ears swiveled to track my progress while I stroked and brushed away dust. His deep coughs sounded as ragged as ever. Every time he coughed, I winced. The barn door scraped against the floor and Ben walked into the stall.

"How's he doing?"

"Pretty much the same. He drank a little water which is a good sign. I'll fix him another conditioning mash when I get back."

"What's that? Is he going to be okay? Is it okay if I pet him? I'll be careful," he promised.

I translated his run-together questions and answered the third first. "Yeah, just be careful of the straps. And no sudden moves. The vet left a recipe for a mash that should help him gain strength. It has minerals, essential oils, glucose powders, fiber—it even has ground sugar beets in it."

Ben grimaced. "Yuck. Beets. Is he eating it? I wouldn't eat anything with beets in it."

I joined my brother at Star's side. "They're really good for him and, no, he hasn't eaten much. The vet said to keep trying. He needs the extra nutrition to help his body recover."

I kept my eyes on my hands stroking Star. "Did...do you know...did Mom and Dad..." My voice trailed off. I glanced at Ben. His face and neck were red as the beets in the mash.

He looked at me then quickly away. "They said...they told me a little bit. Are you...are you going to be okay?" Ben's voice cracked. He looked down at his feet and cleared his throat.

My throat thickened. I shrugged my shoulders. "I'm going to be okay," I assured him. "I just need to work some stuff out."

In an awkward rush, Ben threw his arms around me, pinning my arms at my sides. "I'm sorry about bugging you all the time. I know I get on your nerves. I'll stop, okay, Sara? And you tell me if I'm getting obnoxious, okay?" His arms tightened to a death grip. "Just don't...don't try to hurt yourself again, okay?"

I squirmed in Ben's tight grasp and pulled each arm out of his grip. I turned, put my hands on his shoulders and gave a gentle shake. "Ben. This had nothing to do with you. It wasn't your fault and you don't bug me. Well," I continued, a smile curving my lips, "you don't bug me much." I peeked up at him until his smile answered mine.

"Yeah, right. You lie like a rug." His arms dropped away from me.

"Yes, indeed," I agreed with a laugh. Then my tone sobered. "But none of what happened had anything to do with you. Got it? I just let a bunch of stuff get to me and felt completely overwhelmed. And I'm going to be all right. I promise."

Ben blew out a breath. "Okay." He turned his attention to Star again. "Do you need me to do anything while I'm here? I can brush him or do that mash thing or whatever."

I shook my head. "No. He has what he needs. I just don't want him to be alone. Dr. Heins said he's fine in the sling, but I feel better knowing he's not by himself. I'm going to sleep out here tonight, but I really need to talk to Kev if you can take over here."

"Sure." He lifted his phone out of his pocket. "I'll play a game."

"Okay. Thanks."

I walked down the trail that led to Kevin's house while trying to figure out what to say. Everything I rehearsed in my mind sounded awkward. After about fifteen minutes, I spied Mrs. Richard's work shed. The lights were on, so I knew someone was working. I walked up to the door and peered in. Kevin and his brother were shifting bags of potting soil from a garden cart to a low work table. They both looked up when I stepped into the doorway.

"Hey, Sara," Chase greeted me. "You're just in time. We could use some help." He grinned and nodded toward the half-loaded cart.

"Don't be a jerk," Kevin rebuked his brother. "I'll finish here. You can beat it."

Chase's eyes widened and he blinked several times. Hand curled into a fist, he pulled his arm against his waist and back with a "Yessss." He hurried past me.

Kevin set down the bag of soil he was holding and pulled off his work gloves. He regarded me steadily, but didn't say anything. All the rehearsed words played on fast-forward through my mind, but in the end, I looked at him and simply said, "I'm sorry."

Kevin leaned against the work table and folded his arms. "What for?"

I shrugged and jammed my hands in my jean's pockets. "Lying to you, misleading you, ignoring you—take your pick. I've been so rotten to you I'm not even sure where to start."

"Tell me one specific thing you're sorry for." Kevin's voice sounded hard.

"Kev." There was pleading in my tone.

"One thing," he repeated.

I swallowed hard. My tongue worked against my teeth until I had some moisture in my mouth. I looked at the bundles of lavender and other plants I didn't recognize hanging upside down from racks in the ceiling. I brought my gaze back to Kevin. "Mostly I'm sorry I didn't realize what a true friend you are. I've been selfish and mean. I haven't cared who I hurt and I took advantage of your friendship. I'm sorry. I hope you can forgive me."

Tears threatened and I so did not want to cry in front of him. I backed out of the doorway, turned and hurried back the way I came. I ignored Kevin calling my name. But then I felt his hand on my arm and slowed to a stop. His hand gently tugged me around to face him and then he dropped my arm.

"Want to go for a walk?"

I couldn't read his face or his tone. I nodded. We headed toward the beach path.

"Wait." Kevin took my hand and turned me to face him again. He held my hand, palm up, and with his other hand pulled a sprig of lavender out of his pocket. He rubbed it along my palm hard enough to release the pungent sweet smell, then repeated the action on his own hand. He half-smiled. "Lavender's supposed to be calming. We'll probably need this."

We turned and silently followed the path toward the beach.

Kevin broke the silence. "Why'd you come over tonight? I mean, why now?"

Remembering the words I read in the Bible, I laughed. "You wouldn't believe me if I told you."

"C'mon. I'm serious. I want to know why you came over tonight. We haven't talked since that night I found you with Travis."

Great. That's a memory I wanted to revisit. Not. I pushed the thought out of my mind and answered Kevin. "Okay, you asked for it. I came over because I was reading the Bible and it said I should."

"What? Be serious."

"I am. That's why I'm here. No lie."

Kevin rubbed his hand along the back of his neck. I could smell the lavender and wondered if it had transferred to his hair.

"You read in the Bible you should come and talk to me?"

"Sort of. It said that as much as possible, I should be at peace with everyone, or something like that."

"Yeah. It does say that. In Romans. But why were you reading the Bible?" Kevin sounded confused.

"Good question. Not exactly what you'd expect, right?

It was something Dad said, but it's kind of the end of the story. Can I start at the beginning?"

"Sure. I guess you better because I have no idea what you're talking about."

We reached the beach, chose a spot facing the water and each squirmed a seat into the sand. I picked up my story from when I told him about my diagnosis and we had argued about my reaction. And he got preachy. He totally did.

I told him about my increasing feelings of depression and loneliness complicated by the decision that I couldn't ride Star. I acknowledged my desperation to keep up with Travis and the disastrous result of being ostracized at school. I even told him about my awful confrontation with Robyn in the cafeteria. I asked him if he'd heard the rumors about me at school.

Elbows propped on his knees and hands lightly clasped in front of him, he turned his attention from the waves to me. "Yeah."

I sifted sand through my fingers. Listened to the crash of waves on the shore and the gurgle of retreating water. "I've just felt so crummy in so many ways, and my grades kept going down until Mr. Salz called my parents and me in for a meeting. Well. He ambushed me. I guess that was the last straw." I shrugged and leaned back, planting my hands in back of me. "I couldn't figure out any reason I should keep living if my life was so rotten."

"You still believed your parents were lying to you about lupus being fatal?"

I nodded. "Yeah. I believed a lot of other stupid things, too. Like Tawny wasn't my friend anymore. Or you." I risked a quick look at him to gauge his reaction. Then I took a deep breath, swallowed hard and resumed my story.

"So, a couple days ago, I tried to kill myself."

I leaned forward and hugged my knees to my chest, resting my chin on them, and stared at the sand. I knew

Kevin watched me, but wasn't ready to face him yet.

I sensed him tip forward then felt him turn to face me. He lifted my chin and turned my head so I met his gaze. That was uncomfortable so I shifted around and nudged a new seat in the sand facing him. He kept his hand on my chin, forcing me to look at him.

"What happened?"

I couldn't, for real couldn't, tell the story looking into his steady gaze, so I brushed his hand away and talked to the sand.

"I decided to drown myself because it seemed like a peaceful way to die." I half-snorted; half-laughed. "Just one more thing I got completely wrong. But the worst thing is, I used Star to get me out beyond the waves. I rode him bareback into the surf beyond the waves, then slipped off his back and turned him back to shore. It wasn't peaceful. It was cold and terrifying. The waves would wash over me and I'd choke on the water. I got caught in the riptide and felt like I was inside a washing machine." I trembled at the memory. "I thought I wanted to die, but when it became real, I panicked. The very worst thing was when I realized Star was coming after me."

"What?" Kevin cried. "He what?"

"He came after me. He wouldn't let me go." I reached for Kevin's hand and gripped tightly when I remembered the sight of Star fighting his way toward me through the waves.

"The water kept breaking over his head, but he fought his way to the surface and kept coming. His eyes were scared and I could tell he couldn't breathe, but he just kept coming."

I kept hold of Kevin's hand because telling him the story made it all real again. When I got to the part where Mom met me in the yard, I concluded with, "I finally talked to my parents. Really talked. I've been so stupid."

Kevin didn't say anything; he just let go of my hands,

put an arm around me and gathered me up against his chest. His other arm moved around me until I rested in the safe cage of his arms. I snuggled against him and nestled in. Then I giggled.

"What?" Kevin drew back and looked at me.

"You smell like lavender. It's calming." I relaxed briefly, then said, "There's more."

He waited.

"Star's really sick." My voice caught and his arms tightened. "Dr. Heins says he has bronchitis and pneumonia. Star is too weak to stand so he's in a sling. Right now, he's holding his own, but it's possible he won't make it. Because of me. Because he saved me."

This time my grip tensed around Kevin while I struggled with the reality of Star's condition. Grief and regret threatened to consume me, but I concentrated on the steady beat of Kevin's heart against my ear until I gained control. Falling apart wouldn't do my horse any good.

Kevin kept a tight hold on me, his chin resting on the top of my head. After a few minutes he suggested, "Let's go see how he's doing."

I nodded and sat back. Kevin pushed up from the sand and held out a hand to me. I grasped his hand and let him pull me up. He kept hold of my hand when we turned to walk toward my house. After a few steps, he stopped and turned to face me once again. His steady gaze met mine. "I forgive you."

My hand gripped his hard and my eyes widened. "Really? But I've been such an idiot."

"True," he agreed.

"Hey!" I protested with a laugh.

"Well, you have been an idiot. I get believing I wasn't your friend anymore, but Tawny? Tawny would probably run into a burning building to help you. I wish I had a friend like that. I could tell you weren't happy, but I also got the message loud and clear that I wasn't going to be the one who could talk to you about it. Sometimes we just have to find out stuff on our own. But I was praying for you. Even when sometimes I didn't want to."

"What do you mean?"

"C'mon, Sara. Do you have any idea how hard it was to see you go back to Travis and brush me off? I was hurt and mad and that made it hard for me to pray for you. But I learned when Dad died that staying angry only hurt me. I had to let it go." He shrugged. "So, I did that with you, too. I still felt bad, especially when the guys at school started giving you such a hard time, but you had to learn for yourself what you wanted."

Kevin dropped my hands and turned to continue up the path. I walked beside him, kicking at leaves.

"What I never expected is that you would decide suicide was your best option. I just don't get that," he admitted.

I wasn't sure how to answer him. I had trouble believing it myself. I didn't blame Kevin for being confused.

"I wanted to matter," I tried to explain. "The attention I got from Travis made me feel like I matter. Being chosen as cheerleader made me feel like I matter. But it wasn't real. It was just feelings. And I'm finding out feelings can be different than the truth. Like, being a cheerleader made me feel cool, but I still felt lonely and like I didn't belong. And the attention from Travis? That was even more of a lie because all he ever cared about was himself. I wanted to believe he cared about me so much that I just ignored everything that didn't match what I wanted to be true."

We reached the barn and I pushed the door open. "Hey, Ben. I'm back."

Kevin and I headed toward Star's stall and found Ben perched on my hay bale thumbing through his phone. He looked up and a flash of surprise crossed his face when he saw Kevin.

"Oh, hey, Kev. What's up?"

"Just came to see how Star's doing."

I went up to Star and stroked his nose. "Has he been okay?"

Ben shrugged. "He's coughing, but he did drink a little more water. I filled it back up so it would be fresh." He pushed up from the bale and walked past us out of the stall. "See you guys later."

"Thanks, Ben," I called to his back.

I went to the tack room and gathered the ingredients to make the mash. After I got it mixed, I took it and placed it in front of Star. He sniffed at it, but wasn't interested in eating.

"C'mon, big guy," I coaxed. "You've got to eat."

I picked up the pan and held it close to his muzzle. I continued to plead with him while I stroked his nose with my free hand. Kevin stood beside me, patting Star's neck.

My spotted monster lipped the mixture, but didn't eat. We continued to encourage him until, finally, he lipped up a mouthful, then another. I could tell that was his limit, and set the pan by the stall door. I returned to Star and my heart sank when his head drooped lower and lower. A deep cough occasionally shook his whole body. I pulled Kevin back to my hay bale.

Kevin rested a hand on my knee. "At least he ate a little. That's a good sign, isn't it?"

"It's better than nothing," I agreed. "I wish he'd eat more, but the water is the most important thing. Dr. Heins said Star has to drink so he doesn't get dehydrated. If that happens, they'll have to start an IV."

"When will the doctor be back?"

"He said he'd stop by tonight after office hours. Should be any time."

Kevin nodded and we both fell silent, our attention focused on my exhausted horse. Kevin interrupted the silence with a question.

"You said you wanted to know you matter. What did you mean? How could you not know you mattered to me?"

I picked at stems of hay and felt my cheeks get warm. "I guess I knew I mattered to you. I just...I don't know...it was like..." I had trouble getting it out. Kevin did it for me.

"You wanted to matter to Travis more."

"Yeah." I shrugged. "I'm an idiot, remember? I honestly don't know what happened to me these last few months. You said after the Turnabout that you guessed you really didn't know me. The thing is, I didn't really know me anymore either. All the stuff I thought and did kinda freaks me out. I kept getting these thoughts in my mind I couldn't get rid of. It felt like a dark cloud was taking over my brain. Eventually, all I felt was depressed. What kind of person am I?"

"I don't know. I think you better find out though. Ever thought about a counselor? I went to one after Dad died. Mom made me. I only went a few times, but it really helped."

"Everybody keeps asking me that. I think I'm going to ask Justine for some names. I trust her."

"Good idea."

We were comfortably quiet for several minutes. Star seemed to be dozing, though I could tell he relied on the sling to support his weight. Kevin asked another question.

"You said you knew you mattered to me. How did you know?"

"Mom challenged me to figure out how I would know if I mattered to somebody. You and Tawny helped me figure it out. With you I decided it was several things. Mostly how thoughtful you are in little ways. Like when you brought me the essential oil to help me sleep. It did, by the way." I bumped his shoulder in thanks.

"I really appreciated that and I like how you're always encouraging me." I searched for words to describe how I felt. "It's like—you notice me. You pay attention. To what

I do, what I like, what I need. I matter to you," I concluded.

"Cool. I never thought of it that way. I wonder how I know I matter to people? I'll have to figure that out."

"You matter to me." I turned my head to watch his reaction.

He shook his head. "Now that I'm not sure about. I'll have to figure out why, but my gut reaction says no freaking way. Sorry. Just being honest."

I clasped my hands between my knees and stared at my boots. Finally, I asked, "Do you think you'll ever trust me again?"

He hesitated. "I don't know. Forgiving you and trusting you again are two different things." He paused and his heel scuffed at the straw on the floor. "It's hard…like…I think if I hadn't cared about you so much it would be easier, you know? Like, if you were just somebody to hang out with. But you were a lot more to me. And, I'm sorry, I know this will make you feel bad, you betrayed me, Sara. And I think it hurt so much because I cared about you so much." He lifted his gaze to mine. His was absolutely sincere. "You know?"

I swallowed hard and nodded.

He stood. "I should probably go. Let me know what happens with Star, okay?"

I got up and we walked in silence to the door where Kevin turned to face me. "I'm glad you came over. That was probably hard to do."

Out of words, I nodded. Kevin walked out the door, but had only gone a step or two when I went after him.

"Wait. I get that trust is hard to build again, but am I still your friend? I'd like a chance to show you I can be trusted now."

Kevin smiled. "Still my friend. I don't stop caring about somebody just because they've lost their way."

Relief washed through me like warm cocoa. "Okay. Good. See ya."

I watched him walk away then returned to Star. I stood in front of him and adjusted his halter, smoothing the hair under the straps. I put my hands on his cheeks and brought my forehead to his. "Get better, boy. I love you so much. And I can't believe how much you love me. Fight hard, Star. Fight hard."

I stayed in that position, willing my horse to get better. Gradually my thoughts returned to Kevin. "Friends," I murmured to Star. "I can build on that."

Chapter 26

I'm turning back from my guilt trip to nowhere.
Sara's Diary

The next few weeks at school were the same nightmare, but now I had solid support to help me through. Ryan, Tawny and Kevin checked in with me during the day and, after talking to Justine, I found a counselor who helped me talk through the last several months. It felt good to talk without hurting someone's feelings or making them feel guilty, and Ms. Woods gave me useful tools to help through the drama at school. We did a family session one time, which was interesting. It was both helpful and difficult to talk about the last several months, especially my Aquaman imitation, as Ben called it. He made us laugh, but I noticed Ms. Woods relentlessly guided Ben toward naming and accepting my action for what it was: a suicide attempt.

I tried to brush off the attempt, too, but the counselor kept nudging me gently back around to the subject. Gradually, with the help of Ms. Wood's insightful questions, I solved the riddle of what got me to the point where I acted on such a drastic solution. Once I figured out that letting untrustworthy people's opinions shape my own opinion of myself gave them power over me, I recognized the handful of people who I knew I could trust.

Ms. Wood said, "You can be like a window with the people you trust. They have the honor of seeing inside you. The good, the bad and the ugly. The people who aren't trustworthy?" She shook her head. "Those people don't get the window. They see the protective wall you put up. You can mingle with them; you can be polite; you can even be kind when they are not, but they don't get to see inside. You protect yourself just like you protect anything you value."

I considered the counselor's words. "You mean I protect myself like I'm valuable?"

"Exactly," Ms. Wood approved.

"There's this song I've always liked but never believed called *Priceless*. Do you think valuable is the same as priceless?"

The therapist steepled her fingers together and cocked her head at me. "I think it's more important what you think. Are you priceless?"

I looked out the window and considered the last several months. "I wish I could say it, but it sticks in my throat. I can admit I have value, even if the kids at school don't think so, but priceless? I can't quite go there yet."

Ms. Wood smiled. "That's an excellent foundation to build on. I'm proud of the growth in your self-confidence. Remember, confidence isn't just to stop caring what others think. It's about caring what you think about yourself more. How about we meet together a couple more weeks and reassess?"

I nodded. "I'd like that."

We wrote out a crisis plan for me in case I felt depressed again. I signed two copies, kept one and returned the other to the counselor. It was awkward to talk about what I did, but I'm glad Ms. Wood persisted because I felt confident I would never go down that road again.

The best news of all came four weeks later when the veterinarian snapped his case shut with an air of finality. "That's it, Sara. I don't hear any congestion in his lungs. I believe he's going to be all right." The doctor slapped Star on the shoulder. "A fine animal. Good thing he's so strong. I doubted he was going to make it there for a while."

"Is it okay to ride him now?"

"Yes, but take it easy at first. Build him up slowly. And remember I said he might have permanent damage from the pneumonia. You may not be able to jump again, but he should be okay for trail rides and such."

"I'm just glad he's alive, Doctor Heins. Thanks for all your help."

"You're welcome, Sara."

I texted Tawny and Kevin as soon as the vet left the barn. I had promised to let both of them know what the doctor said.

Vet says S seems fine. Won't know about permanent damage til later. Okay to ride. No jumps.

That is totally dope, SJ. Hang out later? (Tawny)

Good to hear. Happy for you and Star. Headed to beach. C U there in 20? (Kevin)

I answered affirmatively to both friends. I brushed Star and saddled him for the first time in weeks. While I finished fastening the cinch, Ben wandered into the barn.

"Hey! The big S back up to speed? That rocks. Can I give him the rest of my apple?"

"Sure. You know his love affair with food."

"Yeah. He's a lot like me. We bonded while you were going through your hard time. Me and Star are tight now."

"So, can I ask you something?" I fiddled with the saddle strap to avoid looking at my brother.

"Sure. What's up?"

"You remember Ms. Wood?"

"You're kidding, right? How could I forget the human bloodhound? She tracks emotions and bogus ideas like she's Spot on a scent. That counselor is one determined lady." He stroked Star's nose, but had his gaze fixed on me. "Why?"

I stopped fiddling with the strap and looked at Ben. "She really nailed me on something…"

"Doesn't surprise me," Ben interrupted under his breath.

"…and I'm curious what you think?"

"Okay, shoot." Ben turned toward me and gave me his full attention.

"I realized after a few sessions a change in how she talked to me. She gradually switched from telling me, 'You matter,' to getting me to say, 'I matter.' Not in a sneaky way, she just changed up our conversation. It's like she helped me shift from needing to know I matter to other people so much to just owning it and being able to recognize I matter to myself. Ah," I face-palmed in frustration. "I can't explain what I mean." I took a breath to try again.

"It was like…"

Ben interrupted. "Like she wanted you to value yourself rather than counting on other people's opinion of your worth."

"Yeah. She talked to me about the danger of letting my whole sense of identity depend on what other people think about me. Other people don't get to tell me if I matter or not. Relationships are important, but confidence in myself has to come from inside. Like what matters most is self-acceptance."

"I get it. Sort of. What's your question?"

"Question? Oh yeah, I wanted to ask you, so, do you, like, do you have a problem being able to say, 'I matter'?"

"Nope," Ben answered cheerfully. "Remember in fourth grade when those kids started trolling me because I was so tall? Called me beanstalk and stuff?"

I nodded.

"I came home crying one day because they'd been calling me string bean and Great Dane, skyscraper and freak, stuff like that, and Dad sat me down and talked to me about how God has a reason for creating each one of us the way we are. To God we're each like a one-time masterpiece."

"Sort of like priceless?"

"Totally. I get twitchy when people squelch me, like Travis does, but I try not to let it stick. Dad told me to pretend I was Teflon and let it slide off. Dad said I don't have to listen to what people say, and I don't have to *believe* anything but the truth. We good?"

"Yeah. We're good." My thoughts completely side-tracked, I barely noticed him leave the barn. Star interrupted my reflections with an impatient stamp.

"Okay, okay, I'm coming."

When I led him out of the barn, Star sidestepped and switched his tail, full of energy. His antics helped cheer me up.

I ran my hand along his neck and scratched his chest. "What I said is true, Star. I'm ecstatic you're alive, and if you can't jump anymore, it's because of what I did and I'm so, so sorry. That will be all my fault."

Star bent his head and nibbled on the toe of my boot. Then he raised his head and nuzzled the hair on my shoulder before he snorted forcefully, blowing hair in all directions.

"Hey! Don't like my hairstyle?" I grabbed the scrunchy from around my wrist, smoothed my hair and pulled it into a ponytail. "Guess you don't want to talk about what happened, huh?"

I stepped in front of him and placed my hands on his cheeks. "We won't talk about it again, but thank you. Thank you for coming after me. You saved my life." I rested my forehead against his. He stood quietly for a moment, in tune with me as always, but then he shifted his feet to remind me it was time to go. I mounted and we headed for the beach.

I thought about the last few months. What the doctor promised about SLE had come true. I felt better. My hands bothered me some, but I could manage most tasks pretty well. No more dizziness, feet and hands not so swollen, and my weight had stabilized at a place I felt comfortable. Star had suffered more lasting consequences.

Ms. Wood helped me tackle guilt and regret, but so far, I still had trouble letting go of blaming and punishing myself for Star's illness. Nightmares of him drowning instead of me tormented my nights. The counselor encouraged me to talk back to the blame voice that accused and instead, concentrate on forgiving myself.

"It might be a slow process," she warned. "Just keep reminding yourself it's in the past. You can't change the past, but you can leave it there and move on."

The ocean breeze and sound of waves broke into my thoughts. We ambled along the beach, well up from the water line. I couldn't handle being near the water. My heart started to race every time I tried. Dr. Adams told me that was natural and to give it time.

I breathed deeply of the fresh salt air. Contentment settled on me like my favorite fleece blanket. "It's like I finally get who I am." Star's ears twitched at the sound of my voice. "I guess when I tried to get closer to God, it was a step in the right direction. I don't understand everything the Bible says, and I'm not completely sure what I believe, but I don't feel alone anymore."

Star shied when some foam blew past his feet. I patted his neck and laughed. "You're feeling good, too, boy. I'm glad." I pulled him to a stop to enjoy the fresh smell of the ocean and the sound of gulls calling to each other. The empty place I felt for so long was filled with peace. It's like a little warm fire right in my middle. Could that be hope? I considered this possibility and decided absolutely, it must be hope.

Star snorted when a gull swooped in front of him to snatch something off the sand. Then his ears pointed forward and his head jerked up.

I looked in the direction of Star's ears and saw a figure in the distance. I squinted until I recognized Kevin. I pressed Star's sides with my heels and urged him toward my friend. When we closed the distance, I slid off Star and his reins dropped to the ground. I knew he wouldn't wander when he was ground-tied.

Kevin and I climbed onto a rock. He held out his hand and pulled me up the last little bit.

"First ride?" he asked while we found comfortable spots.

"Yep. I'm supposed to take it easy for a while. What's up with you?"

"Not much. Mom has me really busy with her business. She has a lot of new customers. The times you've come over to help have been great. In fact, I realized something."

"What's that?"

"I've been thinking about what you told me a few weeks ago. About wanting to figure out how you know you matter to people."

I nodded. A new life quest.

"I've been thinking about how I know when people care about me. I realized the times you've come over to help make me feel like I matter to you. I guess it's important to me that people spend time with me."

"That's epic, as Tawny would say." I nudged his shoulder with mine. "It's true I come over because I care about you."

Kevin nudged me back. "Truth?"

"Truth," I confirmed.

"Good."

We sat, shoulders touching, watching the waves.

Kevin reached over and took one of my hands in his. I turned to him and smiled.

"Man. I love it when you smile, Sara."

I turned back to the ocean. The little flame of hope in my heart suddenly burned bright as the sun.

Questions for discussion

1. Sara says throughout the story that she wishes she could know when she matters to someone. How do you know when you matter to someone? How do you let people know they matter to you?

2. One theme from *Riptide* is how important it is to belong and be included. Sara is willing to compromise what she believes is right so she will belong in a certain group. How is the sense of belonging a struggle for you? How far would you change your behavior just to be accepted?

3. Do you have someone in your life who has your back, as Sara and Tawny describe it?

4. Describe a time when it seemed to you that even God didn't care about you. What did you do?

5. Some of the girls in *Riptide* are mean. Have you ever experienced someone being mean to you for no apparent reason? Have you ever been mean to someone else? What did you do in both cases?

6. Have you ever known someone who has been active in sexting activity? Do you believe this should be against the law? Why/why not?

7. Why didn't Sara believe the truth about Travis even from people she trusted? Have you ever wanted something to be true so badly you ignored what people you trusted said?

8.   Kevin talks to Sara about trust. He says he can forgive her but that's not the same as trusting her again. Do you believe forgiveness has to include trust? Why/why not?

9.   Do you believe it's easier to believe negative things about yourself than positive things? Why or why not?

10.   Sara learned that while it's important to know you matter to others, it's also important to be able to say, "I matter," about yourself. Are you able to say "I matter" about yourself? Why or why not?

11.   Have you, or someone you know, ever struggled with ideas of suicide? If you, or someone you know, ever have trouble with thoughts of self-harm, please find someone you trust to talk to. If you don't know someone or are afraid to talk to someone you know, please call the National Suicide Prevention Lifeline at 1-800-273-TALK (8255) or go to their web site at https://suicidepreventionlifeline.org/ *Or you can text 741741, write home as the message and a crisis counselor will text you. Another option is to simply dial 988 for the suicide hotline.*

12.   You're welcome to visit my web page, doimatter.org, for more information and resources. Follow me on Instagram and Twitter at doyoumatter1

Watch for the continuation of the story about Sara and Star in the upcoming book, *Undercurrents.*

For parent or youth group speaking engagements, please contact the author at thodesm@gmail.com

Susan Thode lives in Enumclaw, a small town at the base of Mt. Rainier in Washington State. She enjoys the rural setting dotted with many horse farms…and the beautiful mountain.

A former high school English teacher, Susan has been a licensed mental health counselor and certified trauma/crisis counselor for twenty years. She helps people answer tough questions about God's plan and purpose for their lives in spite of pain and confusion. She also gives them tools to navigate emotional journeys of discovery through trauma and crisis.

As much as Susan enjoys her writing and counseling responsibilities, her greatest joy is being Grandma to her 14-year-old granddaughter, Moxy, from whom she is learning Tik-Tok dances.

Visit Susan at

Instagram   doyoumatter1

TikTok   suethode

Web page   doimatter.org

Facebook   Susan Thode

Made in the USA
Columbia, SC
15 July 2024

38425698R00139